Re:ZeRo

-Starting Life in Another World-

Beatrice & Puck

"Yeah,
I know."

"I—I tried. I really tried. I did everything I could. I desperately tried to do everything right...! I did! Really, really, I've never tried to do anything that hard before!"

"—A demon."

"Ah-ha...
ah-ha-ha—"

She laughed.
It was loud
laughter like
that of a little
girl but
overflowing
with naked
cruelty.

Re:ZERO -Starting Life in Another World-

The only ability Subaru Natsuki gets when he's summoned to another world is
time travel via his own death. But to save her, he'll die as many times as it takes.

CONTENTS

Re:ZeRo

-Starting Life in Another World-

VOLUME 3

TAPPEI NAGATSUKI
ILLUSTRATION: SHINICHIROU OTSUKA

YEN ON

NEW YORK

RE:ZERO Vol. 3
TAPPEI NAGATSUKI

Translation by ZephyrRz
Cover art by Shinichirou Otsuka

RE:ZERO KARA HAJIMERU ISEKAI SEIKATSU
© TAPPEI NAGATSUKI / Shinichirou Otsuka 2014
First published in Japan in 2014 by KADOKAWA CORPORATION, Tokyo.
English translation rights reserved by YEN PRESS, LLC under the license from
KADOKAWA CORPORATION, Tokyo, through Tuttle-Mori Agency, Inc., Tokyo.

Yen On
1290 Avenue of the Americas
New York, NY 10104

Visit us at yenpress.com
facebook.com/yenpress
twitter.com/yenpress
yenpress.tumblr.com
instagram.com/yenpress

First Yen On Edition: March 2017

Yen On is an imprint of Yen Press, LLC.
The Yen On name and logo are trademarks of Yen Press, LLC.

Library of Congress Cataloging-in-Publication Data
Names: Nagatsuki, Tappei, 1987– author. | Otsuka, Shinichirou, illustrator. |
ZephyrRz, translator.
Title: Re:ZERO starting life in another world / Tappei Nagatsuki ; illustration by
Shinichirou Otsuka ; translation by ZephyrRz.
Other titles: Re:ZERO kara hajimeru isekai seikatsu. English
Description: First Yen On edition. | New York, NY : Yen On, 2016– |
Audience: Ages 13 & up.
Identifiers: LCCN 2016031562| ISBN 9780316315302 (v. 1 : pbk.) |
ISBN 9780316398374 (v. 2 : pbk.) | ISBN 9780316398404 (v. 3 : pbk.)
Subjects: | CYAC: Science fiction.
Classification: LCC PZ7.1.N34 Re 2016 | DDC [Fic]—dc23
LC record available at https://lccn.loc.gov/2016031562

ISBNs: 978-0-316-39840-4 (paperback)
978-0-316-39841-1 (ebook)

1 3 5 7 9 10 8 6 4 2

LSC-C

Printed in the United States of America

CHAPTER 1
SUBARU NATSUKI'S RESTART

1

—Subaru Natsuki experienced only a single moment between losing consciousness and reviving.

"_____"

His head had smashed against the hard ground, bathing his world red just an instant ago.

The moment after he lost all five senses, Subaru found himself on top of the soft bed.

"Whew—"

He exhaled. His body relaxed as the shock of death retreated from his soul.

It was enough to make him pull up the sheets and cower, forgetting even to breathe.

Of course it was. He'd never leaped off a cliff and taken his own life before.

His fourth death in this loop was suicide. Without a manual for how Return by Death worked, or any precedent, that could have truly been the end of Subaru's life for all he knew.

But—

"I'm...back..."

Subaru clenched his trembling fist, smiling thinly at the white ceiling that filled his vision.

The soft bed, the sweet-smelling pillow, the well-furnished suite—all of it belonged to the guest room that had greeted Subaru on his first day at Roswaal Manor.

And more importantly—

"Sister, Sister. Our Dear Guest appears to be slow to wake."

"Rem, Rem. Our Dear Guest seems to be slow in the head for his age."

The twin sisters were clasping the other's hands, their eyes side by side as they looked at Subaru from the foot of the bed.

They wore little black dresses with white aprons on the front. Both had dazzling white lace headpieces on top of their short bob hairstyles, one with pink hair, the other with blue. Their faces were young and lovely.

They were the maids who took care of the mansion, and also the reason Subaru had made his Return by Death.

Subaru's heart shuddered at hearing their familiar voices speaking in familiar ways, during what would be the fifth round of meeting them for the first time.

He had a mountain of things he wanted to ask. But he felt like something was lodged in his throat; the words wouldn't come out.

Seeing Rem alive and well, while Ram behaved with her typical rudeness, everything felt so ordinary and natural that it was hard for Subaru to keep his emotions down.

"Dear Guest, Dear Guest. Is something wrong? Are you unwell?"

"Dear Guest, Dear Guest. Are you sick? Perhaps a chronic illness?"

Subaru put a hand on his chest and lowered his head before the bewildered twins.

The maids went to one side of the bed and separated slightly, reaching out with one small palm each as if to touch Subaru from both sides.

Those hands—

"Let me borrow those for a sec."

"Eh?"

"Ah."

Subaru, not waiting for them to say yes, grasped their hands, entwining his fingers into theirs.

With the sisters frozen in surprise, he got a good feel for their slender fingers and the warmth of their palms.

"Yeah, I knew it... There's no mistaking it."

Subaru remembered the feel of their hands and how their warmth had saved him in his time of need.

He wasn't wrong about what had given him the determination to throw himself off that cliff.

Both pulled their hands back and poured scorn on Subaru's rude, insolent behavior.

"No, Dear Guest. You are surely mistaken. About everything."

"No, Dear Guest. It was surely a mistake that you were born."

But Subaru nodded as if even those cruel words were music that refreshed his soul.

"All things considered, I probably shouldn't smile at that...but right now, it feels good."

"Sister, Sister. Might Dear Guest actually enjoy being insulted?"

"Rem, Rem. Might Dear Guest be a perverted masochist?"

These were odd accusations to throw at a "Dear Guest" so quickly, but he smiled and let them slide.

If it meant he could really do things over with the two of them, everything else was unimportant.

Faced with an attitude that was less caution and more blatant, visceral distaste, Subaru hopped off the bed. He pressed a hand to his butt as he double-checked his body's condition before turning toward their two suspicious faces.

"Sorry for doing that earlier without even saying hi. There's something I want to say beyond apologizing, though."

Subaru crossed his arms, dramatically puffed his chest, and sat back down, directly facing Ram and Rem. Feeling the rather sharp gazes that both trained upon him, Subaru absentmindedly mused, *They're probably already starting to assess me.*

If Subaru Natsuki could not win their trust, indeed, the trust of

everyone under the mansion's roof, he could not hope to regain the peaceful, tranquil time he had lost.

So he chose to throw caution to the wind, hoping to assuage their suspicions—

"I mean, geez, I'm not some kind of delinquent who can't get along with anyone..."

Hearing Subaru's murmur, both of them tilted their heads a little, as if they had their doubts about that.

Finding it funny that even now their gestures were syncing up, Subaru felt the tension and stress drain from his body. He already knew what he wanted to say, as well as what he needed to do.

"—I trust you, so let's get along, okay?"

Just like in the first loop, he'd do his best to earn the girls' trust.

Having a little knowledge of the future didn't change Subaru's core nature, nor did the mere possibility he might be able to change things. All he could do was address the situation before his eyes and live every day to the fullest.

Subaru's request made the twins look at each other and trade a silent conversation between their eyes. Their back and forth was still going on when they abruptly looked toward the door, having noticed a lone girl entering at just that moment.

She had skin so pale you could almost see through it, with silver hair she wore down to her hips. Her violet eyes seemed to emit a bewitching magical spell that lured you in. It was Emilia, a girl of inhuman beauty.

Emilia, noticing Subaru staring at her, broke out in a small smile as she looked among the three in the room.

"I heard a ruckus, so I came to peek... You seem pretty lively, Subaru. I'm glad."

"I felt kind of conflicted there, but seeing Emilia-tan blows all that away. You're like a compassion pill that works extra strong on my heart."

"Sorry, I don't really know what you're saying..."

A troubled look came over Emilia's beautiful face because Subaru was speaking even more glibly than usual.

"Even your sad look is cute… You're always fresh, and that makes me feel refreshed."

"Somehow, that sounds kind of creepy. But good morning. I'm glad you're safe."

The grimace she had made quickly softened into a charming smile and she beamed at Subaru.

As far as Emilia was concerned, this was their first reunion after the events in the royal capital. Subaru sincerely accepted Emilia's words of relief at seeing him come back from the brink of death.

"Yeah, good morning. Well, let's start again, shall we?"

The three girls in the room, not understanding what Subaru meant by that, tilted their heads slightly with puzzled looks.

Seeing all three of them react like a trio of sisters made Subaru break out in laughter.

"What I meant was, it's time for me to start clearing the Roswaal Manor level."

His goal was to reach the morning he wished to see for him, and for everyone at the manor.

—*Now, let's get this show on the road.*

And so, he began his first day at Roswaal Manor for the fifth time.

2

He needed to surpass two major obstacles to get through his first week at Roswaal Manor.

The first was to win the trust of everyone living there. This meant not just Ram and Rem but their master, Roswaal, as well.

If the girls saw any part of him as even remotely dubious, the chances they'd commit murder to silence him were exceptionally high.

The second obstacle was bringing down the shaman attacking Roswaal Manor.

But he didn't have any real leads for doing that as of yet.

His opponent was a tough one, his true identity remaining concealed even as Subaru was taking his fifth crack at it.

Subaru needed to earn the twins' trust and deal with this unknown, evil magic user. Those were the victory conditions he had discovered by his fourth death.

However, Subaru still lacked many of the elements he needed to fulfill those requirements. In spite of his Return by Death, he hadn't been able to lay his hands on anything solid.

His head felt stuck between a rock and a hard place, but Subaru threw off his negative emotions and looked to the future.

He had to confront the wall standing before him no matter how high it was.

It was Subaru's choice to come back and do this, not knowing if he'd even make it. He decided that, having once experienced death by his own hands, he would do it…even if it killed him.

3

The moon was rising in the nighttime sky as a private discussion took place in the study on Roswaal Manor's highest floor.

The man sat at the desk, posing his question in his slow, exaggerated manner of speech.

"So hooow is he, Ram? How would you raaate him from what you have seeeen?"

He was a man with long indigo hair with ghastly pale skin, and he would look something like a classic variety pretty boy—if not for the clown-like makeup covering his face. That, combined with his peculiar speech pattern, made him a hard man to forget.

He was Roswaal L. Mathers, lord and master of the manor.

Participating in the conversation were Roswaal and a maid—Ram—facing toward him and the desk.

Roswaal crossed his arms and made a broad smile while Ram tilted her head, deep in thought. He raised an eyebrow, finding her hesitance to make her report a rare sight.

"Hmmmm, to see Ram, prone to snap judgments about everything, so conceeerned, it is quite a siiight, is it nooot? Perhaaaaps one day is not sufficient to get to know him?"

"That is…not the case. However…"

Though she immediately denied it, her words revealed a lack of clarity. Ram put a fingertip to her own lips and still seemed a little unsure as she began to speak again.

"Let me grade him first. He…Barusu…has no ability. His workmanship as a servant is completely amateur."

"My, my… Is it not somewhat puuuzzling that he himself asked for this role?"

Roswaal grinned as he recalled the exchange over that morning's breakfast. He remembered, too, what words the freshly awakened guest employed as he sought a reward for his exploits.

What stood out was Subaru's claim of being *a teenager with good health, a half-decent education, and a not-terrible head.* It was a robust self-assessment that, by the same token, merited a certain level of caution.

Accordingly, he had commanded Ram to oversee his education, as well as to observe his actions and report her findings, as she was doing that moment. He had not thought the matter would be resolved in a single day, but Ram's hesitance in making her report was a problem in itself.

Roswaal rested his cheek against his hand. Ram held her silence for a little while before opening her mouth.

"There are some mysterious things about Barusu."

"Yes, yes, do teeell. Speak of anything that stands out."

"He can be said to be completely without talent, but Barusu seems to be…a little too quick-witted when it comes to particular things."

"What do you mean, a little toooo quick-witted?"

"These are very minor things, but…in the middle of work, he seems overly familiar with minor details about the mansion, things I have yet to teach him. When putting dishes away, he opened the drawers in the proper order. Also, our…tastes in tea leaves."

"_____"

Roswaal said nothing in reply to Ram's words, instead silently running a fingertip across his chin. Seeing Roswaal do this, Ram added, "Of course, these are all quite minor details. After breakfast,

I gave him a brief tour and explanation of the mansion. I noticed his eyes drifting to various places. That is really all, but..."

"I see, too much to be a set of simple coincidences... That is rather iiinteresting."

Suspicion begins from the smallest things. If he was not over-thinking it, Subaru could have checked out the mansion before infiltrating it in earnest.

But what made that possibility difficult to fathom was...

"His feat was protecting Lady Emilia in the royal capital, was it nooot...?"

"It seems too...blatant a means to infiltrate the mansion. At any rate, he might well have lost his life had Lady Beatrice not been available."

The memory of his being carried into the mansion was still fresh in Roswaal's mind. Though he had not healed the boy personally, it was impossible that Beatrice would participate in such a scheme. Furthermore, Ram had nursed the wounded Subaru the entire way back from the royal capital. Slipping something past both of them was very unlikely.

"All things considered, such thoughts seem sooomewhat excessive in light of the faaacts."

"The Bowel Hunter' who attacked Lady Emilia... I imagine it is possible he conspired with her to infiltrate the mansion, but..."

Ram's words lacked conviction, suggesting even she viewed it as unlikely. For his part, Roswaal shook his head.

"No, that is not pooossible. Surely we need not even suspeeect that the Bowel Hunter would team up with him?"

"...Is...that so?"

"More importantly, are there any other issues of concern?"

Prodded by Roswaal to move on, Ram lowered her eyes.

"I suppose that...putting aside his being too quick-witted from time to time...Barusu is so optimistic, it is rather nauseating."

"Eh?"

Roswaal raised an eyebrow at Ram's statement. She seemed to be not so much choosing her words carefully as she was searching for the right ones to use.

Surely even Ram knew she'd said something off topic. Ram continued, looking frustrated at her own inability to find a more accurate explanation.

"At this rate, he will speak himself to death. His smile never falters when he bumbles, and he seems exceptionally attentive to how he behaves toward us…"

"…What do you thiiink of that?"

"…It is different from how Lady Emilia describes him… Namely, how he's honest about his own desires like a little child, genuine in a likable way…"

Ram tried to keep her response to the subtle question short.

Roswaal, having had little contact with Subaru, couldn't understand what made Ram so doubtful. But these were the words of a loyal retainer who had a long record of service. Roswaal tugged on his chin as he digested Ram's analysis

"It seeeems we shall have to keep an eye on him for some tiiime. His first day made for difficult viewing, but it cannot be heeelped. It is aaalso a fact he deserves a commensurate rewaaard in thanks for saving Lady Emilia."

"…And if…it becomes necessary?"

Ram's hesitation made it seem like she didn't want to hear what would come next.

The expression on her face remained the same, but Roswaal had spent long enough around her to read what she was feeling inside. Roswaal beheld Ram's moment of weakness with his yellow eye as he made a small shake of his head.

"This is a matter we must handle with great deeelicacy. Above all else, see to it that Rem does not get ahead of herself."

Ram nodded crisply in response to Roswaal's command.

The maid not participating in the conversation, Rem, had a tendency to act according to her own ideas from time to time. Usually, her rushed judgment could be met with just a cute little scolding.

At times like these, however, independent action was likely to push things in a very poor direction. She might well eliminate the danger beforehand, worsening his relationship with Emilia in the process.

The thought did not amuse him.

"Yes, I shall…endeavor that Rem does not act on her feelings of distrust toward Barusu."

Roswaal leaned back with a creak of the chair. His voice felt tired somehow as he murmured.

"I am deeply grateful. This is a time of great expectations… Indeed, time to put them all to the test."

Ram started to say something to him, but she closed her mouth and held her tongue. Silence descended between the two as the cool night air drifted in.

"So, Ram, shall we concluuude your report here?"

"…Yes. I apologize for not being able to convey a great deal."

"I shall not scooold you for such a thing. Now, then, shall we proceed? After nothing for two days, you are aching rather considerably, are you nooot?"

"Ah…yes."

Ram somehow seemed bewitched as she obeyed Roswaal's beckoning finger. From her standing position before the desk, she seemed to wobble as she stepped close to Roswaal and meekly sat on his lap.

"Once again, if you will…excuse me."

"'Tis merely exercising a natural right. It is the same as always, nooothing to be embarrassed about. Your precious body does not belong to you alooone, after all?"

He stroked her cheek. She gently closed her eyes as he tilted her head up. Stroking her pink hair with his other hand, Roswaal closed one eye, gazing down upon Ram with his golden iris.

"Now, theeen, given what you are to us…we should get along nicely, yes?"

Roswaal murmured mostly to himself as his consciousness switched to a different gear. He stared at Ram before him, his consciousness sinking into Ram and Ram alone.

The first night at Roswaal Manor grew late as the suspicious conversation between master and maid came to a conclusion.

4

"Good morning! The weather's great today, perfect for laundry! Let's make this a happy day!"

Subaru raised a shrill *hip, hip, hurrah!* to welcome the arrival of the rising sun.

It was his fifth go at his second morning in Roswaal Manor.

He stood in the middle of the garden, his body bathed in morning sunlight as he twisted his upper body all about. He used the popular morning warm-up exercise to get blood circulating through his whole body, making full use of the energy he had gained from sleep.

"Yes, victory!"

Finally, he thrust both hands into the sky and shouted in triumph as he finished the start to the start of another day.

Subaru vigorously wiped away the light sweat on his brow and turned around with a smile. Emilia smiled back, albeit tersely, standing in the corner of the garden as she engaged in her daily conversation with lesser spirits under the shade of a tree.

"You really are energetic in the morning…"

"Hey, don't talk like it's all me here. Put your back into it, Emilia-tan!"

Puck, Emilia's little cat spirit, was hovering alongside her, cleaning his face with his paw.

"When I see him clean his face like that, I'm like, he's seriously a cat. I guess spirits get sleepy, too, huh? He looks half asleep there."

"You sleep when you're tired, too, don't you? When mana, the source of our vital power, fades away, well, it's close enough. If we're not getting enough mana…"

Puck yawned generously. Emilia put her hand to her mouth and yawned a little, too.

"Both up late, huh? You were staying up talking to a boy you like, weren't you? Let me in on it! Huh? Which girl do I like…? That's, ah, embarrassing to say, you see…"

Subaru folded his arms, looking down as he glanced a little at Emilia.

"All right, all right," Emilia said, waving casually at Subaru's act. "I like Puck. Puck likes me. The end."

"Mutual love?! Is there any room for me in there?!"

"Not even a little, meow. My charm sets Lia's heart a-flutter. You might not be a bad catch, Subaru, but all that is wasted before me. You should just give up on Lia right...meow, meow!"

Subaru closed on Puck, glaring down at him with reproach, but Emilia's fingers caught one ear on each of them before they could start anything.

"Don't get carried away. I'm going to be upset if that's all you two do."

"Ow, ow, she's upset, ow!"

Subaru and Puck meekly endured Emilia's punishment together.

When Emilia let go of their ears, they both rubbed their aching heads as she stood before them, hands on her hips.

"I'm glad you two are getting along, but no taking advantage of people just so you can play. Say yes if you understand."

"Yeees."

Both of them raised a hand and nodded firmly.

Strangely, though being treated like a child should have bothered Subaru, seeing Emilia's pleasant, satisfied smile made such minor concerns irrelevant.

Emilia, not noticing that Subaru had completely fallen for her smile, abruptly clapped her hands.

"Oh, right, now is good. Subaru, sit over here for a moment?"

Emilia sat on the grass with her legs out to the side, patting the ground beside her to invite Subaru over.

"You call, I come running! What, what? The timing's good for what exactly? No matter what your request, Subaru Natsuki leaves no itch unscratched. If there's a place you can't reach, just command me to scratch it and I shall obey!"

"All I said was to sit beside me. That's a bigger reaction than I expected. What should I do?"

Unsurprisingly, Emilia made a pained smile at Subaru's fierce enthusiasm.

"Err...yesterday was your first day at work. How did it go? Did you do well?"

"Ah, yeah, failed at eighty percent of it!"

"I see; you're certainly full of confi... Eh? Failed? Eighty percent of it?"

"Er, maybe eighty's overstating it... Maybe more like six, no... seventy-five."

"That still means you flunked a lot of things..."

Emilia acted like she felt responsible somehow for Subaru's unexpectedly low rating of his own work. But she immediately lifted her face in a show of concern.

"Ah, but, hey, that meant you got twenty percent of work right on your first day, huh? That's fine; I'm sure it's all right. Be confident, now."

"Hey, you're right! It's a long road, but if I start at twenty percent, I can raise that little by little from here!"

"Don't be conceited. Reflect on it properly."

"If you're going to start sweet, why can't you end sweet?! Ah, no, it's nothing, very sorry."

Subaru, cowed by the pressure of Emilia's glare, shrank and nodded meekly.

In any case...

"I do feel like I'm eating Ram's and Rem's dust somehow. Getting twenty percent right while trying my best means that's just where I'm at, so no helping it. I'll just expect better from myself going forward."

"If you're going to be that optimistic about it, there's nothing more I can say, but..."

Upon hearing Subaru's positive declaration, Emilia tapered her lips into something that resembled a pout. The cute childlike behavior she indulged in from time to time never failed to light a fiery yearning in Subaru.

But he restrained himself, smothering the embers.

Subaru pointed at Emilia with a finger from each hand in a comical gesture.

"So, so, you see, I'm spending every day with maid sisters tutoring me while I devote myself to life as a servant. If I get tired of that life I'll just come running to Emilia-tan's lap, so leave it open, okay?"

"...I was only half listening to that, but it sounded kind of all right."

"Harsh assessment with a cute face! Well, if that half was the lap part, that's A-OK! Like I said, leave that lap open for me for tonight, Emilia-tan... Don't steal my spot, Puck!"

Subaru thrust a finger at Puck, calling out his name. Puck reacted to the declaration of war with a casual flick of his own whiskers.

"It doesn't matter what you say, Lia's pact with me means her heart and body are already mine. There's no changing our relationship meow, meow!"

Emilia grabbed Puck's ears for his incorrigible behavior and tossed him into the air to make him ponder the error of his ways.

"Goodness, don't change the terms of our pact behind my back."

Maybe Puck was just used to it, for despite that, he simply landed in Emilia's hands and happily wriggled in them with a look of complete calm. Subaru couldn't help but feel envious of their relationship.

"Well, now that I've energized myself I'd better start the morning work."

"What do you mean, 'energized yourself'?"

"By teasing Emilia-tan."

"There you go again. If all you do is tease people, they won't trust anything you say when you're actually telling the truth, you know?"

"That sounds like something out of a fairy tale. If that happens, guess I'll be reaping what I sowed..."

"Wait, *you're* telling *me* that...?"

With Emilia giving him an exasperated look, Subaru sent a bright smile back her way as he rose, brushing off his backside.

"They'll be seriously ticked if I don't get going, though. I'm supposed to help them with this morning's breakfast. Emilia-tan, you don't like eating green beppers, do you? I'll make sure they're not on your plate."

"You have to eat even the veggies you don't li— When did I tell you I don't like green beppers?"

Emilia tilted her head with a questioning look as Subaru departed with a little smile and a wave.

She actually had talked to him about it; he'd even seen her distaste for them with his own eyes.

He focused on staying on the path, always joking whenever Emilia set eyes on him.

—He had to focus, focus, always focus, to keep the smile on his face.

5

Emilia watched Subaru wander off until he was out of sight before letting out a small sigh.

Puck, watching Subaru from her palm, abruptly looked up when he realized Emilia was now watching him.

"That's a gloomy face. What's wrong?"

"I just feel down somehow. I can't really put it into words."

Emilia cringed at the wishy-washy attempt to express her internal unease. But what caught in her throat didn't have a chance to become proper words as she sighed again.

Puck's pink nose twitched as he watched Emilia's conflict.

"You're worried about Subaru? It's not often you worry about other people like this."

"Don't go off and phrase it like I'm some sort of klutz at dealing with people. I'm not bad at getting close to others… I just haven't had many chances to do it!"

Emilia puffed out her cheeks, an expression she refused to show to anyone save Puck.

Though it looked like the act of a spoiled brat, it was a testament to Emilia's absolute faith in Puck. The spirit, fully accepting her trust, smiled up at her like she was his own daughter.

He offered a nod toward the delicate emotions Emilia couldn't put into words.

"Well, it's no surprise it's throwing you off. Because this has become a little bit of a problem."

"Bit of a…problem?"

He'd said the words in a casual manner, but Emilia's face grew tense; she couldn't miss the tone behind them.

By nature, Puck behaved exactly the same no matter how high-pressure the situation. She didn't know if it was because he was a spirit or if it was simply his personality that made him that way, but he reserved grave observations as a spirit to provide input for hard, important decisions—namely Emilia's.

Seeing Emilia's breath catch, Puck casually toyed with his whiskers. He still spoke in his peculiar manner to the end.

"I only touched him a little, but Subaru's mind is all scrambled. What he shows on the outside doesn't match the inside. At this rate, it won't be long before he reaches the end of his rope."

6

The high-pitched *ting* and the sound of pottery breaking made Ram's eyebrows shoot up in surprise.

The young manservant prancing around like a dancer—Subaru—raised his voice as he grabbed hold of a broom and dustpan.

"It's okay! It's okay! Don't worry! I've got this!"

He quickly cleaned up the ceramic fragments scattered at his feet and pretended to wipe sweat off his brow.

When he looked at Rem, who'd stared at him during the entire sequence, he flashed his teeth in a fiendish smile.

"Don't worry. I took care of it super fast, and there wasn't even one casualty."

"I think your concern is praiseworthy, but were you not the one who dropped the vase, Subaru? I need to get a replacement vase, wipe the floor, put the flowers in order…"

"No, it's all right! I can get a vase and put the flowers in myself! Go ahead and focus on your own work!"

Driving Rem off almost like he was ordering her, Subaru headed to the storage for furnishings and returned several minutes later with a proper vase. He promptly put the new vase in the same place as the old and added water and the flowers, returning things to as they were.

"Whew. Feels good to get a job done, Remrin."

"It is extra work you made for yourself, but at least you took care of it... Subaru, where did you hear where the spare vases are? From Sister?"

"Mm, ah, er... Right, your big sis! It's me we're talking about here—she was pretty sure I'd break one at some point. So she told me in advance exactly where to get a new vase!"

Listening to the clumsy excuse, Rem did not think, *That is Sister for you, such foresight.* She was less concerned with the vase and more with the fact that Subaru had such a grasp of the mansion's layout that he'd retrieved the broom and dustpan to clean the broken vase with, then gone to grab a spare, without any hesitation.

Rem really doubted someone working for only a day or two would do such a thing.

That said, rather than raise her suspicions...

"You all right? You're so swamped with work, go ahead and send some my way. I'll do it; I'll do anything."

...He was so friendly about it that she just couldn't put a finger on the problem.

It was not the behavior of someone bearing malice or hostility, but neither was it how a guileless person behaved. More to the point, for someone hiding something, his facade was riddled with openings.

He looked like he was genuinely trying to get used to the job and attempting to get along well with Rem and Ram.

Rem knitted her brow, looking like she was warding off the emotions bearing down on her at his earnestness.

The sight of Subaru striving so hard, even when no one acknowledged it, stirred up a throbbing ache in her chest.

"Subar—"

"Oh, I forgot the work Ramchi asked me to do! Sorry, I'd better hurry up and take care of that! I'll hook back up with you right after!"

Subaru rushed into the hallway faster than she could call out to stop him. Rem withdrew the fingers she'd reached out to him with, looking over her shoulder as if she should discuss her misgivings with her older sister, but—

"—No, it is not enough to trouble Sister over."

Rem walked toward her own work space, trying to wrap up her remaining work and reduce the lingering ache in her chest in the process.

7

—I feel sick.

"Oh, Ramchi! Did you see me? I'm doing pretty well with a kitchen knife after just one day learning it, huh? Maybe my talent is taking bloom!"

—I feel sick I feel sick I feel sick.

"Remrin, look, look! Right now, my fingers are miraculously imbued with the skill that makes such fine workmanship possible! The power of illusion!"

—I feel sick I feel sick I feel sick I feel sick I feel sick I feel sick.

"Meeting Emilia-tan really puts my heart in a jumble! It's too sinful! I feel *so* guilty!"

—I feel sick I feel sick I feel sick I feel sick I feel sick I feel sick I feel sick I feel sick I feel sick I feel sick I feel sick I feel sick I feel sick I feel sick I feel sick I feel sick I feel sick I feel sick.

He kept a smile nailed to his face as he continued trying to sound playful. He wrestled with his entrusted tasks full force, resolutely attacking problems with no fear of failure, and when he was done, he wandered around looking for more to do.

He had to. He *needed* to.

He didn't have a single second to waste. It was like a video game where you simulated in your head every potential outcome to a particular event. He had to manage the event flags. That was his specialty, right? The more he encountered them, the better his odds.

—I should be able to make them smile more. I should be able to make them laugh more.

His actions were meaninglessly exaggerated. He tried to convince them he was an oblivious fool. He tried not to make them think he was useless. His head spun and spun, always weighing his actions.

Subaru constantly kept watch for anything that seemed remotely out of the ordinary. He couldn't let his guard slip for a single instant, never mind a second.

—*I can't make a mistake. I just can't. I can't.*

Warning bells rang without pause in his head at repeating things over and over.

Danger, danger, they announced.

He hadn't advanced an inch since reaching this other world, but he felt his sensitivity to peril, at least, had grown more acute.

"See, Ramchi? I'm not slacking off here. I'm totally doing so much work. Almost enough that my superior could just go back to her room and take a nap, you know?"

He evaded the situation with an irregular approach, casually glossing things over with a charming smile.

He wondered if he could really do it. Could Subaru Natsuki really pull this off? He hadn't given them reason to doubt him, had he? He paid ten, no, a hundred times more attention, not only in front of Ram but Rem as well.

He played Subaru Natsuki, erasing the unnatural with the natural.

It was simple. It was all up to him. He had to pay not the slightest bit of attention to what anyone living at the mansion really thought, bathing himself in innocence and lack of restraint, until he seemed like a lazy pig who took whatever was given unto him.

As far as the world was concerned, he knew nothing, could do nothing, noticed nothing, and that was all there was to him.

He continued to loiter about, wearing his charming grin like a mask.

He was inside the mansion. He didn't know who would pop out or when. His free time wasn't free. He spent all his spare time examining his past actions and forming plans for what he'd do in the hours to come.

"Wh...o...a..."

He suddenly felt the urge to throw up.

A slight moan slipped from the corner of his mouth, but Subaru's smile did not falter whatsoever.

He kept his expression steady, skipping as he walked, practically dancing his way as he slipped into the nearest guest room. And he stepped over to the room's lavatory when…

"…Blehhch. Uuogh, uuuuughnn…!"

The contents of his already-empty stomach poured out.

He vomited up every bit of the food and drink that had entered his body. That time, everything came out as sickly yellow stomach acid. And the internal pain that had made him spew it all continued to ache.

The nausea wouldn't go away. He gulped down running water until he was full, then expelled it immediately afterward. This repeated several times, his stomach heaving like it was cleaning itself out.

"Haaah…haaah…haaah…"

Subaru roughly wiped his mouth with his sleeve, his face pale and his breath ragged.

The pressure was killing him. If he kept this up without any time to rest his mind, he felt like he'd waste away and expire from that alone.

He wanted to laugh at himself for putting himself in this situation, but not even the faintest smile would form on his lips.

All that welled up from within his chest was anxiety and despair.

—Am I really pulling it off?

The time he'd gotten along with everyone best was during that first loop, when he knew nothing.

From the second loop on, he'd been so obsessed with the first loop that it caused problems in his work and personal relations. That was probably a major reason why he hadn't earned the sisters' trust.

Consequently, Subaru was using the first loop as his model this time around. That said, he'd failed in the second loop by trying to copy the first. That meant he had to do things better than the first time.

Meaning, all he had to do was put everything into any work he found in front of him and do well at it.

"But that still only gets me fifty points... Can't get a hundred if I don't figure out who the shaman is..."

Merely evading death by the sisters' hands wouldn't protect Subaru from the menace of the shaman.

On the morning of the fifth day, someone in the mansion would be crying. It might be over Subaru; it might be over Rem.

Subaru really wanted to get information on the shaman, to turn it over to the others so they could plan a counterattack, but he could not. Even if he suggested courses of action, they didn't trust him enough to act on them yet; he also couldn't divulge the source of his information.

And Subaru would get a little taste of hell if he broke the prohibition on speaking to others about Return by Death.

Pain scared him, but what terrified him even more was meeting the fingertips of that black cloud.

He had to win the others' trust and expose the shaman's identity.

Time was extremely short—enough to make him feel like the walls were closing in.

He had to do something, but he was rushing down a blind alley.

The night before, he'd been held captive by that vortex of helplessness, unable to get a wink of sleep, no answer forthcoming. He felt powerless, having well-founded reasons for his anxiety but being unable to find any solution for it.

He'd paid with his life to come back, yet there he was, an incapable fool.

"Ah, damn it... I'm being pathetic."

He couldn't fail here. His back was against the wall.

Even if it was a life he'd thrown away, a life that ought to have been over, he was afraid of losing it again.

It was his fifth time. Even Subaru wasn't optimistic enough to think he could come back again.

His spirit was in tatters from his mind continually being bashed. If he wasn't at the brink, he wouldn't have made the decision to struggle with all his might.

He simply lacked the courage. He was mediocre. Ordinary in every way.

The more he learned how small a person he truly was, the more he grew to despise himself.

"Stupid, stupid. This isn't the time to whine and cry…"

If he had time to complain, then he had time to run his frivolous mouth and make a better impression.

Shaking off his nausea, Subaru slapped his stiff cheeks in self-rebuke and headed out of the guest room.

It was free time right now, but he didn't have a moment for a break. He couldn't waste a second on rest.

He had to find where Ram and Rem had gone and—

"I've finally found you."

He was putting his thoughts in order when he heard someone call to him from behind.

When he looked back, he saw Emilia standing there, breathing slightly heavily.

The instant Subaru set eyes on Emilia, his mind clicked and switched to a different gear.

He forgot all about the pain in his stomach, the ache in his chest, and the stifling feeling, turning everything toward Emilia. His cheeks bent into a smile.

"Oh, Emilia-tan calling me by name. I'm happy, embarrassed—it's so rare! Your word is my command! I will pass through fire and water for you, even loot sellers!"

Subaru shoved his emotions to the back of his mind for Emilia with a lot more verve than was necessary.

He prided himself on quick comebacks, but Emilia had a different reaction to seeing it than he had expected. He expected an exasperated look and a sigh or something, but instead…

"…Subaru…"

"Wait, now, if you're the Emilia-tan I know, you should be… *Hurk!* Are you an imposter?! But could someone else really copy a beautiful girl wrapped in such an adorable package?!"

His ridiculous humor invited amazement, but Emilia's reaction to even this was muted.

Defying all his expectations, Emilia looked at Subaru, her eyes filled with…pity.

—*Not good*, his instincts warned him.

"Eh? You've gone quiet. This isn't some sort of prank you're playing on a guy who gets carried away on tangents, right? You know, like me!"

This is wrong, said a voice inside his brain, over and over.

Emilia wasn't shocked or angry; she was simply staring at Subaru with pained eyes.

—*I wonder if the comedian's mask I'm wearing slipped somehow.*

The instant worry wormed its way in as Subaru remembered the kitty cat always hovering by Emilia's side. That cat was also a spirit able to read the subconscious thoughts of others.

It was only then that Subaru realized that the jig was up.

The charming smile plastered onto his face vanished, replaced by a look like that of a child fearful of being scolded.

What a joke. She'd seen through him time and time again while he danced in an effort to hide it all. More than that, Emilia was the one he least wanted to know; his tiny bit of pride at pulling the wool over her eyes was destroyed.

A silence fell between them.

Subaru could no longer find words to say. Emilia looked like she was trying to find some herself, without success.

—*I'm disappointing Emilia. I didn't want that to happen, above all else.*

But Subaru didn't know what excuse he could form. He opened his mouth several times, stopping each time, unable to find the right words.

Seeing words fail Subaru, Emilia abruptly murmured "all right" to herself quietly before continuing.

"Subaru. Come with me."

"…Ah?"

"Just come on."

Emilia grabbed Subaru's arm, dragging him along into the guest room right beside them. A questioning look came over Subaru about going back to the room he'd just left. But Emilia left Subaru hanging as she put her hands on her hips and looked around the room. When she pointed at the floor, her voice rang like a silver bell, as always.

"All right, Subaru. Sit."

He followed her finger downward. The carpeted floor belonged to a room no one was using but was cleaned regularly nonetheless. Granted, it was soft enough to sleep on, but…

"If I'm going to be sitting, why not the bed or a chair? Why the floor specifica—"

"Just sit already!"

"Yes, with pleasure!"

Cowed by the strong tone she had never used, Subaru dove onto the floor without hesitation and sat properly on his knees. Emilia nodded, apparently satisfied, and stood right beside him.

Naturally, this left Subaru looking up at Emilia from a submissive position, but wicked thoughts never entered his mind. Instead, he was desperately trying to figure out what her intentions were.

Emilia's voice sounded quietly from her throat.

"…Okay."

She seemed to have said it for her own benefit. Emilia took a deep breath and sat right beside Subaru, kneeling just as he was.

Subaru's heart thumped at Emilia sitting within touching distance, but his sideways glance at her pale face could not tell him what she was thinking. He belatedly realized that her cheeks were flushed; even her ears were red.

"This is a special occasion, all right?"

"—Eh?"

Something pressed against the back of Subaru's head faster than he could properly voice his doubts. Already kneeling, his body offered no resistance as it bent forward—until a very soft sensation hit him.

"The position's a little awkward, and, mm…kind of prickly."

Something shifted around under his head as he heard Emilia's fairly bashful-sounding voice from right overhead.

In surprise, he looked up; the sight before him made his eyes go wide.

Right above him, Emilia's face was so close that they were almost touching. His eyes reflected a beautiful face that was inverted. Subaru belatedly grasped, *Oh, I'm upside down looking up at her.*

This distance, her upside-down position, the soft sensation under his head…

—Subaru mentally searched for terms to describe it and found exactly one.

"Lap…pillow?"

"It's embarrassing, so please don't say it out loud. And you're not allowed to look this way. Close your eyes."

She gave his forehead a light slap, using the palm of her hand to cover his eyes, obstructing his field of vision.

However, Subaru moved Emilia's resisting hand aside and dragged the words out.

"Emilia-tan, you're the best when you're embarrassed…but what is this? When did I do something to earn a reward like this?"

"You don't need to put up that front right now. "

She smacked his forehead again. But this time Emilia left her hand on it, stroking Subaru's hair with her fingers. He squinted at the ticklish feeling.

"You asked me to let you rest on my lap when you were tired, didn't you, Subaru? So that's what I'm doing. It won't be like this all the time, but today's special."

"Special? Come on, it's not even the end of the second day here. My body's not weak enough to keel over from overwork that fast…"

"I can tell you're beat-up just by looking at you. You won't go into the details and tell me, will you? I don't think this'll make everything better, but…it's the only thing I can do, so…"

Her compassionate gaze made it hard to brush her off. Her fingers had parted his black hair; she began to gently stroke his forehead like he was a little boy.

Subaru burst out laughing and tried to twist away from Emilia's fingers.

He had promised himself to stay strong in front of Emilia. To say this was all a misunderstanding. To say he wouldn't do anything as unseemly and uncool as that.

"Ha-ha… Emilia-tan, you, doing that…for…me…"

Yet his voice was shrill. His throat caught, and the next words wouldn't come out.

Subaru couldn't switch mental gears when he felt her soft fingertips stroking his forehead.

"You're tired, aren't you?"

"I—I can still do…more. I'm totally…all right…"

"Have you been having trouble?"

"You're being so nice to me, I mean, I'm gonna blush. If you keep doing that, I'm…gonna… Ha-ha…"

Subaru's reply to her brief question sounded like complete lies. Even *he* could tell that his words sounded hollow and empty.

Then Emilia gently drew her face close to Subaru's.

"It's been hard for you, hasn't it?"

"—!"

She sounded like she pitied him. She sounded like she sympathized with him. She sounded like she cared for him.

That was all it took for Subaru's walls to collapse.

They crumbled, fell apart, and came crashing down all at once.

All the powerful emotions he'd tried to keep bottled up hadn't gone away in the slightest and came rushing out.

"It was…hard. It was really, rough. I was really, scared. I was really sad, enough that I thought I was gonna die. It hurt so much…!"

"Yeah."

"I—I tried. I really tried. I did everything I could. I desperately tried to do everything right…! I did! Really, really. I've never tried to do anything that hard before!"

"Yeah, I know."

"It's because I like it here… This place, it's precious to me…! That's why I was dying to have it back. I was afraid. I was so afraid to see that day again…and I hated it. I hated myself for that!"

He couldn't control his emotions.

The initial explosion had blown the dam wide open, a deluge of tears marring the smiling mask over his cowardly face.

The tears wouldn't stop. His nose was runny. His mouth was awash in some sort of weird liquid as Subaru's sobbing became harder to listen to with each passing moment.

It was a sorry sight: a grown man with his head on a girl's lap, bawling his eyes out. It was pathetic enough that he could die, but the warmth filling him might just kill him, too.

Emilia made gentle sounds of understanding as she listened to Subaru weep.

There was no way she actually understood what Subaru was saying. And yet, the kindness of her voice brought relief to Subaru's heart.

He didn't understand why. Maybe he just wanted it to be so.

But it was true nonetheless that Subaru felt saved by her warmth.

And so, a flood of tears flowed from Subaru as he continued to cry on Emilia's lap.

He cried, he cried, he wailed, and at some point, the sobs faded into the distance.

—The only noise that filled the guest room after that was the sound of quiet sleep.

8

As Subaru sank into slumber, he felt the presence of heat deep inside his chest.

Subaru knew now what that emotion was.

The throbbing in Subaru's chest had grown stronger each time he looked at Emilia, spoke with her, felt the touch of her fingertips—but he hadn't had a name for it before.

When he thought of her, his body was afflicted by the hot pangs of that troublesome illness known as *love*.

Once a person became aware of it, he lost all will to fight against the disease.

Subaru was no exception. After all—

No matter how much he got hurt, no matter what pain he endured, no matter how often he tasted despair, it was all to save Emilia.

Everything was so he could spend his days walking by Emilia's side.

—Even if Subaru Natsuki died again and again, that love would live on.

9

Emilia was gently stroking Subaru's hair as he slept when Rem arrived at the guest room.

Opening the door without a sound, Rem saw Emilia inside and opened her mouth, but she closed it when Emilia put a finger to her own lips.

"Shh."

Rem narrowed her eyes a bit, walking over as she looked at the two of them nestled close together on the floor.

"Subaru is merely asleep?"

"Yes. Hee-hee, he's like a little boy. He looks so peaceful when I stroke his head like this."

Emilia seemed to enjoy petting Subaru, as she prodded Rem for agreement. Rem replied with a quiet shake of her head.

"It seems Subaru will not be able to work any further today."

"Yeah, he gets the rest of today off. He's a *very* naughty boy for taking time off on his second day. When he's all better, make sure to punish him, okay?"

Emilia made a small smile and returned to toying with Subaru's head.

She appeared to have no intention of moving the sleeping Subaru to free up her legs. Rem, reading Emilia's intent, quietly looked down at Subaru, who seemed to be deeply asleep.

He looked so innocent. There was not even the slightest trace of tension on his childlike face.

It was completely different from his strained attempt at light-heartedness when last they had spoken during work. It was enough to make her earlier suspicion seem incredibly stupid.

"It is hard to think of that when you see him sleeping like this, though."

Rem seemed to be murmuring that more to herself than to Emilia as she gave Subaru's hair a light caress with her fingers.

His ignorance of the world, like an innocent babe, made Rem's lips slacken just a little.

"I will inform Sister that Subaru is of no use for today. We must reallot today's chores."

Rem left things at that, bowing politely as she turned to leave.

She started to go find her sister. Around this time, she would still be cleaning up the dining hall. There, they would rearrange their schedule for the day.

"Rem…"

Abruptly called, Rem stopped and gently turned her whole body around.

Emilia was sitting below her on the floor. In spite of that, Rem mysteriously felt a powerful pressure coming from Emilia's gaze, like Rem was the one who stood lower.

Emilia, not noticing Rem's small measure of surprise, spoke in a quiet voice.

"Subaru is a good boy."

"—"

Rem responded with a single, solemn bow.

Then, without another word, she headed to the door and left Subaru and Emilia behind in the guest room.

She mulled over Emilia's statement as she walked down the hallway.

Even Rem did not notice the slight tremble on the side of her neutral visage.

—But the faintest trace of a vile odor remained lodged in a corner of Rem's mind.

CHAPTER 2
I CRIED AND SCREAMED AND WILL CRY NO MORE

1

"Borrowing a girl's lap, letting her caress my head, and falling into a peaceful sleep... By itself you'd think it was awesome, but man..."

Subaru said things like that over and over, red to the tips of his ears as he plucked a bit of hair from his head.

He thought back to the scene several hours before, when he'd spectacularly laid bare his soul.

"So I was a big crybaby in front of my sweetheart, fell asleep with tears on my face and a runny nose. Plus, I had her lap to myself for hours on end... This is like a humiliation game."

He thought back to the sensation of Emilia's knees, as well as the price they had paid to convey it to him.

The spectacle had left Emilia's skirt all a mess from his runny nose. No matter what problems Subaru had been going through, this was inexcusable, even if just from a hygienic view.

Still, Emilia hadn't rocked him awake in all that time, nor did she hold it against Subaru as he earnestly apologized for dirtying her clothes.

"That's fine if it makes you feel a little better. Besides, you really don't understand, Subaru."

"Eh?"

"It's more satisfying for the other person to hear a single thank-you than a dozen apologies. I don't want you to apologize for something I wanted to offer you, so there."

The way she pressed a finger to his apologizing lips and winked at him would bowl over any man. Indeed, Subaru bowled over right on the spot.

Now that Subaru knew he loved her, everything she said and did, that included, seemed covered in glitter and gloss.

Emilia headed off to change clothes in her room. Subaru kept wandering around the mansion in a dreamy state for a little while before finally regaining his senses and clutching his head at what he'd done.

"Oh man, I've totally done it now. Emilia's the one I didn't want to look weak in front of. Is there anything more embarrassing I could've done? I seriously can't look her in the eye now!"

"...Is that what a person says when entering someone's room late at night, I wonder?"

The way Subaru pressed the middle of his thigh against the stool and writhed around it put the girl in the dress—Beatrice—in a particularly bad mood, bringing a dreadful scowl over her adorable face.

After parting ways with Emilia, Subaru had it in his head that he couldn't let anyone else see him, so his feet carried him to the archive of forbidden books, and thus beyond anyone's reach. Though, he liked tweaking the nose of the girl in charge of it, too.

"Don't say that, Beako. We're friends, right?"

"What kind of relationship do you think— Wait, what did you call me just now, I wonder?"

Beatrice raised an eyebrow with a twitch of her cheek when Subaru clapped his hands.

"Beako. I think nicknames are an indispensable way to show my friendship. You're the only one in the mansion so far who didn't like it even a little bit, though..."

He thought back to the last loop, when the loneliness and despair had been driven home.

One could even say he was cajoling her into bringing sophistry and threats at him. It was from such humble beginnings that a firm pact had been established between them.

In the end, Subaru had unilaterally severed the deal. But Beatrice had exploited the vagueness of the details to continue to protect him.

Even if Beatrice had forgotten, Subaru would never forget how he felt back then.

"—So I don't care what you think of me, I'm going to call you Beako. It's the greatest sign of affection I can give you!"

"That does not please me *whatsoever*! What is with that overbearing goodwill?! Is it merely distasteful or completely disgusting, I wonder?!"

"Hey, what's with that way of talking?! I'm thanking you from the bottom of my heart here. This is no time to make fun!"

"If you're going to insist that what you said just now was not meant in jest, you and I are no longer engaged in conversation. It may look like dialogue, but it is not!"

She informed him that if conversation was supposed to be a game of catch, this was more like rugby.

He was showing considerable affection in an appropriately Subaru-like way, but that seemed to be lost on Beatrice.

"Well, I'll set that aside, but I'll still call you Beako."

"Such single-minded resolve is quite unnecessary. What would happen if I simply do not respond to that name, I wonder?"

"Don't say cold things like that, Beako."

"..."

Subaru called out to Beatrice, but silently keeping her gaze lowered to her book, she made no reply. Apparently she meant what she had said earlier.

While Beatrice acted stubborn, Subaru grudgingly walked over and paced around the stool.

"What's wrong, Beako? You look glum, Beako. Are you all right, Beako? If there's something wrong, you can talk to me, Beako. Mm? What is it, Beako? We can do this, Beako. Beako, Beako!"

"I have never seen *anyone* as annoying as you! What is with you, I wonder?!"

Someone as thin-skinned as Beatrice was natural prey for someone born with a talent for getting on other people's nerves like Subaru. He pumped a fist, the corners of his lips twisting as Beatrice's shoulders shook in anger.

"Actually, I've got an admission to make. I'm backed into a corner and really need your help."

—He explained to the curly-haired girl the conclusion he'd formed after pathetically bawling his eyes out.

2

While on Emilia's lap, all the ugly feelings and tears built up inside Subaru had come pouring out. What remained were Subaru's pure personal desires.

—He loved Emilia.

He'd thought he loved her before, but now he truly knew what falling for someone meant. It was love at first sight. Just hearing her voice made his heart skip a beat. Just talking with her was so pleasant it felt like a dream.

He couldn't leave this girl who put herself in harm's way for others.

That's why I love her, he had thought, but now he sincerely understood what he'd felt. She was the first one to save Subaru when he was summoned to another world without anyone to depend on.

And, when he'd been backed into a dark alley of despair, it was she who had saved his dying heart. She'd saved both his life and his heart.

—He could no longer think of living in a world without Emilia.

He loved spending his days with Emilia at the mansion. He loved learning all sorts of things about the world. He loved Ram, who'd taken such care of him in spite of her blunt tongue. He really loved Emilia. He loved Rem, who insulted him with polite language but always showed him how to do things. He was enveloped by goodwill toward everyone living at the mansion. Subaru wanted to stay there forever.

Those overflowing feelings filled his chest to bursting.

But on the other side of that happy coin—

He loved Emilia. He despaired at lacking the power to protect her. Life at the mansion had grown stale. He didn't know where or when he'd be found out. He feared Ram, who commanded Blades of Wind that could slice his throat. He was terrified of Rem and her skull-crushing iron ball. Roswaal's disturbing madness could lead him to command the twins to eliminate Subaru without mercy. Every time he woke up, he checked whether he was still alive, and he could sense himself cracking under his own constant vigilance against despair.

These, too, were Subaru's true, indelible feelings.

Emilia had saved Subaru before the friction in his mind had roasted Subaru from the inside out.

By consoling him, Emilia had pulled his heart back from the brink.

Thinking about her filled him with life and energy. Emilia was what kept his urge to flee in check.

"In other words, E M D (Emilia-tan's Majorly Divine)!"

Beatrice responded to Subaru's declaration by acting astounded and shooting him an annoyed grimace.

"Did you say something exceedingly stupid just now, I wonder?"

"Not at all. I'm putting my top priorities back in order."

"Let us return to the topic at hand… You say you want my help? What do you mean, I wonder?"

"Yeah, I'm pretty serious about that, like enough to beg God for help. I can't think of anyone else I can go to."

In the present situation, Emilia was, of course, the member of the mansion he could place the most trust in—but she was also the most important part of Subaru's life. In other words, the absolute last thing he wanted to do was put her in danger. To Subaru, who normally prioritized his own life, Emilia's life weighed much heavier than his on the scale.

That being the case, he couldn't go to Puck for help, either, which left—

"Beako. She's actually pretty sweet. And softer than she looks."

"I don't understand your meaning, but I do sense that you are mocking me."

"That's not my intent at all... Actually, the way things are in the mansion right now, you're the only one I can rely on."

Of course, he couldn't come clean to Ram and Rem, let alone Roswaal.

Except for Emilia, Beatrice was truly the only person in the mansion who he could trust.

"Please. I'm begging you."

Subaru was kneeling on the floor before Beatrice, bowing his head as he petitioned for aid.

Subaru needed a lantern to light the way so that he could bring an end to the chain of despair.

"I need your help. I want to set everything right and protect the place where I can be happy. And that's no good if it doesn't include everyone here."

"—"

Subaru, touching his head to the floor, looked up at Beatrice after a long silence.

"...Beatrice?"

The conflict he saw in her eyes made his breath catch.

Beatrice knit her brows and bit her lip as she glared at Subaru. And yet, despite the ferocity of her gaze, she looked on the verge of tears.

"—"

She opened her mouth to speak, but her gaze wavered as she found herself unable to find the words.

Beatrice's heart had been shaken. He had to make her speak to him.

"Listen to me, Beatrice. I understand why you don't want to help me out of hand. To you, I'm a weirdo and a stranger who wandered in just the other day."

"…If you know that much, you do not need to hear it from my lips, do you?"

"You're the one who patched me up. Thank you. I know you don't know this, but I have a mountain of other things I need to thank you for. And here I am asking you for help again… It's pretty pathetic. It's a miserable sight, really, but you're the only one I have."

He laid out all his cards on the table.

It was the lowest form of begging—pushy and self-centered and with no regard for Beatrice's feelings whatsoever.

With Subaru lowering his head in nothing but earnestness, wearing sincerity on his sleeve, Beatrice made a very typical snort.

"You are a worm crawling on the ground, wailing about your own powerlessness. Do you have any pride at all, I wonder?"

"I know what's important to me. I'll bow my head ten times or a hundred times and pound the floor if that's what it takes."

He was too much of a weakling to obsess over petty pride.

Subaru kept his head down as he continued to plead for her aid.

He knew it was a cowardly way of doing things. During his five loops, he'd continued to quarrel with Beatrice during their encounters along the way.

That's how he knew.

Beatrice acted like she was blowing him off, but—

"You may…raise your head."

The moment the soft voice reached his ears, Subaru believed his craven request had been granted.

He was acutely aware of his own pettiness and he resented himself for his insincere behavior toward Beatrice.

But even that had been necessary to make the girl named Beatrice come to her decision.

That was how the rather simple man named Subaru Natsuki had seen it, but…

"Bea…"

"Take this, would you?"

"*Bwah!*"

But that miserable, heartfelt face met the merciless sole of a shoe.

Subaru was still prostrate as his head alone lifted from the floor, with his formless sound of anguish echoing around the archive.

Subaru remained in that awkward, bent-back position, making an incoherent yell as she stomped him a few more times.

"Hey...this is...!"

"You could think on it a hundred times and you would never comprehend the work I go through. No matter how many silver coins you gather, they will never equal the sacred glow of a gold coin. Do you understand, I wonder?"

"Er, if you get a few thousand silver coins they'll equal it, I'm sure. It's just a matter of comparable value, right? Or maybe you're just bad at math?"

"Will you stop looking at me like a pitiable child, I wonder?! Are those the eyes of someone who was just begging me?!"

And so, Beatrice and Subaru resumed their bickering.

It was a pointless battle that had begun for no particular reason, repeated several times across different worlds. As he continued his familiar banter with Beatrice, he thought on some level that the pathetic stubbornness inside him was pretty moronic.

"All right, then, I'll play my trump card. If you cooperate with me, I'll give you a reward of equal value, you hear?"

"Do you think the likes of me would be lured by any reward you can muster, I wonder?"

"How about this? Because I saved Emilia at the capital, I get to borrow Puck. And Puck said if I want to swap that for something else, I only need to ask... You see what I'm getting at here?"

Beatrice's expression changed. Subaru smiled unpleasantly as he brought all his negotiation skills to bear.

Now that it involved a reward, she agreed to reluctantly cooperate with Subaru.

Subaru thought it was pretty silly to settle things by offering up Puck on a silver platter. He knew the little magic user would go for it, but still...

3

It hadn't exactly been a warm and fuzzy process, but Subaru had finally managed to win Beatrice's cooperation.

He'd repent of pushing things on to a little girl because of his own powerlessness *after* all the problems were cleared up.

"…You want to know more about shamans?"

Subaru's cut-and-dry statement caused Beatrice to raise her shapely eyebrows with an air of disgust.

His top priority was to deal with the menace of the shaman's attack on the mansion without a moment to lose. A large part of why he asked Beatrice for help was so that her magic could counter the deadly curses.

Explaining as much as possible to Beatrice without getting to the heart of the matter was crucial for Subaru.

"I'll probably pay a price if I let too many cats out of the bag, so…"

When he'd tried to confess his Return by Death to Emilia, time had suddenly stopped all around Subaru as a black cloud took the shape of a hand and inflicted immense agony upon him.

Subaru's silent screams and the torture of having his heart crushed had robbed him of any notions of easy defiance.

As a result, Subaru was immensely wary of the black cloud, choosing his words very carefully as he continued to explain.

"I know there's such a thing as curses, but I don't know anything else beyond that they're different from magician and spirit stuff. I want to know more about them."

"It is rare for someone to ask about that. I wonder, does paying that bunch any heed get you anywhere?"

Like before, Beatrice's distaste toward even forming the word *curse* on her lips was considerable. Back then, he'd avoided pushing deeper into the matter, but that would not be the case this time.

"Curses are magic spells that exist only to cause trouble for other people and come from some country up north, right?"

"Is it not sufficient to know that much, I wonder? Curses invade their targets like a disease, limiting their movements and robbing them of their pure life forces... A tradition in very poor taste."

"Normally I'd say it depends on how you use them, but looks like you can't use them except to hurt people, huh?"

Reason enough to call these *curses*.

If curses were supernatural powers that existed to bring down others, the practice in his home world of putting needles into voodoo dolls probably counted. Well, not that he actually accepted the existence of the occult in *that* world...

Subaru sat up more, thinking about the things Beatrice had mentioned in a grave tone of voice.

"So, let me ask this... How do you defend against a curse?"

It was pretty tough to aim a counterattack at the shaman without knowing his identity. Subaru's one advantage was knowing in advance that an attack would take place. Consequently, figuring out a way to stop the shaman's attack in its tracks was a wonderful idea...in theory.

"You do not."

"—Eh?"

"No means exist to defend against a curse once it is activated. Once activated, you are finished. Isn't that what a curse is, I wonder?"

"I-isn't there any kind of Instant Death Resist...?!"

In a video game, you dealt with Lv. 1 Death type spells by casting Instant Death Resist in advance.

With the light at the end of the tunnel growing ever distant, Subaru pulled his hair, his brain on fire as it tried to come up with a new plan. He'd underestimated the situation. That reality sent Subaru's mind into free fall.

"—However, that is limited to curses that have activated."

"—Huh?"

The words spoken to Subaru a moment later made his eyes go wide.

Beatrice grinned with what seemed to be great delight.

She got me good, thought Subaru as the look on her face confirmed it; all he could do was open and close his mouth like a flounder in a mix of surprise and anger.

"Just as I said, there is no way to defend against a curse once it has been activated. However, an un-activated curse can be blocked. It simply requires a cleansing rite prior to activation, so anyone with the requisite skill would find removing it rather simple."

"I'll save getting angry for later... So, who can do that?"

"In this mansion, there's me, and of course Puckie. Beyond that, Roswaal and...the three little girls do not have the requisite experience, so no. Oh, and of course you cannot."

"I know that one only too well..."

He'd gone through hell because of his lack of resistance, not once but twice.

Subaru put aside his unpleasant memories as he raised a hand and asked Beatrice a question.

"So how would you know to use a rite before a curse activates?"

"Powerful curses place a commensurate burden upon the body. Perhaps magic and curses share that in common? The side effects of a curse are considerable. Could I say that they are deeply flawed, I wonder?"

"So...is there something you can do in advance to protect yourself?"

Subaru asked his question like he was hanging from a thread. In response, Beatrice closed her eyes for a while, licking her lips.

"Though it depends upon the specific details...there is an iron rule for curses."

"An iron...rule?"

With bated breath, Subaru prodded Beatrice to continue from where she'd left off.

And so she did.

"—Physical contact with the target. An absolute prerequisite, I wonder?"

"_____"

Subaru's brain spun round and round the instant that detail entered his skull.

The caster of a curse needed to touch his target. In other words, both times Subaru had suffered from the effects of the curse, he had made physical contact with the shaman beforehand. That narrowed the possibilities to—

"If it's no one here at the mansion, then…it's gotta be the village…"

Subaru had walked to the village both times he'd undergone Return by Death from suffering the effects of witchcraft.

When he thought about it more, he'd gone to the village midway through the fourth day both times.

At the village, the shaman had performed the rite for the curse, and that curse activated that night at the mansion—resulting in his death. That had been the pattern.

The shaman being at the village would explain why Rem had fallen prey to the curse during the last loop. That time, Subaru had never gone to the village, so Rem became the shaman's target instead. If Ram had gone, she would've been the target; if Subaru had gone there with her, no doubt he would've been the target again.

It connected. It connected *everything*.

The shaman was in Earlham Village. It was unclear whether the shaman was a resident or a visitor. If he was the latter, finding him wouldn't be all that hard. It was a village with a small population. A stranger's face immediately became known to all, just like Subaru's had. If the former, it'd have been a carefully premeditated crime, but…

"That doesn't seem likely."

In the prior incident, someone tried to throw a monkey wrench into Emilia's royal candidacy. But that candidacy didn't exist before the royal family suddenly died out only half a year beforehand. Emilia's name popping up on the candidate list probably took time, so that meant only three or four months to prepare at absolute most. A shaman would have had to infiltrate the village years beforehand to be considered a native.

"So the shaman's an outsider. Finding him won't be all that hard, either…"

Subaru voiced his thoughts out loud as he began to search for holes in his logic. It wasn't a bad idea to raise a hypothesis, even if you amended it as you went along.

As far as the shaman was concerned, he hadn't actually done anything yet. Short of his opponent being God or the Devil himself, it was impossible for his existence to be exposed as of yet.

Subaru mulled over the fact that he was still on the night of the second day. He had a long grace period before things were due to take a turn for the worse on the fourth.

In other words, it meant he could do his own preemptive strike on the shaman.

"I've got you by the tail now, damn it. I didn't die twice at your hands for nothing!"

Subaru, finally able to see his situation brightening, clenched a fist as his voice quivered with joy.

While Subaru delighted in the change in circumstances, Beatrice looked quite dissatisfied at having been dropped from the conversation. Her lovely cheeks reddened to emphasize the sourness of her gaze.

"What is that attitude in front of someone you asked for aid, I wonder? If what I spoke was of service, I think you should say as much to my face."

"Yeah, you're right! You saved my bacon; I can see the light thanks to you! I love you, Beako!"

"Wha—?!"

Subaru leaped over to Beatrice, picking up her very light body and twirling all around with her on the spot.

Despite her elaborate dress, the girl's body was as light as a feather. Subaru's spinning increased in synergy with the buoyancy of his mood.

"Let g— Would you put me down, I wonder?!"

"Ha-ha-ha, I could just fly in the sky right now! Nah, how 'bout we fly together, Beako?!"

"Fly all by your lonesome—!"

"Bwah?!"

She released magical energy from right above him, slamming him

hard enough to make him do a full leg split on the floor. The impact he felt on the top of his skull transferred to the rest of his body. Subaru's internal mana was all a jumble. His eyes were spinning as he continued to rest on his butt.

For her part, Beatrice landed with an elegant flutter of the hem of her skirt, turning her head and sending a snort Subaru's way.

"Do you see what happens when you get carried away with frivolity, I wonder?"

"That's not the only thing I saw. They're white!"

"—. —?! Take this, would you?!"

"Brfhh!"

Subaru took the second shot right between the eyes, sending him flying into a corner of the archive like a rag doll. He rolled head over heels before slamming into a bookshelf, bringing heavy books down upon his head.

He crawled his way out of the mountain of books, tears in his eyes from the many bumps and bruises.

"The friendship gauge goes down just a little and I get this?! If you're not happy with something, just say it, geez!"

"Being picked up like a little child, spun around in midair, having my panties seen, you speaking superficially lovey-dovey words, all of it! Is your entire existence a nuisance, I wonder?!"

"Hey, don't put down my existence; that's really sad stuff! I'm trying not to be a masochist here!"

Subaru hoped to find ways to improve himself, just like he'd found a chance to improve his circumstances.

Just because I'm powerless doesn't mean I have to be helpless, too, Subaru thought, nodding at his own internal rebuke.

"Anyway, the situation's a lot better than it was. It'll be hard waiting out the night, but tomorrow I'm heading to the village."

Let's find out who this shaman really is, he thought.

That'd probably mean going with either Ram or Rem. Considering they both had combat strength, it was a natural choice in case he ended up duking it out with the shaman then and there. If he could get rid of the vile shaman and raise his friendship gauge with both girls in the process, that'd be the grand finale bringing his first week at Roswaal Manor to a successful conclusion.

"Now that I think back on it, I sure went through a lot..."

He knew it was speaking too soon, but it was a light at the end of the tunnel even so. Surely no one could blame Subaru for feeling that way.

Shouldn't you be thinking of something else? he wondered. Looking up meant missing that which was right at his feet, didn't it? Subaru, a man of little nerve and much wariness, suddenly remembered...

"The scent...of the witch..."

"What do you mean, I wonder?"

"Right, the witch. Rem mentioned her. You did, too, Beako."

The moment the word *witch* formed on his lips, he remembered the various places he had encountered it. The witch was often treated as an abominable being by the residents of that world, but Subaru's only clue as to why was the broad outline given in the children's story "The Witch of Jealousy." That really bothered him all of a sudden.

After all, the road traveled by Subaru Natsuki had been peppered by references to her.

Subaru lifted up his face and looked at Beatrice, who was knitting her eyebrows.

He wasn't sure she'd even answer the question he was about to ask. It was grave enough that Ram had refused to answer it entirely, while Rem had used it as one of her justifications for attacking him.

He felt that even Emilia strongly resisted the topic.

"Beako, you know about the witch, right?"

"—"

The reply didn't come immediately. The word thrumming in her ears made Beatrice close her eyes, sinking into silence as if making sure she'd heard correctly. Her reaction left Subaru with no option beyond trying to keep calm and waiting.

When she suddenly murmured the words, Subaru's breath caught as his eyes went wide.

"She who drinks the world itself. Queen of the Castle of Shadows. The greatest of all disasters—the Witch of Jealousy."

Upon seeing Subaru's reaction, Beatrice let out a gloomy sigh.

"In this world, there is only one being indicated by the word *witch*. Should I add, it is even considered taboo to speak her name aloud, I wonder?"

"So everyone's in awe and fear of her, and no one defies her?"

"Yes, precisely. Rather, why would you even ask if I know her, I wonder? In this world, aren't the names you know best those of your parents, then other family, and finally, the name of the witch, I wonder?"

"Oh, come on…"

Subaru tried to poke fun, but he swallowed his words when Beatrice's expression made plain that she wasn't the slightest bit joking.

And if she was serious, that meant the witch was an unparalleled darkness in the world.

"The Witch of Jealousy, 'Satella.' She consumed the great sinners of yore known as the Six Witches, swallowing up half the world in the process, the vilest of all calamities."

Beatrice's words, spoken with emotions suppressed, brought a short, hard breath out of Subaru.

The name, one he'd heard before, bore much more gravity in the context of the rest.

"It is said that the witch desires love. It is said she does not comprehend human speech. It is said she envies everything in this world. That none have seen her face and lived. That her body is untouched by the ravages of time, unable to grow old or decay. That the Dragon, the Hero, and the Sage combined their power to seal her away, because even they could not hope to destroy her."

Beatrice spoke point by point, not allowing Subaru to get a word in.

"It is said…"

Finally, as if reaching the end of her tale, she paused after her pre-
amble and said,

"…she is a half-elf with silver hair."

4

—Satella, the Witch of Jealousy.

The Six Witches had made the world scream, but this witch wiped
them out in one fell swoop, ushering in a calamity that destroyed
half the world.

A hero had sealed her flesh within a crystal, where she continued
to sleep, even then, in some corner of the world.

That's an absurd story, Subaru's sensibilities as a child of moder-
nity made him think.

Crimes so vile that people spoke of them centuries afterward were
already bad enough, but the fact that the perpetrator continued to
exist, sealed away somewhere out there, would be unthinkable in his
world.

Subaru began to cite a rather extreme example as he sat cross-legged
with his chin on a palm, watching a corner of the garden.

"Well, I can't really go by that. Even if people don't know the name
of their own prime minister, they know the name of, say, the nation's
most popular idol group…"

It was morning as Emilia sat on the grass of the inner garden, conversing with the flickering lights surrounding her.

The scene never lost its mysterious, surreal air no matter how
many times he set eyes on it. Seeing Emilia like this every day was
one of the most beautiful sights that world had to offer.

Subaru was watching at a distance so as not to interfere with
Emilia's conversation. He was still wearing his servant's outfit as he
suppressed a yawn, letting out a long breath as he sank into a sea of
contemplation once more.

It was now the morning of the third day, for night and sunrise had
passed since his conversation with Beatrice in the archive of forbidden books.

As the night had crept toward morning, Beatrice had suddenly scowled.

"I suppose my skin shall be compromised if I do not get my beauty sleep. Staying up late like this is quite a bother."

After being roughly evicted from the archive, Subaru managed to get in a morning bath before meeting up with Emilia in the garden. The sight of her so diligently carrying out her daily routine made him clench a fist with renewed determination.

A gray fur ball—in other words, Puck—popped his face up in front of Subaru's eyes and called out to him.

"Well you seem to be doing better now."

Puck continued to hover in the air as he began grooming his face with his short paws like any normal cat. He continued, "To be honest, you were not much to look at yesterday. I'm a little relieved."

"That so? Sorry to make you worry. But my naive heart still isn't completely over everything, so I want the feel of your fur to comfort me. *Ahhh...*"

"Well, if you can bluff like that I suppose you're fine. Lia did lend you her lap and everything."

Subaru's fingers wrapped around the palm-size cat and, searching for something beyond even the surprising sensation of his ears, arrived at Puck's tail. From base to tip, the feel of it was beyond even Subaru's expectations, making his breath catch.

Subaru savored the supremely comfortable touch in his hand as his eyes met Puck's.

"Did you see the lap pillow, too, by any chance?"

"Only because she did it for so long. It was quite difficult to stay kneeling in that position for hours, and I offered to take over several times, but... Relax, Lia saw it through to the very end."

Puck's metaphorical seal of approval abruptly made Subaru, still shy about the awakening of his love, red in the face.

Puck nodded at Subaru's schoolboy reaction. And then—

"*Ei!*"

"Ow—! Why did you just scratch me?!"

"You had an explosion of complex feelings of affection for my daughter. Maybe I ought to explode *you*?"

"You ought not!! That daddy mind-set's a complicated thing, geez!"

Puck's "explosion" of fatherly concern threatened to put distance between Subaru and Emilia. Subaru plaintively bowed his head before Puck, somehow managing to keep the situation in check. When this process was finished and he glanced back at Emilia, he saw that she seemed to still be immersed in conversation with the spirits, never noticing the comedy routine between man and beast that had ruptured the calm of the morning.

Subaru watched the side of her face, gazing at the gentle, charming smile so beautiful that you could drown in it, when he abruptly murmured to himself.

"—A silver-haired half-elf, huh?"

It was one of the things Beatrice had said about the Witch of Jealousy.

The witch had shaken the world to its core, and even now, her name was synonymous with terror. He wondered how great a burden it must be to have similarities with such a being.

Even Subaru, who had never felt hardships like this, could imagine it was no easy road to travel. And yet, Emilia had been raised to be an honest, benevolent person... No doubt in the hope that she would live as a lovely, untainted flower.

"Either she grew up in a real friendly environment, or..."

Puck looked back and smiled, one paw on his hip, the other toying with his whiskers.

"Or maybe she was raised by a good father. Mm-hmm."

The cat could read his emotions. He'd no doubt discerned Subaru's thoughts to work out the context of the soliloquy from a moment before.

"Well, to a large extent she was just born that way. Not to harp on it, but that girl had a much, much harder time than you can imagine. It's adorable how she's like this in spite of it all, though."

As Puck squinted, the thought of contradicting him never crossed Subaru's mind.

The plain fact was that Subaru didn't know anything about Emilia, while Puck had spent an enormity of time with her. Subaru's knowledge of how hard it'd been for her barely scratched the surface.

Puck was driving home that Subaru had no right to act like he knew.

Men were helpless in the hands of Fate. Subaru knew that powerlessness all too well.

"Hey, Puck, do you know about the Witch of Jealousy?"

"There is little that I do not know."

"Okay, I wanted to ask you this… Under what circumstances would you use the Witch of Jealousy's name as an alias? Wait, *alias* doesn't sound very nice; it's more like…borrowing the Witch of Jealousy's name temporarily."

The back of his mind recalled an occurrence in the midst of the loop in the royal capital on the first day of his summons.

In the very, very first loop, Emilia had called herself "Satella" to Subaru, who knew nothing at all at that point.

Subaru had vaguely guessed what she must've been thinking, but he wanted a second opinion on the matter. There was no one better than the person who knew Emilia best.

Not knowing Subaru's intentions, Puck swayed his tail and inclined his head a bit.

"I think that would be a reckless thing to do. There are still many people with undiluted hate toward the witch, with fear and despair still carved into their souls. A person would have to be soft in the head to use the name of the witch as an alias around people like that."

"I'll take that as a 'never.'"

"Meow meow?"

Puck made a skeptical sound as Subaru poked him with a finger. Subaru then snapped his fingers, for Puck's support for his hypothesis made him put aside his own doubts.

In this world, using the name of the witch as an alias would obviously be insane. It was only Subaru, there by chance without the slightest clue about what passed for common sense, who would think it was normal. So why would Emilia, who certainly knew better, claim the name of the witch as her own?

"So she was trying to creep out a weirdo to keep him out of this royal selection business..."

She had tried to protect him, a boy she had met only in passing.

Emilia's thoughts behind claiming the alias had already vanished into another dimension. Only Subaru knew she had ever done such a thing. And Subaru would never have the chance to ask her what she truly intended by it.

But he couldn't help but imagine that that was what it meant. All he could do was believe.

Subaru, struck by the tenderness of that Emilia in another dimension, was caught off guard as the current one sat next to him with a strained smile.

"That's quite the distant look you have. What's wrong?"

He could no longer see the flickering lights frolicking around Emilia, so her pleasant conversation with them seemed over. Puck, having waited off to the side with Subaru until then, landed on her narrow shoulder to replace them.

"Back in my proper place. Ahh, this is where I'm most at ease. Home sweet home."

"Oh, so now you're Daddy back home from a trip, are you? Poor you, driving home all tired like that."

"That's because my eyes were wide open protecting my daughter from a wolf's poison fangs. Those poison fangs won't come near her, you see?"

"Hey, don't stare at *me* and talk about 'poison fangs'—twice! You'll ruin my reputation here."

Subaru forced a smile as Puck's big black eyes beheld him. Playing with the little cat like this meant he was kicking down the road a bit one of his opportunities to speak with Emilia, even though she was right there.

It wasn't that he hated talking to Emilia. He just couldn't look her in the eye. After all, he'd bawled his eyes out on her lap and spent untold hours with her stroking his head. It'd been only a single night since then; he didn't know how he could face her.

That he had gone to meet her even so proved only that Subaru had a severe case of Emilia poisoning.

Faced with Subaru's extreme confusion, Emilia hesitated, too, running an unhurried finger through her long silver hair. After a brief silence, Emilia made a determined breath and smiled.

"Err, this is a little embarrassing… Are you feeling all right?"

"I was in a tight spot until I heard Emilia-tan's voice. And, er, also, sorr—"

The apology died on his lips. Subaru swallowed back the word he was about to say and changed his approach.

"…Thank you. For everything. After all that, I think I have my head on straighter."

"It doesn't seem you're completely over it, but I'm glad you think you're getting there. Mm, if I was able to help a little, that's just fine. If you feel whittled to the bone again, just tell me. Your sister will gently console you."

Emilia teasingly put a hand to her chest and winked.

Surely she was acting this way to lighten Subaru's feelings of guilt. But when he gazed upon her happy, older sister–ish look, the fact that she kind of seemed serious made him tremble a bit.

"The main thing is that you're feeling better. You have to work hard today, you know? Are you sleepy? You slept at such odd times."

"No need to worry. A shut-in like me holding down the fort sleeps all day and is up all night to begin with. Well, it got a bit healthier as of late."

"Just to ask, what is a shut-in anyway?"

"He is the Guardian of the Culture, always immersed in an ocean of information about the state of the world and the global economy to better protect the home day and night… The upper ranks never set a foot outside the house and even commemorate their lovers' birthdays through their screens."

To be blunt, the souls of those who did that had long risen to a higher plane of existence.

The oddness of Subaru's explanation seemed to tug at Emilia a little as she made a lovely smile. Seeing Emilia's reaction, Subaru suddenly had a thought.

"Hey, Emilia-tan, what kind of magic do you use, anyway?"

"Err, strictly speaking, I'm not a magic user. That's because I'm a spirit mage, including my pact with Puck here. What I use isn't magic but spirit arts. The principles are largely the same, though…"

"So how are magic users and spirit mages different?"

Subaru turned his neck and looked at Puck sitting on Emilia's shoulder. The little cat, realizing the conversation had shifted in his direction, stroked the fur over his belly as he explained.

"Magic users use the mana inside them when they use magic. In contrast, spirit mages use the mana in the air around them. The process is fairly different, even when the effects are the same."

"So what kind of differences are those, sensei?"

When Subaru raised his hand and asked his question, Puck, sitting in the lecturer's role, grinned like a cat in a good mood.

"Technically, it's whether a gate is used or not. The size of a gate depends on the individual magic user, but that doesn't matter much for spirit mages. That's because you're using external mana."

"I see. So magic users bring in mana from around them through the gate, then send it back out the gate when they use magic, but spirit mages can cut out the middleman." Subaru was digesting the explanation when he tilted his head halfway. "Mm? But then that makes spirit mages way too powerful. Magic users are limited to the amount of fuel they can store inside them, but spirit mages have a free pass to use as much as they want. There's no contest."

"You understand quickly. But it isn't quite that convenient. In the first place, the mana in the air isn't infinite…"

Puck's words trailed off as he looked up at Emilia. The girl nodded as she took over.

"And the strength of the spells a spirit mage can use is dependent on the spirit you've formed a pact with. The predisposition needed to form pacts with spirits is rare to begin with, and powerful spirits are even rarer. It's difficult to say which is better."

Subaru replied, "Mm-hmm…but it must feel pretty good to get a pact with a strong spirit, right? You must really be hot stuff, Emilia-tan. Seems like Puck is hot stuff himself, though…"

"Well, I can't really deny that I'm above average."

"Man, you just said that with a straight face; no hesitation at all rating yourself like that?"

Subaru thought his self-consciousness outclassed most, but Puck's bluntness was a level higher.

No doubt it was the age difference. A greenhorn had seen many fewer years than Mr. Great Spirit. Though, judging from the rather merry, blushy smile the Great Spirit was making, maybe he wasn't as used to flattery as he pretended to be…

"Oh, by the way, what kind of spirit is Puck, anyway? He made ice come out at the loot seller's place, but…if my memory's right, there's no ice affinity to begin with."

With the bath serving as a lecture hall, Roswaal had explained to him that the four orthodox magical affinities were fire, water, wind, and earth. The annoying light and dark affinities rounded out the six.

It was not Puck, still making a blushy smile, but Emilia who replied to Subaru's question.

"My specialty is ice, but it's actually fire mana. Fire relates mainly to temperature, so cooling that which is hot is classified as part of fire, apparently."

"Huh, is that so? Magical logic…? Magic…? Magic, huh?"

Upon hearing Emilia's explanation, Subaru felt a fondness for magic bubble up within him. Having withdrawn momentarily, Puck twitched his ears as he looked at Subaru's face once again and nodded.

"Hmm. By any chance, do you want to use magic?"

"Can I?! I mean…if I can! Super-powerful stuff, like calling down a meteor shower and—"

"Ah, well, no. Fundamentals are important, both for magic and spirit arts. Magic is not something you can learn in a day."

Subaru's hopes suddenly leaped up, only for Puck to smack them back down. Subaru wilted on the spot, then Puck twirled a whisker and added, "But…if you simply want to experience it, we can do that."

"Meaning…what?"

"Meaning, if you want to use magic, Lia and I just have to support you. We'll use the mana inside you to use magic through you. The magic we use from the atmosphere is different from the mana inside you, so the magic itself will come out of your gate. How about it?"

Emilia rebuked Puck for his invitation.

"Puck, wait. Don't make it sound so causal. It might be dangerous."

However, Subaru's feelings were set in stone.

"Sorry, Emilia-tan. I'm super happy you're worried about me…but I'm gonna do it!"

Subaru gave Emilia a congenial smile, complete with a glint of his teeth and a thumbs-up.

Subaru's action, meant to drive away all unease and anxiety, made Emilia's eyes go wide.

"Wh-why do you want to do it so much…?"

"That's obvious—so that I can live as the man I was born to be!"

Subaru clenched a fist as he made the manliest cry he could.

To anyone born a man, ceasing to pursue your dreams was the same as death itself. Since arriving in another world, Subaru had never displayed as much courage as he had then and there.

—Besides, being able to use magic gave him one more option. Perhaps it would increase his chances of protecting Emilia and the others during the current loop.

Faced with Subaru's strong spirit, Emilia shook her head, abandoning all thoughts of stopping him.

"If you think it's getting dangerous, you *will* stop right away, understand?"

And so, with that warning, she resolved to see Subaru's battle through.

Subaru accepted Emilia's words of caution with a nice smile before turning back to Puck with bated breath.

"So what should I do first? Draw a magic circle? If you need a sacrifice, can I volunteer Beako?"

"I'm happy you seem to be getting along better with Betty. Yes, first, how about I see what affinity you are, Subaru? That's the first step to knowing what kind of magic you can use."

Subaru's expression, buoyant until that moment, instantly died when he heard Puck's suggestion. As Puck and Emilia blinked in surprise side by side, Subaru shook his head in robotic fashion.

"My...affinity...is probably...'fire'...?"

"Why the sudden pauses...?"

When Emilia asked, Subaru simply lowered his eyes. He didn't want to remember any further.

But Puck leaped off Emilia's shoulder and hovered in front of Subaru's face as he stretched his tail.

"All right, let's check. *Myon myon myon myon...*"

"I know the weirdo nobleman did the same thing, but isn't that, like, overkill?!"

The tip of Puck's long tail swished across Subaru's forehead as his mouth made the accompanying sound effects. Subaru wallowed in apprehension as he awaited the scan's verdict.

"Wait, I should think positively about this. Thinking back on it, Roswaal's behavior was unnatural, wasn't it? Right, he was jealous of the hidden magical talent within me. Yeah, it was jealousy. That's why he tried to convince me to just give up—"

"Wow, this is rare. Your affinity's pure Dark."

"Farewell, my magic-using life—!"

Subaru wailed at crossing into another dimension only to be blacklisted by someone else.

His glittering future was now closed, with the curtain rising on Subaru's life as nothing more than a debuffer.

"So all I need to do is practice saying, 'I've turned their defense to paper! Go, NOW!' Ha-ha-ha..."

"Ah, you have no talent at all, either. Your gate's small; at least the number is kind of okay...? But there's barely any opening, so not much is coming through."

"Shut up, I know that already! Incidentally, what does that talent thing mean, by the numbers?"

"If you spent twenty years in daily training, you might become a high-end second-rate magic user."

"So I'd devote half my life and still come up short of top tier... I think I'd better give up now..."

Emilia finally wore an exasperated look when she heard Subaru hold back tears as he gave up on his dream. But it couldn't be helped. Yes, *effort* and *trying your best* were words prominently featured in Subaru's lexicon, but whether to give up on a man's impossible dream or not was a different subject.

"I just want to try the magic demonstration. What do I have to do?"

"Since it's Dark affinity, Lia can't handle it. How about something simple, like Shamak?"

"Ah, a magic smoke screen? I've never seen it myself," Emilia replied.

Apparently, it was something of such a trivial level that she'd never encountered it professionally.

The two continued their magic talk while leaving Subaru aside as he sank into deeper despair about his tiny skill tree.

"It's not fair you're in a world all by yourselves. I mean, we're talking about *my* magic, right? I mean, can I actually use that Shamak thing? That's kind of important here."

"Good point. Unknown magic is a scary thing. All right, this is Shamak."

"—Eh?"

Puck, nodding in concession that Subaru had a point, made a brief incantation and waved a paw.

The next moment, Subaru's vision was shrouded in darkness. Instantly, the scene before his eyes was buried in pitch-black.

Startled, he abruptly raised his voice, but the sound never reached his ears. The profound darkness had cut off his vision from everything outside him. A shiver went up his spine at being severed from the outside world.

"There, all done."

When Subaru heard the clap of hands, he realized that he had returned to reality. Seeing Emilia in front of him when his sight returned put him at ease.

"That was just a moment, but he broke out in such a sweat… Subaru, are you all right? Do you want me to hold your hand?"

"I-I'm all right. I just lost my senses for a moment… Ah, I lost my chance to hold your hand."

While making his typically flippant comment, Subaru touched his own eyelids to make sure nothing had changed there.

"So that's a Shamak, huh? It's simple, but it's pretty strong stuff, isn't it?"

"Not at all. Anyone but a lower-grade opponent can brush it off with skill, and it can't be maintained for long. Although I could cast it on the likes of you so that you'd spend your entire life in darkness…"

"That's a scary thought!! I'd go crazy if I had to live one day like that, let alone the rest of my life!"

Subaru made a strained smile. He quietly hid his trembling fists behind him.

He didn't want to convey how the feeling of being momentarily cut off from the world had filled his entire body with terror. The instant he thought that he was alone in the world, with no one on his side, the sheer loneliness made Subaru's heart quake.

I'm pathetic. He bit the thought down and smiled to conceal his inner turmoil.

"Anyway, whether it's any use or not, I can use that magic, too, right? I wanna try that right away! I want to, but, um!"

"That's fine. I'll assist you. Lia, if his mana runs wild, it might blow up, so please move back. I don't want to get your clothes dirty."

"It's not like that's gonna happen, right?! That's, like, a super-rare case that basically never happens, right?!"

Puck smiled in silence. Emilia made a slightly sad face, counseling, "Don't be reckless, okay?" as she really did move away from him. The very outpouring of concern deepened his unease. Left in the lurch, Subaru was in an exceedingly uneasy position as events proceeded.

Puck sat down on top of Subaru's black hair and adjusted the position of his tail.

"What a prickly and uncomfortable head to sit on."

"Hey, it's not like I thought someone was going to sit on it someday! No one warned me to bring a cushion, but just, uh, help yourself, okay?"

"Nah, I'll be done and back to Lia's lovely hair in no time. So, ready to begin?"

When prompted, Subaru hesitated for just a moment, but a smile quickly came over him as he nodded. He was on something of a knife's edge of unease, but he just couldn't deny his curiosity. Having received Subaru's assent, Puck made a large nod of his own.

Then, Subaru suddenly felt his entire body get hot. He felt something besides blood running through his veins—no doubt it was the formless gush of mana stirring inside him.

He could tell that the energy inside his body was moving in accordance with Puck's hand.

"Subaru, try to picture it in your mind. Move the mana inside your body, flowing through me, by your own will. Push a portion of it out of your body through your gate. Picture it as a black cloud."

"Picture, picture. Trust me, daydreaming is totally my thing."

Subtly distorting Puck's advice, Subaru tried to picture where the energy wriggling inside his body was supposed to go.

He tried to picture the gate—the doorway at the center of his body. He pictured himself carefully opening a heavy door to make the energy inside flow out. Once outside, Subaru would generate the phenomenon by his own will—

Right around the last part, Puck murmured abruptly, "Huh, this isn't good. All of a sudden, the gate..."

Subaru didn't even have time to ask, *The gate what...?*

The next moment, Emilia cried out—

"Are you two—?!"

A few seconds later, a black cloud spewed out with explosive force, shrouding the corner of the inner garden of Roswaal Manor.

He didn't blow up, but the result was a spectacular failure nonetheless.

5

"If I must make a conclusion, your control of your gate is too weak, so you shouldn't push it, Subaru."

"You see me like this and *that's* the first thing you say, damn it?!"

Puck slapped his head and stuck out his tongue.

"Tee-hee-hee."

"That's not cute, you know!"

Subaru shouted at Puck as his whole body soaked up the sensation of the lawn. Lying atop the grass, Subaru felt his breaths were labored; his whole body felt unusually languid. He was as sluggish as if he had a high fever. His limbs seemed to lack the will to move.

He'd felt something like this before.

Back on what was, in a true sense, his first day at the mansion, he'd felt the same sluggishness after Beatrice drained his mana. That was to say, Subaru was completely out of gas at that moment.

Emilia interrupted.

"For better or worse, Subaru simply isn't used to using his gate. That's why it ignored the user's will and everything inside flew right out."

"So I didn't close the lid right… What am I, soy sauce…?"

He managed to voice his resentment, but the depletion of his strength was nothing to laugh at. He wanted to at least manage to get up, but he couldn't put any energy into his limbs or the rest of his body.

Subaru was still stuck lying on the ground when Emilia, kneeling beside him, met his gaze.

"You mustn't move. You're all out of internal mana, so behave yourself. Maybe you should take today off work, too."

"—That's really bad!"

Emilia was scolding him like a misbehaving child when Subaru raised his voice out of the blue. Emilia blinked in surprise off to the side as Subaru deeply rued his own carelessness.

If he really did have to give up the whole day, it meant abandoning one more day he needed to put this loop in order. That was crazy, even fatal. And now his body felt like it was rusted over.

"*Ughhhh...*"

"Now hold on, I told you not to push it!"

"Now's when I have to push it. If I don't, I'm going to really seriously regret it later..."

It was by no means unusual for him to reap what he had sowed, but the timing was simply too awful.

Emilia, seeing Subaru's brow covered with sweat as he struggled with all his might, slumped her shoulders.

"Goodness, you really can't be helped."

Once more, Emilia's lips tapered as if she was upset with him. Subaru, not grasping the meaning behind Emilia's statement, could only lift his eyes to look at her.

"—? Emilia-tan, what's *mnnff*?!"

Emilia peered down at his face from above while suddenly stuffing something into his mouth. He felt something round and soft on his tongue. Though bewildered, Emilia put a hand over his mouth and nodded to him.

"Bite down."

"—?"

"Bite down...and swallow. Yes, there you go."

With Emilia tolerating no dissent, Subaru located the object in his mouth and bit down on it—hard.

A bittersweet taste swirled all around his mouth. He narrowed his eyes as his taste buds sensed it was some kind of fruit. The next moment...it hit him.

"Whoaaaaaaa—?!"

Subaru, feeling like his whole body was alight, got up then and there, practically leaping to his feet.

He felt like his blood was boiling as it coursed through his entire body, scalding heat reaching all the way to the tips of his fingers and toes. He exhaled hard, as if the air in his lungs was too hot to handle, and his knees were marching up and down all on their own.

It was around that point when Subaru realized he was standing on his own two feet.

There were still vestiges of sluggishness in every part of his body, but the crippling lethargy had vanished.

"Wh…? What was that…?"

"It's called a bokko fruit. When you eat it, it gives the mana inside your body a kick so that your gate powers up again, just enough to feel a bit better."

Apparently, the mysterious fruit was some kind of MP recovery item.

Subaru rotated his arms and, finding that nothing was wrong aside from a little fatigue, breathed a sigh of relief.

"Wow, I'm relieved. I'd never forgive myself if I got another BAD END on account of that. Thanks, Emilia-tan."

"I don't have many of them, and it's not good for the body, so I didn't really want to use it… You weren't bluffing there, were you?"

No doubt it was Subaru's genuineness that had spurred Emilia into using such a precious item on him.

Subaru responded to Emilia's prodding by sticking out his chest and boldly declaring, "Not one bit. I won't let you regret this."

Then he immediately wiped all the sweat off his brow.

"But man, I was an idiot there… When this is all over I'm going to kick myself even more than before."

He carried the burden of having experienced numerous forms of death, something other people would only experience but once, but he wanted to avoid dying from *embarrassment* if he could at all help it.

In fact, he wanted his suicide by leaping off a cliff to be the last death he ever experienced.

The scars of having decided to end his own life ran deep. He didn't want to do that again, ever.

One death was enough for anyone. He wanted death to be the natural end of his life. Of course, the best result would be some crazy event that ended with Emilia embracing him, but—

"Man, I'm such a kid I can't even think about it, huh?"

Even though he was always so glib, he would never again casually speak the word *death*. Surely Subaru could only laugh at his own cowardice because he was reliving the same experiences, literally whether he wanted to or not.

Seeing the change in Subaru's expression, Emilia had a sullen look as she asked, "Are you all right? Do you think you can go to work?"

"I'll do work, and all the other stuff, too. Having you on my side is like riding an unsinkable battleship, so I'll give it all I've got."

"…Riding a… I'm not quite sure what you mean by that, but…"

"Hey, Emilia-tan, how you put that kind of makes me excited. Can you say that again?"

"You have a lewd look in your eyes, so no."

Their usual banter left Subaru laughing as he stretched his limbs and finally his back.

"Well, I'd better go face my seniors and turn over a new leaf!"

"I suppose so. I don't think either has spoken one word about you since yesterday."

"—Ah."

Subaru stretched his back as his hips made their own dull creak.

6

"Sister, Sister. The lout known as Subaru has come."

"Rem, Rem. The wage thief named Barusu has appeared."

"I'm very sorry about yesterday…! Please forgive me!"

Subaru sought forgiveness, bowing his head low in an earnest apology.

He felt like he'd done nothing but bow his head for half an entire day. He'd accounted for everyone at the mansion except Roswaal—meaning the entirety of the female population.

"I'm back to a route with all the girls looking down on me again... I've got some deep karma here."

"Sister, Sister. It seems Subaru is quite the pervert."

"Rem, Rem. Subaru is a masochist who likes being degraded."

"That's going too far, especially for you, Big Sis!"

Shouting in response to the sisters' sharp rebuke, Subaru used his arms as a fulcrum to go from his prostrate position into a handstand, twisting his body around and using the momentum to rise to his feet.

"Anyway, I'm sorry about being pathetic yesterday and annoying the day before... Well, a lot happened, but I've had a complete change in attitude, so it's a new me going forward."

"It was the lap pillow."

"The lap pillow, yes."

"Don't tell me everyone knows?! That's so embarrassing!"

Subaru hid his reddened face and crumbled as the twin maids met each other's gaze.

"It is time to begin the morning chores, Sister."

"It is time to begin our morning duties, Rem."

"No comment?! That puts me down even more!!"

With a wave, the two left behind Subaru and his pleas, heading off to work just as they had declared. As they did so, Subaru called for them to stop.

"Time-out, time-out. There's a favor I want to ask about work this morning."

Subaru's appeal made both twins stop, turn around, and tilt their heads in sync.

"A favor?"

"A hassle?"

"Weird, I haven't heard Big Sis's bluntness for a while and it's getting me all fired up..."

A pained smile came over him. Unlike the little sister, the older sister's unpleasant attitude was a lot easier to deal with, but he was glad he could talk to them like this at all.

He breathed out, trying to brush off the absurdity of it all.

"Actually, I'd like to go see the village. It's nearby, right? Isn't there something you need to buy there?"

Overnight, he'd formed a firm hypothesis in the archive of forbidden books, but he wanted to get to the village that day no matter what. That was what was on Subaru's mind as Rem put a hand to her chest, sinking into thought.

"Certainly, we are running a bit low on spices, so I was thinking of heading to the village tomorrow…"

"Let's change the schedule and do it today, then. Might as well get more before you're running out, and you can't just borrow some from the neighbors out here, can you?"

There were no other mansions in the first place, even if they had wanted to go see the neighbors.

Rem seemed to ponder Subaru's suggestion a little when…

"It's fine, isn't it?"

"Sister?"

In contrast to the little sister's pondering, the older sister stroked her own pink hair with a look of indifference.

"We have to buy them either way, and there are no other pressing matters. It is the perfect opportunity to employ Barusu as a mule."

"I was in bed with a gut wound just three days ago, so take it easy, okay?!"

Subaru had hoped for some warmth from the merciless Ram, but her cover fire still made him tilt his mind's inner head a bit.

He'd thought so, but this was vivid proof that the twin maids were not united in their opinions.

He remembered how, in the loop before last, Rem's coming to kill him had been on Rem's own judgment. Perhaps their thinking was even less on the same page than Subaru had assumed.

Either way…

"…If Sister…says so, then…"

After thinking it over a bit, Rem finally gave her own consent.

The majority of work at the mansion got done only because of

Rem, but Subaru knew from long experience that she let Ram, the less accomplished of the two, make a lot of the decisions.

Whether mere coincidence or not, Ram's intervention had essentially settled the matter.

Subaru pumped a fist as Rem's face went from contemplation back to a calm, neutral look.

"However, either way, going to the village must wait until after lunch. Let us do it after Two Solartime…after we have finished all other outstanding work."

"It will be all right. Barusu has pledged to work until his body is ground to a pulp, yes?"

"Yep. Just watch what I can do now that I've been reborn. I'll work like a hot knife through you know what."

They corrected his corrupted idiom in unison.

"Butter."

"Right. That."

Subaru scratched his face as it sunk in that he'd succeeded in his negotiations. Now that the promise to go shopping had been made, it was finally time to begin servant time.

He watched Rem leave in a hurry, probably sorting out in her head the order of her chores, before shifting his gaze to Ram beside him.

Naturally, Ram had been given orders to stick with Subaru for another day and oversee his education.

No doubt it was best to avoid the tension that had built up the day before—or rather, the day before last. More to the point, finding himself had been so painful that re-creating the tension was a little too much to ask.

"Getting self-conscious of my own bad points in such a short time like that… It's a bigger shock than seeing an infant grow into a man in three days."

As Subaru sank into reflection, Ram folded her arms and gave him a cold look.

"Before we get to the issue at hand…"

For some reason, Ram's gaze made Subaru feel like he should straighten his back. He did so and turned toward her.

"About that magic in the garden earlier…"

"Ah, sorry for the mess. I can't use that thing right, so I'm not touching it for a while. I hear it'd take twenty years for me to learn the fundamentals right."

"A mess it may have been, but do not provoke Rem too much."

"…?"

Not understanding what Ram meant, a virtual question mark came over Subaru's face. Ram watched Subaru's inquisitive look before making a belated *hmph*.

"Rem was quite disturbed by the magic that covered a corner of the garden as well as Lady Emilia. You should be dancing for me in thanks for stopping her, Barusu."

"Ah… Ahhhh… Yeah, you're right…"

In his shock at the failure of his magic, Subaru hadn't noticed, but a third party was unlikely to see that situation as a mere failed spell.

He was truly grateful that Ram hadn't jumped the gun. On the other hand, he was aghast at Rem's willingness to make a snap judgment on the spot.

"Oh man, I was way too careless… I have to think ahead more after four Continues."

"What are you mumbling about…? If we do not get to work soon, both breakfast and dinner shall run late."

"Oh, I was just thinking about the shopping in the afternoon. Which one of you will be going with me?"

Under the circumstances, going with Rem would be a heavy weight on his mind. Either way, though, it made practical sense for Rem to be the one to go with him to the village. Subaru figured that he'd be going shopping with Rem, just like he had on two previous occasions. However…

"What nonsense are you speaking?"

"…Eh?"

Subaru inclined his head. For once, Ram's neutral expression broke into a smile—an extremely cold, malicious, devilish smile.

"You shall go with both of us. You will have a lovely flower on each arm, Barusu."

That would be nice, as long as the flowers aren't poisonous.

Subaru, now aware that the negotiations had gone a little too well, covered his face with a palm, looked up to the heavens, and groaned.

CHAPTER 3
THE MEANING OF COURAGE

1

From Subaru's perspective, it was his third visit to the village.

It was a village named Earlham, practically right beside the mansion, part of the territory belonging to Roswaal in his role as margrave. It was a small village, with about two hundred residents, give or take. In his original world, that wouldn't have been enough to fill an elementary school. And there was Subaru, walking around a village you could do a full lap of in twenty minutes, with two girls, "a flower on each arm."

"I must say, work was finished rather quickly."

"Barusu was so deft, it was revolting. What happened to him?"

"I won't blush, so praise me all you want. The latent potential sleeping in me has finally blossomed!"

Subaru was rather full of himself at the high praise for his work before noon. He'd focused on speedy work for the sake of the afternoon shopping trip, and it worked out well. Apparently, he'd been failing as a result of putting too much stress on himself; this time, a more natural approach seemed to work much better.

No doubt his ability to let go had something to do with the feel of Emilia's lap…

That sure helped me relax, huh…?

Unlike before when he was under so much stress, the lying on Emilia's knees had made him able to smoothly converse with the twins. The remaining nervousness only bolstered his resolve, erasing his carelessness in the process.

Furthermore, at that moment, Subaru was calm enough that he felt like nothing could shake him. That was very fortunate, because he couldn't afford to behave like a troublesome eccentric here.

The Q&A session with Beatrice the night before had established that a shaman had to physically touch the target of a curse. That's what made curses a fairly risky means of assassination.

He compared having to get up close and personal to sniping from long range like someone would do from his world. The risk was probably offset by the curse being such certain means.

"Either way, I have an MO for the perpetrator. It has to be someone who touched me on the trips to the village before."

And if the person had arrived in the village in only the last few days, then his suspect was as good as found.

That said, Subaru couldn't rely on everything in the village being perfectly as he remembered. He'd learned that the hard way back at the mansion. It'd be very hard to go over the same things save for a few specific events.

"The ones who stand out are Muraosa, the acting headman, the granny touching butts in search of her lost youth, the leader of the young men with short haircuts, and the guy with a short cut leading the Ram-Rem Defense Force."

Subaru named all the people whose faces stood out to him and went over each one.

There was the guy who acted like he led the village, Muraosa, and the old woman who engaged in perverse behavior while laughing and saying, "Got me youth back, got me youth back." The two young men wore identical faces; they'd frequently butted Subaru's shoulders, perhaps out of jealousy for being so close with the twin sisters.

"I had to lead Muraosa to the john when he started flaking out…

Now that I think about it, all of them touched me somehow. That's kind of suspicious..."

But all of them were native villagers through and through. They didn't fit the profile.

"That being the case, guess I'd better just hang around the same places..."

Subaru sighed at himself for his lack of any better idea. And as Subaru made that gloomy sound, a series of voices reached Subaru from above.

"What's wrong, Subaru?" "Are you hungry?" "Do you have a tummy ache?"

Subaru twisted his neck to see the multiple silhouettes glomping onto his back.

They were children who had raced to reach Subaru first before he'd even set foot into the village. There were seven in all, not just latched onto his back but his legs and hips, too.

Subaru, not finding the weight excessive for his build, cracked his neck.

"I've got a connection with you across time and space or something..."

"What are you saying?" "Did you hit your head?" "Do you have a tummy ache?"

"Quit it about the tummy ache, geez. You make it sound like I've got diarrhea or something."

As Subaru spoke, the children all burst into laughter. No doubt it was less about his joke than the word *diarrhea* being funny in and of itself.

Apparently, hopping worlds didn't change the fact that kids of that age thought the cruder, the funnier.

"And I've got kids all over me, just like old times..."

The kids on his back were pulling on his cheeks. Subaru could only slump his shoulders at being a brat magnet.

"Why is it I get along great with brats and the elderly? I mean, it's like it's the only good point I have in this world."

He twisted his body to nuzzle the kids riding his back.

Subaru heard merry cries behind him, voices calling, "Me next! Me next!" as he marched around the village, children in tow.

At the time, Subaru was moving around by himself. Not that he actually *was* alone, but Ram and Rem were not with him.

When they'd arrived at the village, the maid sisters hurried off to go shopping, leaving ominous statements behind them.

"Sister, Sister. Let us gather all the light things."

"Rem, Rem. Let us leave all the heavy things for Barusu."

Subaru had said he wanted to have a look around the village, so no doubt they were being considerate, but he really did wish one of them had stayed with him. That way, the kids would have happily jumped onto *her*.

"And I managed to meet all the suspects without being super nervous, even..."

Subaru wiped some cold sweat off his brow, breathing heavily as he continued using himself as a decoy.

Subaru had opted for the extremely risky method of searching for the shaman. It was near suicidal behavior to put himself back on the chopping block, but if he didn't, he wouldn't be able to get a look at the face of the one responsible.

"At the very least, if it's just the rite, I can get Beako to lift it, right?"

As long as there wasn't some mistake and the curse activated right away, just having the rite embedded in him shouldn't be a mortal threat. If he got cursed, he just had to bow his head to the floor before Beatrice and beg her to take it off.

"Subaru, your face looks bad!" "Scary face!" "Weird face!"

"Geez, you make that sound awful. And that third comment annoys me *just* a little!"

Subaru continued strolling around the village, dragging the children along while bearing the brunt of their jokes. It wasn't like he could shake them off him, anyway, and they knew their way around the village, so they were somewhat useful. More importantly, to a shaman trying not to cause a fuss in the village, attempting to harm Subaru while he had a gaggle of children all over him was a poor option. So they functioned as human shields, too.

"Man, I'm getting pretty evil, too. I'm expanding my horizons here!"

"What's wrong, Subaru?" "What is it?" "Did you flake out?"

"Nah, it's nothing."

Subaru rubbed the heads of the children clamped on his legs and laughed at his own expense.

"Well, this is all for my happiness. You'll cooperate a little longer, won't you?"

Incidentally, he didn't think he liked children very much to begin with. They were noisy, way too chummy, and completely self-serving.

—Perhaps that was how he thought about himself, too.

2

Ram ran a hand through her pink hair as she sighed with exasperation.

"Free time was finally over, so we came to look, and *this* is what we see…"

Ram stared at Subaru as he raised both arms to the sky then and there.

"Victory!!"

After Subaru raised his arms and shouted, a chorus of voices rang out in celebration.

"Victory!!"

The people beside him spontaneously patted one another's backs as they voiced their admiration. Subaru, too, wiped the sweat off his brow, exchanging pleasantries and giving high fives as he caught his breath and headed toward Ram.

Subaru's buoyant approach was greeted by Ram's frosty gaze.

"What kind of attraction is this?"

"It's nothing big enough to call an attraction. I figured I'd kill time with the kids, and then the adults saw and jumped on the band-wagon, that's all."

Aerobics was his chosen method for playing with a bunch of noisy kids at the same time. The adults saw and they joined in, with the end result being a huge ruckus with almost half the village's popula-tion pitching in.

"Well, I've gotten so popular it scares even me. It's something fun for the young and old alike. Maybe it really is the secret to living longer!"

"I would not know."

"Geez, that's a cold brush-off."

Subaru gave Ram's unimpressed reply an exaggerated reaction. Upon seeing this, the children copied him.

"That's cold, Ramchi!" "That's awful, Ramchi!" "You're scary, Ramchi!"

"…You taught these children that manner of address?"

"Not so much taught them as, ah, made you more approachable? I mean, if you keep everyone at arm's length, they can't see who you really are. That's a lonely thing… That's what I think, anyway…"

"You certainly have an active mouth. I do not mind, but Rem may not care for it."

"Remrin?" "Remrin." "Remririn."

"—Ah, we kind of…crossed that bridge already."

Hearing from the children that her words of caution had come too late, Ram slumped her shoulders in resignation.

"So, did you look around the village as you desired?"

"—Yeah, that part went off without a hitch."

Subaru's cheeks warped into a grin in response to Ram's question.

His stroll around the village to come into contact with the people on his suspect list was a great success. More to the point, Subaru stood out so much that it was he who had the opportunities to touch them this time.

"The last, last thing on my to-do list was to high-five the guy with the crew cut after aerobics, and that's done."

Having touched all the obvious suspects brought him a measure of relief. Now his time in the village was at an end—in other words, time to say bye-bye to the kids.

"I've got work to do, so get lost, guys. Ahh, what a pity. If I had more time I could've played with you some more. Ha-ha-ha, too bad so sad!"

"He's smiling!" "He's laughing!" "Are you really so happy?!"

Subaru "regretfully" shook loose of the kids, sticking his tongue out in the face of their complaints. He did not consciously recognize the sense of satisfaction filling him at having regained even such mundane ground with his limited capacity as a human being.

Either way, he and Ram were on their way to the rendezvous point with Rem when—

"Ah?"

Abruptly, the girl wearing her brown hair in braids tugged on Subaru's sleeve, her face red.

Subaru was surprised, for until that moment, the braided girl had religiously maintained an arm's-length distance from the other kids while they'd piled onto him together, never entering the fray herself. Subaru crouched so that their gazes were at the same height.

"What is it? If you've got something to say, I'm happy to listen."

"Err, well… Come over here."

The girl led him by his sleeve to another place. Subaru, guided by the slender hand, looked back at Ram.

"—You may do as you please a little while longer."

"Oh, thanks, I owe you one. So, what is it?"

With permission having been granted, he continued to follow the little girl's hand. With her in the lead, the children from earlier followed them to a corner of the village.

"You'll be real surprised." "You'll love it." "You'll break out in a dance."

"Surprise, happiness, dancing? You sure are expecting a big reaction out of me here."

Surrounded by giggling children giving previews of how he'd react, they slipped past the houses of the village to a nook away from prying eyes. Then his eyes followed the children's pointing fingers and saw *it*.

"Ah, yeah, there was this event, too, wasn't there…?"

Out of the blue, Subaru voiced his assent, clasping his hands together and nodding several times over.

The braided girl rushed over, picking *it* up in her arms, out of breath as she returned.

—This was the creature with brown fur that looked like a dog.

Its eyes were round and its fur soft, making it almost seem like a newborn pup. The latter quality appealed to a connoisseur of fur such as Subaru.

But unfortunately, the puppy did not respond to Subaru in kind.

"*Arf!*"

"I figured this was coming…"

The moment Subaru reached out with his hand, every hair on the dog's body stood up as it barked out a warning. The children all wore shocked faces at how its small body shuddered, on guard against him.

"But he's always been so good!" "He's only angry at Subaru!" "What did you do to him, Subaru?!"

"That's what I wanna know—sheesh! This is the third time and everything. Just not compatible or what?"

The children booed behind Subaru as he turned toward the unfriendly puppy with a strained smile.

He'd encountered this puppy on both his prior visits to the village—in other words, during prior loops. Each time it had displayed a severe dislike of him, wounding his animal-loving heart.

"I guess in one sense, having something not change between loops feels about right…but I'd have liked a more friendly reaction, seriously."

In spite of Return by Death, many things had been repeated very differently, but the puppy's reaction was practically a broken record.

But when Subaru made a friendly smile, the puppy suddenly let down its guard. With the puppy curled up in the braided girl's arms, Subaru snapped his fingers, realizing this was his chance.

"Well, if you'll excuse me…"

He'd show this puppy his full range of the fur-stroking skills he had honed on Puck.

He rubbed the puppy in all the important places, like the head, neck, and the base of the tail, with the sensation bringing a big grin over Subaru.

"*Heh-heh*, I've been looking forward to this feeling. Pretty nice stuff for a stray. A little tender, loving brushing and this'll be a long, shiny coat. Hey, there's a bald spot on the head. This a wound? Where did you bump against—?"

Maybe the puppy had a complex about the white scar; the instant Subaru touched it, the puppy's maw chomped hard on his hand. He quickly pulled his hand back, but it had a prominent bite mark on it nonetheless.

Subaru yelped at the sharp pain on the back of his blood-smeared hand as he stroked the wound.

"What an event with which to get a one hundred percent completion rate. You even got me in the same place. What, did you do a time leap just for this?"

Subaru smiled to put it at ease, but the puppy, back on guard, continued to snarl.

Watching relations between man and beast return to the gutter, the children observing the two nodded to one another.

"Yep, he got carried away." "It's because he touched it that much." "The puppy's a girl!"

"I feel like that's a weird tangent at the end there…and what, no one's worried about me? I'm gonna cry here."

Subaru lightly washed his hand at a watering hole and waved good-bye to the puppy and the frolicking children. The braided girl looked like she felt responsible, waving with a frail, bashful smile before returning to the others.

When he got back, he had a maid waiting for him, leaning against a wall with her arms crossed and a big attitude.

"Sorry for the wait."

"I sent you off thinking it would be a brief affair, but you come back with your hair disheveled, your clothes a mess, and bleeding from your left hand, of all things."

"Well, sorry about that! A bunch of things happened. You can tell just by looking, right?"

"I suppose so. One glance and I can largely tell what happened."

He saw a gloomy expression on her elegant face as she sighed a little.

Subaru raised an eyebrow at the odd nuance of her statement and her un-Ram-like demeanor, but Ram instantly gave her usual *hmph*, not allowing Subaru to voice his question.

"Your wound and clothes are both unsightly. We shall quickly rendezvous with Rem, because she can actually heal you."

"Ramchi, you don't use healing magic?"

"I can handle sealing a wound after an amputation."

Subaru could not conceal his shudder.

"That's some really extreme first aid there!!"

Out of nowhere, Ram walked over and tugged on Subaru's sleeve. Subaru blinked, turning only his head to face Ram when she went, "Aren't you coming, Barusu?"

"It's with you, so yeah."

For a single, brief moment, he saw her lips slacken at his reply. Ram proceeded straight to leading him off by his sleeve.

He thought that she'd be really cute if she always acted this straightforward, but that might have been because his honesty with himself kept him spewing lines like *that* all the time.

Perhaps honesty, too, had a time and a place.

That was the thought on his mind as he and Ram walked toward where Rem was waiting for them.

For some reason, he sensed that the girl leading him was walking more slowly, more gently than usual.

3

By the time the three returned to the mansion, the sunrays were heavily tilted, as it was well into the evening.

As they stood before Roswaal Manor, bathed by the evening sun, a lone man collapsed onto the ground.

It was none other than Subaru Natsuki. He set the oversize keg aside and flopped onto the ground, breathing hard.

"I made it… I made it! …Good job, me! Totally good job!"

"Yes, yes, well done."

"Yes, yes, much appreciated."

The twin maids sandwiched the fallen Subaru as they gave him stiff, formal thanks for his labors.

Ram's coolness was entirely normal, but Rem's bluntness was no doubt due to her anger at seeing Ram leading Subaru by his hand when they met up after shopping in the village.

The first words out of Rem's mouth had been, "You and Sister seem to be getting along nicely."

That made Subaru regret the decisions he had made. He wanted to make up for it somehow, so when she'd made him carry a heavy barrel back to the mansion out of apparent spite, he hoped it would improve her impression of him just a little.

Rem spoke down toward Subaru.

"Well, then, we shall return to the mansion ahead of you. Take your time."

She then picked up the large barrel as if it were filled with feathers.

Subaru could bench-press about 175 pounds, but he had serious doubts that he could lift that barrel above his shoulders. And yet, he'd just seen Rem pick up the heavy object with one hand while still carrying miscellaneous objects in her other arm.

Subaru laughed drily at the pretty picture it all made.

"You didn't need me to carry that, did you?"

"As you can see, not at all."

Ram wasn't minded to pamper Subaru's inner boy at all. As he saw Rem casually walk off while carrying the cask, he was painfully aware that his grunt work had been meaningless.

"So why'd you make me do it, then? Was it seriously just a grudge against me? Stop bullying the new guy, sheesh."

"Do you not understand, Barusu? It is out of consideration for you, of course."

"I don't get what you mean by 'consideration' here."

"Barusu, what would Lady Emilia think if she saw you coming back carrying nothing but a small bag full of spices behind Rem while she carried a large, heavy object?"

"You're such a considerate supervisor, it leaves me speechless!"

As Ram knelt, he expressed deep gratitude toward her. If Subaru had come back full of himself carrying a little bag while a girl smaller than him lugged around something huge…and Emilia had seen… Just picturing it was enough to make him want to die.

Rem, who had gone to the mansion ahead of them, returned during their exchange, looking down at the two.

"Sister, Master Roswaal summons us."

Ram responded quickly to the mention of her master on her little sister's lips. Instantly, her usual laid-back attitude vanished; she straightened herself and looked down at Subaru.

"What are you doing, Barusu? Do you intend to make Master Roswaal wait?"

"Just because you two know something doesn't mean I do. Er, what, this is a meeting with all the servants?"

Subaru felt like he was being treated like a child who was slow on the uptake as he followed behind the others. Along the way, he straightened himself in accordance with Ram's lessons and opened the mansion's front doors. As he did so, Roswaal, the lord of the manor, awaited the three with open arms.

"Ohhhh, you were together, were you nooot? That indeed saves me some tiiime."

He had indigo hair and oddly colored eyes, one blue, one yellow. He had the delicate build of a pretty boy, but the clown makeup adorning his face put it all to waste. But all that included, the air he gave off felt different somehow.

"Are you wearing that to go out somewhere?"

"Precisely. I actually do not faaavor formal wear like this, either, but it cannot be heeelped. The other paaarty is troublesome to deal with in normal attire, so I am forced to go out wearing thiiis."

Usually, Roswaal indulged in his eccentric taste in clothing. It had been some time since Subaru had seen him wearing something with geometrical patterns, lacking the usual clownish spirit. Or rather, it was the very first time.

Subaru could think of only two possibilities as to why Roswaal would be wearing such an outfit. Ram and Rem, thinking the same thing as Subaru, aired both possibilities simultaneously.

"Entertaining a guest?"

"Going on a trip?"

Faced with questions from all his servants, a pained smile came over Roswaal as he pointed at Ram.

"Ram is correct… I am heading out. A somewhat trooooublesome message has arrived, you see. There is something I must check in the environs of Garfiel, though I do not plan on being very laaate."

Having never heard that particular word before, Subaru couldn't be certain whether it was the name of a person or a place. But given that the twins seemed to know what he was talking about, Subaru nodded without objection.

"For that reaaason, I do not believe I shall be back tonight, so… Ram, Rem, I leave matters in your hands."

"Yes, if you command it."

"Yes, even at the cost of my life."

Roswaal acknowledged the pair's immediate replies with his oddly colored eyes alone before gazing at Subaru with them. Subaru, feeling backed into a corner by the differently colored glints, squirmed uncomfortably.

"Sorry, I'm not loyal enough to swear even at the cost of my life yet."

"That is fine and weeell. If you swore that all of a sudden, it would feel raaather disconcerting. But I leave things in yooour hands as well, Subaru."

Roswaal patted Subaru's shoulder, one eye closed, so that only his yellow iris was visible.

"This has a fishy aroma to it. I can cooount on you to take care of Lady Emilia, yes?"

"Yeah, you can seriously count on me for that."

That went without saying.

Subaru didn't know how much of a read Roswaal had on the situation. He didn't know, but he'd picked up this much…

—This had never happened before.

Perhaps it truly meant that Subaru's actions had changed the world around him.

Nodding, Roswaal gave Subaru a satisfied smile before giving his faithful twin retainers various instructions.

"Well, theeen, I shall be off. I pray that nothing shall occuuur."

As he spoke, Roswaal went out the entrance, with the three of them watching him go. But Subaru belatedly realized that there was no coach or carriage to whisk Roswaal away.

Surely Roswaal wasn't going to *walk*—

"Well, I leave it in your hands—"

When Roswaal spoke, his overcoat flapped as he made a light leap. And then, Subaru saw: Roswaal's body sailed up into the sky, wind wrapping around it as he soared at high speed. Subaru's mouth opened in surprise as Roswaal rose almost as high as the clouds, heading toward the mountains, growing smaller, and finally vanishing from view.

"H-he flew... Geez, magic's amazing stuff."

Subaru voiced his admiration at the solo flying he had just witnessed. In contrast, the sisters, clearly accustomed to Roswaal's flight magic, quickly switched gears. They instantly established the order of affairs in the mansion in the absence of their master.

"Even if Master Roswaal is absent, our duties do not change. Indeed, the fact that he is not present means we must be even more diligent," said Rem.

"That's a nice professional attitude. Okay, then, let's get this started!"

Rem began divvying up work as Subaru rolled up his sleeves, burning with enthusiasm.

Of course, he wasn't just fired up about work but about the changing situation, too.

The change clearly made the twins expect a potential attack on the mansion. They would be securely guarding the mansion, but Subaru, who knew with certainty an attack was coming, was even more on guard than they.

He needed to discover the shaman's identity without a single moment to lose.

If the other side was acting faster, there was no doubt in his mind that the visit to the village that day had triggered it. In other words, Subaru's decoy plan had worked as he had meant it to.

All Subaru had to do now was confirm his suspicions and smoke the shaman out.

4

"So, it's that time again, Beako!"

Those were the first words out of his mouth when he pushed open the door and entered the archive of forbidden books.

His grand and very pushy entrance made Beatrice, sitting on the footstool as she read a book, slump her shoulders.

"Really...? How do you breach the Passage with such ease...?"

"Intuition. It's all intuition. I've got a sixth sense about these things."

Beatrice wore a very sour face as Subaru approached, and she abruptly narrowed her eyes, no doubt because she noticed the seriousness in Subaru's.

"Another half a day and you have yet a different expression. I suppose you are a busy sort?"

"Hey, I want to take it easy, too. But the world's enough of a mess that it's not exactly giving me the chance."

Subaru, an ordinary person, had been buffeted by one problem arising after another. But he was confident that, at long last, he was catching up to the problems, instead of them purely catching up to him.

"I want you to check something for me, so I finished cleaning the bath in record time."

"If cleaning the bath came first, surely it is no great affair?"

This applied to Subaru as well, but time in the bath was one of the few respites in a world of few pastimes. Just thinking of Rem's reaction if she found out he'd slacked off in cleaning that place of rest was enough to give him chills.

After all, Subaru getting along with her big sister had put his friendship rating with Rem in the dumps. Even if he located the shaman, poor relations with Rem meant Subaru couldn't escape a BAD

END. Having to advance along both routes simultaneously made Subaru feel like he was walking a tightrope.

"If it was just a problem of which girl to get lovey-dovey with, I'd be real happy, but…"

"Are you wandering off topic again, I wonder…? What did you want of me, then?"

"Ah, yeah, about that…"

Subaru sank in thought in front of Beatrice, who at least seemed tentatively willing to hear him out. After hesitating about how to put it exactly, he nodded once.

"I think there's a little curse on me. Can you check?"

"…What are you saying, I wonder?"

"I think there's a little curse on me. Can you check?"

"I did not tell you to repeat yourself! Has it been even half a day since we spoke about shamans in detail, I wonder?! Even gullibility has its limits…"

Beatrice stormed over and yelled, probably thinking Subaru had some sort of persecution complex. But her expression changed midway to one of surprise; she looked up at Subaru as if some doubt had just been answered.

"I sense a curse rite… You truly have been cursed."

"Seriously? I mean, I figured as much, but having it actually said out loud is still kind of a shock…"

The whole point of the decoy operation was to get cursed, but it was still a jolt to know that he really had been. What brought a pall over his face was not only fear but his own thoughts—in other words, the fact that one of those lighthearted villagers had been an assassin.

"Do you know what kind of curse it is?"

"I can say nothing from merely seeing the rite. But as we discussed, the odds are extremely strong that it is a curse to take your life."

Subaru calmly accepted Beatrice's statement when she looked up at him with a blink of her large eyes in apparent surprise.

"You do not look like you think dying is a frightening thing, you know?"

"Huh? What a stupid thing to say. I'm super scared of dying.

There's nothing more frightening in this world than death. People who say there's worse stuff than dying should say that after they've tried death once or twice."

It was the one unshakable truth Subaru had learned from that world: Death was absolute. He could not abide it being treated lightly. Nor could he stand comparing death to other things by those who had not experienced it.

After all, Subaru, having experienced death multiple times, had returned to the world to start over because he had himself tasted despair worse than death.

"That's why I'm going to get through it this time, Fate."

If there was indeed a deity that governed fate, Subaru had just declared war upon him.

Subaru Natsuki would snatch back his happy ending to make up for the agonizing times he had suffered.

Having finished his rant at the supernatural being, Subaru turned back to Beatrice.

"So, could you lift that little curse for me? I'm short on time here."

But at the very moment Subaru was burning from the chance to strike the perpetrator when least expected, the girl who should have been his greatest ally cut him off at the knees.

"…Why do I have to save your life, I wonder?"

Subaru scratched his head as he replied, "I thought you might say something un-cute like that, so I came beforehand with a way to convince you. If I die, it'll make Puck sad, too."

"…Would Puckie's heart be greatly moved by your demise, I wonder?"

"No, no, if I die, it'll be a pretty huge shock to Emilia. If it's a shock to Emilia, that'll hurt Puck, too. And especially you, the one who could've stopped it beforehand!"

"You are completely touched in the head, unable to distinguish begging for your life from using it as a threat!"

Beatrice stomped on the floor, but apparently a rebuttal to Subaru's declaration was not forthcoming. She sighed in annoyance and gave him a reluctant look as she beckoned him with a hand.

"I suppose I shall yield. However, do not bother me any further, ever!"

"To be honest, I can't promise you that, either. If I'm in trouble, I'll be back to ask for your help. I'll pick the scraps from your table if I have to."

"Are you even aware that I am saving your life, I wonder?"

"I'm super aware that I'm annoying you with weakling logic. Sorry."

When Subaru bowed his head in apology, Beatrice shook her head with a look of annoyance. After that, her palm glowed with a white light, which she gently touched to Subaru's body.

"I shall now destroy the curse rite. Bear in mind that it is implanted in the place where the shaman touches your body directly."

"Sure, don't worry, I'm all set."

Subaru checked his own body as he felt the light in her palm convey its warmth.

He'd kept track of where the suspects in the village had touched him. Only the granny searching for her lost youth had touched his butt. So, if Beatrice moved her hand to his butt, he'd know that the granny was the perpetrator. He'd also complain to Beatrice about sexual harassment.

"—Eh?"

But the place Beatrice's palm touched was completely at odds with Subaru's expectations.

He felt a swirling heat where the white glow leaped from her palm into his flesh. There was an itchy feeling where she had touched, but it seemed to ooze right out of his body as a…

"Black…cloud…?"

The light in Beatrice's hand directly caught hold of the black fog that had been the curse.

The itchiness vanished as Subaru shuddered from that wriggling cloud having been inside his own body. Then…

"Must you be so abominable, I wonder?"

Beatrice crushed it in her hand before it vanished, then shook her hand as if having touched something icky. Realizing Subaru had gone silent, she harrumphed.

"It is done. I suppose you will be fine now?"

When she said *it is done*, Subaru realized that he'd stopped breathing. He rued his timid heart, but a more pressing concern came to mind.

"Hey, Beako."

"Would you stop addressing me that way already...?"

"Is the place you touched with your palm the place the shaman touched me?"

Faced with Subaru's grave question, Beatrice set her own complaints aside and reluctantly nodded.

Her nod affirmed in Subaru's mind the perpetrator behind the string of curses.

"I've got to...go to the village—!"

Now that he knew the culprit's identity, he had no choice but to act immediately.

He'd originally planned to wait until the next day, go to the village with Roswaal and the twins, flush the shaman in the village out of hiding, and deal with him. But he couldn't do that now.

Subaru's heart continued to race as he rushed to put his hand on the door. His breath was so ragged as he ran that he didn't even hear Beatrice call out for him to stop.

Fate's irrationality and poor taste in irony, dangling Subaru and the others on a string, filled him with rage. That anger gripped Subaru as he ran, yelling at the top of his lungs.

"Just how far are you gonna take playing me for a fool...?!"

He kept running.

5

Subaru dashed through the hallway, leaped down the stairs, flipped around at the landing of the stairs, the heels of his shoes sliding to a stop at the entry hall as he raised his face and yelled out.

"—Ram! Rem! I've gotta talk to you!"

Ram immediately popped into view, responding to the shout that probably carried throughout the entire mansion. Apparently she'd been working quite close by. She looked at Subaru's red face and ragged breathing with her eyes narrowed in disapproval at the impropriety.

"What is it, Barusu? Your haste is quite unsightly."

"Sorry, I'm heading to the village. You can't stop me; I'll go even if you try. I just thought it'd throw everyone off even worse if I just left without a word."

"The village…? Why would you…? No, more importantly, do you intend to disregard Master Roswaal's instructions? Tonight, Rem and I are in charge of this mansion. Surely you understand this?"

Ram glared at Subaru even more sharply.

Ram's position was that whatever Roswaal wanted came first. Subaru's open disregard of her master's command really rubbed her the wrong way.

But Subaru wasn't minded to retreat an inch even so.

"Time's short, so I'll get right to the point. There's a bad magic user in Earlham Village. I know who it is, so I have to go now."

"…You ask me to accept what sounds like a child's made-up excuse?"

"I can't help it; there's no other way to put it here. Go talk to Beako; you'll see I'm telling the truth… Besides…"

As he pleaded with the increasingly suspicious Ram, the great doors opened behind him as Rem emerged.

"Sister—"

When Rem saw the two speaking in the entry hall, she went to her sister's side like it was second nature.

"Sister, what is…?"

"He says he is heading out to rid us of an evil magic user in the village."

Ram bluntly conveyed Subaru's statement to Rem for him. Hearing it put that way, even Subaru thought it sounded like pure fiction. Apparently that was Rem's conclusion, too.

"Sister, Sister. Subaru's joke is not very funny."

"Rem, Rem. Barusu thinks he has a future in comedy."

"Ram, Rem. I might kid around all the time, but I talk seriously sometimes, too."

Faced with their twin-act lines, Subaru spoke to both at once. He took a step forward as if to emphasize that he wasn't cowed by the sisters' reactions.

"I know it's an unbelievable story, and it's asking too much for you to just take my word for it right now. But I'm not asking you to let me go without any conditions."

To Subaru, this was a crucial fork in the road.

Subaru wet his lips with his tongue, jabbing a finger toward the silent pair as he made his proposal.

"I'm going to the village. If you think that's suspicious, fine, tag along. Watch me and see. But I'm not going with Emilia left all alone, so it has to be just one of you."

"You cannot simply go off on your own... In the first place, neither Sister nor I have any reason to go with you if we are to uphold Master Roswaal's command..."

"No, you don't, if Roswaal's command in the evening is the only one you're upholding. Are those the only orders Roswaal gave about me?"

"—"

Rem was at a loss for words.

Subaru's statement a moment before had been a mere bluff, but her uncomfortable reaction made it plain he'd hit the mark.

Piecing together info from the previous loops, Subaru had guessed that Roswaal had ordered the pair to keep an eye on him.

Rem looked like she was searching for an escape route, but Ram beat her to the punch, exhaling.

"Understood, Barusu. We will accept your independent action."

"Sister?!"

Rem was in utter shock at seeing her sister wave a white flag so easily. But Ram indicated to her little sister to keep quiet.

"However, just as you said, we cannot allow you to go alone, Barusu. Allowing you to act alone here would in itself disregard Master Roswaal's commands."

"I figured as much. So what's our compromise gonna be?"

"Though it pains me, we have no choice but to go along with your prior suggestion. Rem will accompany you."

"Ask and ye shall receive, I guess."

Subaru thrust out a clenched fist to show his agreement with Ram's terms.

Ram sighed a little as she turned to her little sister, shunning Subaru.

"Rem, this is how it is, so, please. I shall confirm matters with Lady Beatrice and protect Lady Emilia myself—I shall be watching you from here."

"Sister, you must not use that eye too oft—"

"This is no time to say that. I will use it if I need to. The same goes for you, Rem."

The way the older sister put it left no room for Rem to question any further. Subaru was glancing toward their conversation, understood by only the two sisters, when Rem shifted an unfriendly glance at him.

"Subaru, I would like to hear the details."

"I'll tell you on the way. Things might've already gotten pretty bad, though..."

If Subaru's worst premonition proved true, there would be damage that simply couldn't be laughed off. Not to Subaru personally but in a much larger sense.

He gave Ram's shoulder a light, grateful pat as he headed to the entrance with Rem, who still didn't look on board. He was figuring it was fifteen minutes to the village if they ran straight there, when—

"—Subaru, where are you going?"

A voice clear as a bell danced down from above the great stairway of the entry hall.

Turning around without a thought, he looked up to see Emilia standing there, her silver hair swaying.

Judging from her heavy breaths, she'd heard Subaru's earlier shout and had come over to see the three of them below.

"I thought I'd come down because I heard a loud voice earlier... Did something happen?"

"Something...might've happened. You don't need to worry. Ah, I'll be happy if you worry a *little* bit."

Subaru was behaving casually on purpose so as not to make Emilia too anxious.

Though Subaru was acting in his usual lighthearted fashion, Emilia seemed to pick up on something.

"Your face says you're going to do something dangerous again."

Emilia had a sullen look about her as she saw right through him.

Subaru wailed inside at how his grand act had been so easily foiled as he covered his face with his palms.

"That's what we were arguing about just now. We finally got everything cleared up, so…"

"There's no point trying to stop you, is there?"

"Well, not really. And if you succeeded, it'd only make things worse…"

"Yes, yes, I understand. I won't stop you."

Emilia walked down the stairs, stopping just in front of Subaru and placing her hands on her hips. Subaru was unable to look away from her glimmering violet eyes.

With Subaru unable to move, Emilia reached out and gently touched his chest.

"Even if I tell you not to be reckless or careless, you probably will anyway, won't you?"

"If that's what it takes… Ah, er, not that I want to do either, mind you."

Whether it was achievable or not, the best thing would be to travel a path free of worry and strife.

If, instead, Subaru was the only one who could change the situation, he had to act, even if it was recklessly.

He wondered where he'd picked up such a troublesome personality.

—*Probably has something to do with the girl I'm staring at right now*, he thought with a strained smile.

Emilia was still touching his chest as she murmured.

"—May the grace of the spirits be with you."

"What was that?"

Subaru tried to decipher the expression without success. Emilia shot him a broad smile.

"Words you say when seeing someone off. They mean 'come back safely.'"

"Ahh, I see. Got it, Emilia-tan. So when I do come back safe and sound, you'll gently hug me to your chest like a baby chick, right?"

"Yes, yes."

Letting Subaru's desire for coddling slide off her, Emilia shifted her gaze to include Rem. Rem, who had been silently watching the exchange, straightened her back in response.

"Be careful, Rem. Also, make sure Subaru doesn't do anything rash."

"Yes, Lady Emilia. As you wish."

Seeing Rem grab the hem of her skirt and make a polite bow, Emilia nodded to her in satisfaction. Subaru waved.

"Well, Emilia-tan, I'm heading off."

Emilia's voice had given him words of encouragement to see him on his way.

"Come back soon."

He pushed the doors of the entrance open and began to run toward the village side by side with Rem as the remaining two watched them go.

"So, I would like to hear the details now…"

"There's a shaman in the village to hurt Emilia's royal selection. He cursed me good, but Beatrice removed it. If we don't act now, the whole village could get wiped out."

Even while running, Rem's breath caught, her eyes going wide as she asked, "Are you…serious?"

Subaru replied with a silent nod as he focused his energy on getting to the village.

He wouldn't have had to imagine a shaman with human intelligence taking such a measure. But if Subaru's deduction was correct, he had to assume the worst.

And so, Subaru ran onward. Rem continued to silently sprint by his side, as yet unaware of the gravity of the situation.

6

By the time they arrived at the village, bonfires burned brightly, pushing back the dark of night.

Normally, there was no way anyone would have so many fires lit just to keep it bright at that hour.

Rem, standing beside the out-of-breath Subaru, picked up on the strange atmosphere; her face showed she understood something was wrong.

A young man from the village recognized the pair and hurried over.

"Hey, it's the two from the mansion. What are you doing here at a time like—"

Rem interrupted the youngster's question. "It seems good that we are. Has something happened?"

The young man seemed a little surprised by Rem's manner of speaking, but he immediately replied excitedly.

"Yes. Actually, a bunch of village kids are missing. We knew they were out playing before it got dark, but…well, that's why a whole bunch of people are looking."

Since the youngster in front of them wasn't being specific, Subaru cut in before Rem could ask further.

"The missing kids, that's Luca, Petra, Mildo, and them?"

"Y-yes, them… Do you have any idea where they went?"

When the young man answered affirmatively, Subaru clicked his tongue and kicked the ground. His gaze shifted outside the village—toward the wall that separated it from the forest.

"Who else is looking for the kids besides you?"

"All the young men in the village, plus Muraosa."

"The kids are in the forest. You'll never find them by looking around the village like this."

Subaru's declaration brought a change in the young man's face. He seemed like he wanted to ask Subaru more, but Subaru patted his shoulder and ran toward the trees.

"I'm going into the forest. Tell everyone that's where the kids are!"

Subaru made a beeline toward the woods, paying no heed to the questioning voice behind him.

Rem hurried to keep up with Subaru, giving him a look wrapped in doubt about how certain he seemed.

"How do you know such a…?"

"I can tell. No, I *know*. If what the brats said was right, they should be this way."

A tall wooden fence surrounded the village. The pair climbed over a section bordering the forest and cut among the trees as they headed deeper in.

Subaru had just been going by his memory of what he'd heard, but Rem, walking beside him, suddenly lifted her face.

"—The barrier has been…severed."

Rem's surprised voice made Subaru grit his teeth, because he had been right.

Rem pointed to a crystal embedded in a large tree right before their eyes. Judging from how it wasn't glowing, it must have been placed there to power a barrier blocking off the spaces between the trees.

Subaru remembered several times when people had pointed to the forest and spoken of the barrier. He couldn't recall exactly when, but Ram had told him point-blank not to go into the mountains.

"What does the barrier being cut mean here?"

"It means that demon beasts can cross the boundary. This forest is their habitat, you see."

"Demon beasts…? Huh? So, um, what are they, anyway?"

Subaru's question made Rem's eyes waver as she delivered a textbook reply.

"They are beasts imbued with dark power, the enemy of intelligent life. It is said that the witch created them."

"More of the witch, even here, geez…"

Subaru grimaced at the piece of vocabulary that stuck out, but Rem's explanation made him certain: He knew who the "shaman" was, and that this was just a prelude to an attack on the village.

Before Rem's eyes, Subaru stepped into the gap between the trees she had called a barrier and headed deeper into the woods.

"—! Subaru, what are you—?!"

Rem, surprised, raised her voice to stop him.

"The kids are in there. I have to save them."

"Do you have hard proof of that? Master Roswaal's permission is required before crossing the ba—"

"The scar on my hand is proof!"

He raised his left hand so that Rem could see the animal bite mark on the back of it.

It was the scar left by the bite he'd gotten in the village that afternoon when the kids had surrounded him and he'd touched the puppy.

Beatrice had pointed to that scar and said that the being that made it was the culprit behind the curse on Subaru. Meaning—

"The kids had a cute puppy with them. It looked like a dog, but what if it wasn't a dog? What if it was a demon beast that curses whoever it bites?"

That puppy had bitten Subaru not once, not twice, but three times. If he hadn't been bitten this time around, he had no doubt Rem would've been bitten instead.

Human hands hadn't cast the curse; it was more like a natural disaster.

Just like rats were the medium through which the Black Plague spread, demon beasts were the vector by which the curse was propagated.

The kids had followed the demon beast into the forest. There was no telling whether or not they were safe within.

"This gets worse the more time passes. We don't know if the kids are already cursed, but for now we've got to bring them all back to the mansion and purify them."

"Hold on. You cannot simply decide that on your... In the first place, the situation is too suspicious."

"Huh?"

Rem pointed toward the village, which happened to be toward the mansion as well.

"To have such a problem occur while Master Roswaal is absent... Are you certain this is not a diversion for an attack on the mansion?"

"So what would you do? Abandon the kids in trouble right this minute, go back to the mansion, and batten down the hatches? I mean, yeah, we can do that, if you're all right with everyone in the village being dead by morning."

Even as he said it, Subaru was well aware of how cruelly he'd put it.

Rem was just trying to do her job and minimize the risks to the people at the mansion. It was natural for her to think that way, and he had no intention of blaming Rem for it. But there came a time when you had to make a choice, no matter how much you tried to push it away.

And Subaru knew only too well that the greatest regret came from choosing not to choose at all.

"Rem, let's go. We've got to do something."

"Why are you that determined to…? Subaru, what connection do you have to the vill—"

Perhaps it was her still being unsure about his judgment, but it was the first time Subaru had heard Rem murmur in a feminine fashion.

Here was Rem, prim and proper through thick and thin, uttering such soft complaints.

If he was being honest, Subaru would've said he was scared to go forward. His legs were trembling from fatigue, but from another reason as well. Who could have blamed him if he'd displayed the face of a coward he was desperately keeping concealed?

But Subaru slapped his own cheeks to make his heart forget its slide toward weakness and escape.

"—Petra wants to be a clothing maker in the capital when she grows up."

"…Ah?"

"Luca wants to follow in the footsteps of his dad, the top wood-carver in the village. Mildo wants to make a wreath from flowers from all the flower beds and give it to his mom as a present…"

"—"

Subaru recalled each face one by one in the back of his mind as he continued, counting with his fingers.

"Meyna's all happy because a little brother or sister will be born anytime now, and those brothers Dyne and Cain are both working hard to get Petra's hand in marriage..."

He let out a small laugh. Then he shook his head to Rem, who stood in silence.

"I know their faces, their names, and what they want to do in life. I'm not some stranger anymore."

Subaru hated kids.

They were noisy, rowdy, and they talked trash with no respect for their elders. They thought nothing of discourtesy or disrespect, were brash and unreserved—it was like looking at himself in the mirror.

"But, Rem, I promised them I'd do aerobics with them again tomorrow morning."

Subaru had thought the same things during the loop on the first day after his summoning.

It'd be easier just to let things go. But he ran forward because he *couldn't*.

He looked at Rem. She was conflicted. She hesitated.

Looking weak, powerless, about to break out in tears—that was Subaru's job.

Seeing her looking weaker than he, Subaru resented himself for hardening his resolve. He loathed that he was a small and petty-enough person to use others to protect himself, even though he was the incurable scaredy-cat.

If his own cowardice could be used as a tool, he'd use that, too.

"I keep my promises and expect others to keep theirs—I'll do aerobics with those brats again, you'll see. That's why I'm heading in."

—He had no idea courage was such a terrifying thing.

Subaru was so focused on keeping his hands from shaking that he didn't even notice the tremor in his voice. From behind, Rem watched all this, then silently closed her eyes. Then...

"Then it cannot...be helped."

"Rem?"

Subaru lifted his face as Rem's tongue abruptly loosened.

It was practically the first time since he'd met her that she'd displayed clear emotion on her face.

"After all, I have been assigned to watch over you, Subaru. I cannot accomplish that duty if I let you go by yourself, can I?"

Rem sounded like she was teasing Subaru, leaving him in shock before he finally shook his head.

"Yeah, I suppose not. Keep a good eye on me to make sure I don't do anything suspicious."

"Yes, I will. So, let us be off?"

Seeing Rem standing beside him, Subaru felt like it was the first time they had *truly* stood side by side.

He had an urge to thank Rem, but before he could find the words, he noticed *it*. As Rem walked beside him, she had at some point taken an iron ball in her hand. Attached to a handle via a long chain, the metal looked much too heavy for the ease with which she carried it.

"Er, ah, Rem, that's…"

"For self-defense."

"Er, but that's…"

"For self-defense."

Subaru and Rem traded words along those lines as they walked into the woods without any path to follow.

He desperately tried to re-harden his resolve and revive the courage he'd wrung out of himself at such great pains.

7

With Rem maintaining her combat readiness with the iron ball "for self-defense" in one hand, the two continued exploring the night-covered forest.

The moonlight was obstructed by the tree canopy, bringing a deep, black darkness over the forest. As they stepped around the trees obstructing their path, plowing forward through leaves and branches, their bodies picked up scratches that oozed blood.

Plunged into a world with just a little moonlight trickling through to light the way, there was only one thing they had to search for.

"—"

Rem stopped, looking all around as she sniffed the air. Her motion was like that of a police dog, and they were indeed relying on Rem's sense of smell to guide them through the forest.

Subaru kept from speaking to her so as not to disrupt her concentration, but his unease was intense. He trailed after her small back as she stepped ahead of him, the long silence whittling Subaru's mental state down further, when…

"—I smell something alive… It is close."

Rem sent a sharp gaze to her left as she murmured, and Subaru followed suit. But he saw nothing there but darkness, the same as all the rest. Seized by impatience, he patted Rem's shoulder.

"Is it the kids?"

"I do not know, but it is not an animal smell."

"That's enough to go on," said Subaru, nodding to Rem as he rushed forward. She ran right behind him.

Even Rem's expression brightened a bit from having a solid lead that cut through the darkness. She subconsciously picked up her pace.

Although, as their expectations increased, so did their unease. That fact was probably part of why Rem was unwilling to say for certain if the scent belonged to the kids.

Rem drove forward, shoving aside foliage to make a path. Subaru chased after her, out of breath as his legs began to grow heavy. But his mind was crystal clear. His eyes had begun to acclimate to the darkness, so Subaru started to make out the outlines of the forest, too—and the next moment, the forest opened up, and both arrived on top of a high little hill.

Moonlight shone down on the green slope in the gap in the forest like something out of a dream. And there—

"It's the kids!"

There, lying on the ground, were the children, arms and legs spread as they slept.

Rem and Subaru rushed over together to check on whether they were safe. There were six on the ground in total. They weren't conscious, but they were breathing, and their bodies were warm to the touch.

"They're alive. They're alive!"

"We made it in time!" Subaru shouted with joy. But Rem, standing beside him, had a stern look on her face.

"No, they are still breathing, but they are heavily debilitated. At this rate…"

"Debilitated…? The curse?!"

When he looked closer, he saw that the children all had pale faces; their breaths were short and ragged, like even that drained their strength. Their brows were covered in cold sweat as they slept with pained expressions, like they were seeing nightmares.

"After we finally found them… Rem, can't you lift the curses?"

"My skill is insufficient. If Sister is indeed watching this place… At any rate, I will use healing magic to put them at ease. We shall carry them once they calm down."

"Got it. I'll… Shit, I'm so useless. I'll keep an eye out for trouble."

Subaru resented himself all over again for his lack of ability. Rem said nothing to him; instead, she infused her palm with a pale light—the light of healing mana—and began to treat the children.

While he kept a lookout, Subaru watched as the wave of healing began to bring peace to more of the sleeping children. At the rate they were calming, they could bring the kids back to the mansion and ask Beatrice to lift the c—

But just as Subaru was mentally putting plans in order, a girl lightly opened her eyes and called his name.

"Suba…ru?"

Her gaze looked troubled, perhaps because her mind was so hazy, so Subaru took her hand.

"You're awake, Petra? Okay, good girl, you're a strong girl. We'll be taking you back real soon and making the reason you're suffering go bye-bye, so right now you need to just rest…"

"There's one in… Still… The forest…"

"—Hey, what did you say?"

Petra was trying to tell him something with her halting words.

The information nuggets gave him a bad feeling, so Subaru called out to Petra once more. But his voice never reached her; her eyes had closed and she'd lost consciousness again.

Subaru patted the sleeping Petra's forehead and urgently rushed to the other children, looking them over. Then...

"Aw, crap... She's right. I don't see the youngest one here."

He knew the faces of all six of the children sleeping there from spending time with them during the day. Setting aside Subaru and the puppy, it left the shy, withdrawn girl missing.

"Damn it all!"

Subaru stood up, tearing at his hair at the turn for the worse.

Rem, who'd seen and heard the entire exchange with Petra, widened her eyes, apparently alarmed at Subaru's behavior.

"P-please wait. It is too dangerous. If she was taken away by the demon beasts, there is nothing—"

"I know what you're trying to say. I know. I know all too well, but you heard it, too, Rem. Petra said to go get the last one of them before anything else."

Petra was suffering to the brink of tears, weakened to the point that breathing was a struggle. Even so, she'd expressed concern for her friend rather than saying the words *save me*.

She was a weak little girl, but the life of her friend came before her own.

"...I want to do what Petra asked me to. If we're gonna pick one up, we might as well do our best to pick 'em all up."

"You are too greedy. If you pick up too much, you might end up dropping everything on the floor."

"You're here to make sure that doesn't happen, Rem."

Rem looked daunted by it all. Seeing her so surprised, Subaru spread his arms wide to make her look at him.

"I can't do anything here, either. I can't use healing magic, and there's no way I can bring the kids back by myself. If so, I should use myself as effectively as I can, right?"

"What does that have to do with m—"

"You need to save your strength to carry the kids, Rem. The young men from the village will…probably be coming in after us soon enough. Just hand the kids over to them and come after me."

The villagers had to be well aware that demon beasts were in the forest. Furthermore, they'd no doubt girded themselves with gear and plenty of light sources. All Rem needed to do was hand the kids over and tell the men to bring the kids to the mansion.

"While you're doing that, I'll go deeper in and look for the last kid… Hey, if it's worst case, I'll come running right back. But if there's still any ray of hope, at least I can buy some time out there."

Rem, unable to accept Subaru's decision, grabbed Subaru's sleeve and argued vehemently.

"You do not know your opponent's strength. There is no guarantee when the villagers will come, and worst case, I may not be able to find you."

Perhaps she was worried about him. Perhaps it was just her nature not to go along with uncertain plans.

Thinking that it'd be nice if it was the former, Subaru pulled Rem's fingers off his sleeve and held her hand.

"I'll be all right. You'll find me."

"What proof do you have of…?"

"I've got proof right here."

Subaru smiled, pointing a finger at his own nose before pointing it back at Rem's face.

"Even if no one else notices, *you'll* notice my scent. I have the lingering stench of a villain hovering about me, right?"

Rem's eyes opened wide in surprise. It was thrilling, really.

He laughed, like seeing this Rem before his eyes was taking revenge on that other Rem from times past.

"Subaru…how much…do you know…?"

"Ah, I'm pretty ignorant about tons of things. It's so bad, I'd never find the answers even if I repeated yesterday, today, and tomorrow over and over again."

He thought back on those days and how repeating them too much had worn him to the bone.

He then realized he'd changed a lot to actually be able to laugh about it.

"Looks like you have some things you want to ask me, and I have a mountain of things I want to ask you. So when this is all over, let's talk it out till our throats go dry. It's a promise."

And, without waiting for Rem, he kept their hands together as he wrapped his little finger around hers.

Rem remained perplexed at the sight of their intertwined pinkie fingers as Subaru moved the fingers up and down in a shake.

"There. Pinkie promise."

"Wh-what did you just…?"

"It's a ritual from my homeland for making a promise. It's a terrible ritual guaranteeing you'll get a thousand sewing needles stuck into you if you break it."

The encroachment of Subaru Space had already exceeded Rem's comprehension.

Rem was befuddled and confused beyond words when Subaru snapped his fingers and flashed his teeth.

"I believe in you, Rem. So I want to act based on that trust. That's why we need to promise here."

"—"

"I told you, right? I keep my promises, and I expect others to keep theirs. Plus I've got Emilia's blessing on my side, so don't worry, be happy."

"H-happy…?"

Completely unable to keep up, Rem made a long, exasperated sigh as she laughed weakly.

Subaru, seeing that Rem was continuing to laugh, kept his voice down as he laughed, too. Then Rem said, "A promise, then. There really is much I want to ask you, after all."

"Sure thing. It's a promise between the two of us that needed making. The same probably goes for the hair, too."

"The hair…?"

"The reason why you keep staring at my hair."

Rem was at a loss for words when Subaru pointed it out. Guilt also seemed to well into her eyes as he watched her open her mouth.

"Subaru, I…"

"It's all right. I'm not getting the wrong idea. You were always watching me while I did my amateur work because the shabby top of my head really bothered you…right?"

On the last day before he'd begun looping again, Subaru and Rem had made a promise—a promise for Rem to cut Subaru's unsightly hair.

Now Subaru understood the truth behind those words.

At the time, Rem had been seized by enormous distrust of Subaru, hence the intensity of her gaze toward him. Ram had simply been trying to cover for her.

That promise had been made on the basis of a lie. He knew that now.

But Subaru would take the promise that began with a lie and make it true, smiling all the way.

"When I come back safe and sound, I'll put myself at your mercy. I'm counting on you to make me look so cool that Emilia will fall for me without even thinking."

"…Given what I am starting with, even I have my limits."

"Could you please put facts like that in a less direct way…?"

This was the Rem who had always left him behind. Her agreeing to go along with his suggestion made him happy then and there.

Subaru made a satisfied nod at how the cheerful days he sought were being born anew.

Rem said, "I shall hand off the children and immediately catch up with you. Please do nothing rash in the meantime."

"Don't worry. After all, I'm possessed by a demon today."

"Possessed…?"

"Possessed by a demon instead of a god. Lately it's my favorite saying!"

Subaru posed with two fingers standing above his head to act as pretend horns.

Regardless of what she thought about Subaru's frivolous behavior, she let his pose pass without comment.

"Please be careful."

With Rem sending him off and turning around, Subaru went down the low hill, going deeper into the forest. He headed in the direction Petra had indicated just before losing consciousness.

"Well, Subaru Natsuki, let's do this."

Speaking to encourage himself, Subaru ran, clenching the hand with which he'd made the pinkie promise for good measure.

—He didn't know if despair or hope awaited him, or something else.

One way or another, the morning of the fourth day seemed far, far away.

8

His heart was in a hurry, but he tread cautiously.

The inside of his mouth was parched; his throat was tense with stress. He kept his footsteps quiet as he guardedly advanced into the dark forest. His steps were hesitant, but not because he was afraid or timid about moving forward.

"I sure flapped my lips in front of Rem there, but…"

It was a dangerous move to go alone, but Subaru thought his odds were far from hopeless. In the first place, Subaru was a weakling; his personality was fundamentally averse to gambling. He was doing this precisely because he had a reasonable basis to think he had a chance.

"If it was that puppy from today that cursed the kids, I've got a shot…"

It bore the frightening title of demon beast, but surely a puppy didn't have much combat ability. Its curse was indeed a frightening thing, but if it came to a clash of man versus fang…

"I won't lose to that thing, right…?"

It was rather pathetic to pin his hopes on his opponent's small size, though.

No doubt it was an optimistic and convenient thought, but he didn't think he was wrong to be optimistic, especially because this world had given Subaru such a raw deal. If he just piled on negative images, he would lose himself, cast into despair too deep for his exuberance to get him out of.

Subaru sighed, slumping his shoulders at how his parents had taught him to look at the warped world around him. Then…

"—!"

Subaru held his breath and stopped his feet at the sudden malaise he felt. The air seemed to shift against his skin. The sweat on his brow suddenly grew much cooler.

The wind carried into his trembling nostrils the thick scent of beasts in the direction he was traveling. Whereas before the air was thick with the scent of grass and soil, it was now full of the stench of some wild animal in nature.

Subaru, unable to quash the feeling that something bad was on its way, stilled his breathing. He poked his head out through a gap in the trees. His breath caught when he saw the cause of the wafting scent.

"—"

At the end of his line of sight, in a tiny clearing, he saw a tree that had fallen due to wind and rot. A slender white leg was poking out beside it.

When he craned his neck and peered in, Subaru saw that the leg had tattered cloth over it, attached to a girl wearing her frayed brown hair in braids. He'd found her.

"—"

He held his breath and thought about this.

There was no doubt this was the girl in question. But the girl's body did not so much as twitch while she lay on the ground. She was not conscious, and of course, he couldn't even check to see if she was breathing from where he stood. He quickly scanned her surroundings, but it seemed like the demon beast that had left the girl here was not close by.

So the beast had dragged back his prey, then abandoned it? That didn't feel right. It didn't, but…

"…It's a golden opportunity… What to do…?"

With every moment he waited during this ideal chance to save the girl, the danger increased, all the more so because Subaru had, at best, a 50 percent chance of actually handling his potential opponent.

—Why was Subaru Natsuki the one here?

What if it had been Roswaal? Or Beatrice? Or Reinhard?

If it were one of them, blessed with power worthy of heroes, the situation could be easily resolved.

But it was Subaru Natsuki who stood there. It was Subaru Natsuki who yearned for a miracle. And it was Subaru Natsuki who most assuredly could not bring a miracle about.

His rational mind pleaded for him to play the sure hand and wait for Rem. And yet...

—*Emilia wouldn't hesitate.*

The instant he thought it, Subaru's legs stopped shaking. His pulse, quickened by the decision pressing upon him, calmed along with his ragged breath.

Subaru rushed through the grass, flying into the clearing in front of him, and made a beeline toward the girl in the shade of the fallen tree. He sat up her tiny, light body and checked to see if it had a pulse.

—Her breathing was frail, but he felt a faint, steady pulse through her veins.

"...I'm so glad."

He was truly relieved that he hadn't decided to abandon her.

The faint breathing and pulse might have meant she was being affected by a curse as well. If that was the case, he needed to get her healed by magic and have the curse lifted without a moment to lose.

He wasn't exactly confident about his endurance, but he figured he could carry a single girl out of the forest...but as Subaru rose to his feet with that judgment in his head...

"—"

The sudden chill running up Subaru's spine made him gasp and look over his shoulder.

—The bushes rustled as a four-legged beast crossed the grass and stepped onto the bare soil.

It was a beast with short black fur. At a glance, it seemed similar in size to a Doberman from his world, but it was built twice as thickly as the dogs Subaru had seen. The clawlike paws were sharp; slobber was dripping out from its fangs even with its maw closed. It made a low growl as its bloodshot eyes glared at Subaru.

It was a demon dog, or rather, a demon beast. Such a name suited its malevolent appearance.

"...This is, uh...not what I had in mind here."

He didn't even realize his cheek was twitching as a smile and a dry laugh came over him.

The demon beast before his eyes was clearly not the little puppy-size one Subaru had expected. In addition, the timing with which it had showed itself meant that...

"...You used this girl as a decoy and waited for her to lure me out...?"

Subaru shuddered. Perhaps it was only feral instincts at work, but the beast's unexpected intelligence disturbed him. Either way, he didn't have any time to ponder the matter.

His eyes roamed the area, but he saw neither any sign of Rem catching up to him nor any avenue for escape from the demon beast. Indeed, the latter had already lowered its head, clawing the ground.

He had no time to hesitate.

"Tch... Shit, if you're gonna come, come!!"

As Subaru vented, he stripped his jacket off, wrapping the well-tailored garment around his left arm.

In a confrontation with a wild animal, the thing you had to worry about the most was its sharp fangs. Wrapping thick fabric around your arm to limit the damage was the least you could do against a four-legged beast.

He'd remembered seeing police dog training on TV in his old world and instantly copied that. He thrust his left arm out, glaring at the demon beast as it tried to figure out when best to leap at him.

The way the demon beast kept its center of gravity low, not moving a muscle, unnerved Subaru.

"Hey, what's with the laid-back attitude here?! Hey! Come on! C—"

It vanished.

Suddenly, the demon beast that should have been right in front of him melted into the darkness.

Fright froze his throat as an indistinct black cloud headed for Subaru's outstretched left arm. The next moment, he felt sharp fangs punch through the thick fabric, with the demon beast biting deep into his flesh.

"That—!"

In an instant, he felt a jabbing pain, intense enough to turn his vision red, slam directly into his nervous system.

But…

"—Didn't hurt!!"

He poured strength into his left arm, tightening the muscles so that the fangs sunk into his muscles wouldn't come out. As a result, the demon beast clamped on at an angle was now completely unable to move.

Its two red eyes met Subaru's gaze. Subaru bathed in the beast's overwhelming enmity as he said, "You bit me, you mangy mutt—!"

Wrapping his whole left arm around the demon beast, Subaru whipped his body around, hard. Centrifugal force sent the demon beast floating into the air, spinning it backward toward the fallen tree—and slamming against an outstretched branch.

"—!"

The sharp branch ruptured its hide, making a dull sound as it rent the beast's flesh. Its dying howl echoed throughout the dark forest.

The demon beast, impaled through its back, kept Subaru's arm clamped in its maw for a while, but it finally relented as it stopped moving. Subaru, for his part, fell to his knees.

"I…won?"

Seeing that it was not breathing, Subaru murmured as he yanked the demon beast's fangs from his arm. His forearm was in horrid shape under the bloodstained jacket. Upon actually seeing the wound, Subaru made a soundless whimper as pain assailed his nerves. Even so, he made a sigh of relief, grimacing all the while.

Even without Rem's strength, he had been able to get out of that crisis. He took the time to retie the jacket around his arm, using it as a bandage.

He made sure his arm could still move before walking back to pick up the girl for real this time.

"Hurts…but that means I'm alive. Crap. Anyway, gotta get back to the vill—"

He cut his words off there because he noticed that the grass had rustled once more. His hair stood up as his entire body was gripped by the sense that something bestial still lurked.

He looked back. Then Subaru murmured, "Oh come *on*…"

Red eyes flared through the dark forest—a horde of them gazed at him through the trees ahead, their numbers virtually beyond count.

Not that he really wanted to count, but all his fingers and toes put together probably wouldn't cut it.

Before he knew it, Subaru had thrust his arms out wide. Not to surrender to the countless points of light—but to shield the little girl behind him.

"—"

The beasts were unimpressed by his silent resolve. The red points of light ignored Subaru's wishes and leaped at him all at once.

"*Ooo—!*"

Subaru realized his own throat howled. He roared, unwilling to give in.

His spirit kept up the facade, telling him that he would not lose, no matter how many red eyes were before him. He was, of course, bluffing; his tiger's mask was nothing more than paper. As Subaru yelled, a demon beast rushed up to rip out his throat—

"—"

—when the head of the demon beast before his eyes exploded like an overripe melon.

Bludgeoned to death at point-blank range, its fresh blood showered Subaru's face. The demon beast's headless body sailed forward and crashed into Subaru. Blown backward by the force, Subaru rolled and, feeling unpleasant from the pain and blood, he shook his head and stood up.

—What just happened?

A blue-haired girl had descended onto the field of battle, one hand lightly grasping the hem of her skirt as it made an elegant twirl, the other wielding a malevolent iron ball.

"The children are safe and are returning to the village. I see your efforts to buy time have gone well."

"Rem, look o—!"

Subaru's elation over the arrival of his awaited reinforcements was short-lived, for now that the vanguard of the demon beast force had been cut down, two more leaped toward her slender body.

"*—Hah!*"

Her right arm, wielding the iron handle, whipped sideways; the iron ball followed in the wake of the whirling chain.

The destructive weapon, which ought to have been slow and unwieldy, turned with incredible force, following the arc of the swing of her arm to utterly pulverize everything in its path. Its might mowed down branches and snapped tree trunks before slamming straight into the demon beast's body. The weapon connected with such power it split the torso in two, turning it into fertilizer for the forest.

And, as the comrade beside it fell in a single moment, the other soared to angrily sink its fangs into Rem's left flank—but just before it reached her, Rem smashed her left fist into its snout from above, pummeling it out of the sky. The might of her fist caved the beast's skull in, slaying it instantly with a blow powerful enough to bury its head into the soil.

Her skill was crystal clear. Subaru had thought he appreciated Rem's destructiveness, but now he truly *knew*. That made his head hurt.

"Y-you're so strong!!"

"Are those appropriate words to speak to a girl, Subaru?"

"That's the only thing a weakling like me can say! You're really out there!"

Ecstatic that Rem proved far more reliable than he'd imagined, Subaru leaped as if to embrace her. He then skirted around right behind Rem as the remainder of the pack spread out and surrounded them.

Having lost two more of their number, the pack moved sluggishly. The beasts crouched, awaiting their—well, Rem's—next move; Subaru could tell that there was bitter enmity in their eyes.

"...Incidentally, Rem, do you plan on wiping them out by yourself?"

"There are too many of them. Alone, they can overcome me with numbers."

"Well that figures. In that case..."

Before the beasts could recover their bearings and come leaping at them, Subaru and Rem had the same thought. Their eyes swept the surroundings before settling on the same place—a weak point in the encirclement with only three of the beasts.

Subaru yelled in concert with Rem's attack.

"There!"

The iron ball ripped through the air, with the howl heralding the slaughter. A moment before reaching the cluster of demon beasts, the iron ball smashed into the ground, kicking up a huge cloud of dirt. Subaru sensed that the cascade of soil had thrown the beasts off.

Rem was the next to yell.

"Now—!"

Subaru ran like his body had been shot out of a cannon.

The blow from a moment before had opened a hole in the barricade, a narrow area that he could break through—

As Subaru flew through the gap, the demon beasts howled at how they had left open a path. But when they rushed in pursuit, they became easy prey to the iron snake lashing behind them.

"Whoa, traumatic sound alert—!"

As he sprinted full force, Subaru recalled the sound of the dancing chain sending his left arm flying off. Behind him, the iron ball swung ferociously, making numerous bloody flowers bloom fresh in the dark forest.

Subaru vaulted over a tree root, getting smacked on the cheek by a branch as he yelled, "Rem, I can't see where I'm going!"

"Straight...straight ahead. This will be settled when we pass through the barrier. Head for the bonfires in the village!"

Straight ahead, she'd said, but Subaru couldn't even tell which way was the front. He never imagined that the darkness, leaving him able to see only a little ways in front, would ruin his sense of direction to this degree. Nor could he grope ahead with his hands when he had a little girl weighing down his arms.

He was out of breath. He was full of anxiety that he had lost his way or that the beasts were about to catch up to him.

His left arm was going numb. The bleeding had never stopped; the fabric of his jacket was drenched in blood. He could picture in his mind how blooddrops were falling to the earth, leaving a perfect trail that led his pursuers right to him.

He saw what looked like the same scenery over and over, as if he hadn't made a single step of forward progress. A sense of irritation burned in his chest; he felt like he was about to fall to his knees. Yet, all the while...

...he heard the sound of a chain whipping behind him.

"Aww, shit! My side really hurts—!"

Forward, forward—!

Then the darkness before Subaru suddenly lifted.

His field of vision broadened and, as his eyes instinctively narrowed at the suddenness of it, he saw man-made light off in the distance.

"Rem! I see light! Someone from the village is...at the barrier!"

Subaru looked back in joy at the appearance of a literal ray of hope. But a moment later, his eyes silently went wide.

He could describe the sight of Rem fighting to protect him from behind only as heroic.

Her perfectly sized maid outfit was ripped and gnawed to shreds; the white flesh below it was marked with countless cuts. Her vivid blue hair was all a mess, and there was too much fresh blood in it to make out the original color.

He saw Rem in a ferocious battle worthy of legend. And at that very moment, the same Rem was fast approaching Subaru as she reached out to him with a hand.

"Rem—?!"

Rem's outstretched hand shoved on Subaru's back, adding enough forward momentum to send him sprawling. He instantly protected the girl in his arms from the shock, but in exchange, he was unable to protect himself as he hit the ground face-first, banging up his body.

Subaru felt the pain and tasted the dirt in his mouth; he wanted to ask Rem why she'd done something so violent just then—but he was at a loss for such words.

"...You're kidding me..."

Subaru murmured as, right before his eyes, the soil was sweeping from right to left.

Wind enveloped the earth, sand and mud rose in a vortex, and trees were torn from their roots as the very terrain of the forest changed. Faced with the violent scene before him, Subaru caught his breath when he shifted his eyes to the point from which the flowing soil originated.

—For there, he saw the little demon beast, surrounded by a golden glow as it unleashed magical power.

—Demon beasts were enemies of mankind that possessed magical energy.

This was no curse. Curses couldn't be wielded the way that energy could. In other words, it was using *magic*.

"—R-Rem?!"

When he belatedly understood what was happening, Subaru realized that Rem was no longer behind him. He also realized that Rem had shoved him to protect him from the river of dirt.

And in exchange...

"—"

...the dirt and stone had launched her uniform-clad body high into the dark sky.

The ground gave Rem a rough welcome, buffeting her small body like a fallen leaf. The way blood scattered from her and how she flew helplessly in the air proved with crystal clarity that she'd taken more damage than she could bear.

Rem was unable to soften the blow when she made a hard landing. The saving grace was that she hadn't cracked her skull on the ground left bare by the flow of the soil.

"Re... You idiot! How can you...? What have I been...?!"

Doing this for, Subaru was about to yell, but in that instant, his spine froze.

No doubt they'd all felt it, too. The little demon beast making the current of earth and the pack chasing after them...they all stopped moving.

He could feel it. He was sure of it. What hovered in the air was the heavy presence of death.

—Slowly, Rem's fallen body rose up.

Even though she'd taken such a spectacular blow, Rem didn't show any sign of injury as she stood up. Indeed, as far as he could see, all her wounds had closed.

The incredible healing energy emitted a high temperature, and her very blood boiled, rising as red steam.

Rem turned her head, slowly looking around the area. Her eyes had lost all trace of reason. Her face, covered in blood spatter, twisted into an ecstatic smile.

Then, Subaru saw.

"—A demon."

—With her headdress now off, he saw a white horn grow from Rem's forehead.

"Ah-ha...ah-ha-ha—"

She laughed. It was loud laughter like that of a little girl but overflowing with naked cruelty.

Twisting herself, Rem's body moved like the wind as it charged the demon beast pack. Faster than the unmoving demon beast in the vanguard could react, Rem smashed it with her heel. She kicked its body at the demon beasts ahead of her, slowing them down as she swung her iron ball, leaving a large quantity of bloody blossoms and beast corpses behind it.

"Demon beast! Demon beast! Demon beast! —Witch!"

Rem continued to yell with each overpowering blow as she slew one demon beast after another.

Blood scattered, skulls caved, and innards and gray matter scattered around the forest with great force.

Subaru fell to his knees, forgetting all about his pain as he took in the scene.

He didn't have the courage to raise his voice. That ought not have been so, but somehow, Subaru knew that if he appeared on Rem's radar right then, he'd have been killed in a heartbeat.

Rem's behavior was so far off that he couldn't imagine he was wrong.

Subaru was taking in the fact that Rem had gone berserk. But the demon beasts didn't simply sit and wait for death.

Unfrozen after the initial shock, the demon beasts surrounded Rem to take advantage of any opening. The corpses slain by single blows grew in number as they whittled Rem down by fang and claw.

The horde was endless. By now, she ought to have crushed at least the number that had initially pursued them, but the numbers of red eyes had increased along the way; they came in waves that seemed as constant as the tides.

"Even if she's in her Ultimate Mode, there's no way she can hold out against enemies with infinite spawn…!"

The circumstances had undergone a dizzying change, but Subaru and the others were still at a steep disadvantage.

Subaru, grasping the situation objectively, looked back when he felt another spike in magical energy.

The demon pup kept its distance from the melee between Rem and the pack while deploying a magic circle. It was sucking the air dry of its mana, preparing to release yet another force to warp the space around it.

Rem's face whipped up, apparently sensing the vortex of energy, sending the iron ball flying high so that she could whirl it to dispose of the new menace. But when Rem stopped moving, the pack of demon beasts seized their chance, leaping at Rem's back all at once.

"—!"

It was instantaneous. He was reaching for Rem's back before a single thought entered his mind.

Rem's breath caught at the impact that pushed her out of the way. Her face stiffened in shock and unrest. Her empty eyes regained the luster of reason, her monstrous smile dropped away, and her emotions spilled over.

—*Ah, you can make a face like that, too*, he thought in a corner of his mind.

"—*Gaaaaah!!*"

The next moment, something crushed the wrist of his outstretched arm.

He screamed. His right leg, his left flank, and his back felt fangs sink into them simultaneously. His vision was dyed red. He couldn't register the pain. His ankles were crushed. His belly was rent. Blood and intestines flowed out, a waste of blood and flesh.

"Subaru—!!"

He thought he heard a shriek.

Even though he tried to lift his face toward it, his body no longer moved as he wished. His balance was wrecked. His crushed ankles were unable to respond at even half normal strength. He collapsed to the ground as such wounds demanded. Right before him, a maw lined with fangs was rushing at him. It went for his windpipe. Also right before him, the iron ball rent the earth and smashed it. Blood scattered. Was it his blood, or...?

His mind was wandering. He didn't know when it would vanish altogether.

He felt his life drain away. He, too, thought it was a stupid thing. He'd put the cart before the horse. What was the point of redoing it all now?

Pain. Suffering. Everything was so far away—invisible, inaudible. Dwindling.

His life was oozing out of the hole in his side like grains of sand from an hourglass.

I'm fading. It's over. It's all...over.

"Don't die, don't die, don't die—!"

A voice on the brink of tears.

A cry.

I—

CHAPTER 4
THE DEMONIC METHOD

1

His consciousness floated on a distant wave.

His mind, in a daze atop the shifting tide, floated back and forth between dream and reality.

"—no other way to save him?"

"—all, I wonder? You should do as you please, then."

Far away—no, close by—at the border neither here nor there, he heard one person conversing with another.

A clinging voice. A blunt voice. A crying voice. A voice with frozen emotion. Voices.

Abruptly, he felt an embrace of a soft hand.

He remembered whose it was, because he had felt it several times before.

He craved that warmth. He wanted to go back. He didn't want it to be simply a dream.

The sensation of the hand suddenly grew distant. Far, far away, unreachable and untouchable.

"—I will…save you."

Only those words of iron determination remained.

Everything vanished. It all left, leaving him far, far behind.

And then—

2

How many times had he been knocked out cold, only to wake up like this?

Subaru stared at the unfamiliar ceiling as such thoughts hovered in his mind.

"Unngh, ow…"

His side spasmed the instant he sat up in bed. That *really* woke him up.

When he tried to touch his painful belly, he felt something very wrong with his left arm. The ill feeling remained as he brought his arm before him, seeing with his own eyes what a sorry state it was in.

There were white scars covering him from the tips of his fingers up to his wrist.

It wasn't just his arm that felt off.

He yanked up his shirt and saw that he had similar scars on his right side. He had more on both ankles, on his right upper arm and shoulder, and lastly, one on his butt.

They all seemed to be scars left from the demon beasts' fangs.

"I was sure I was a goner…"

He'd been bitten all over when shielding Rem.

The maws of the ferocious beasts had made mincemeat out of Subaru's flesh. He felt how low his life had dimmed in his blood and internal organs; he'd been more than half sure that it was over.

"So I barely held on to life and got patched up after…?"

Subaru carefully looked around the area as he made sure his fingers were moving properly.

The ceiling was unfamiliar; the bed, crude. The room was far too cramped to be one of the rooms in Roswaal Manor. Then he noticed the girl sitting in a wooden chair right next to the door, her head down as she slept.

"—Emilia."

She showed no sign of responding to his call.

Emilia was breathing quite deeply, matching the depth of her sleep. Her beautiful silver hair was disheveled for once; more than that, her clothes were still heavily caked with blood and mud.

He was wounded. He'd slept close to morning. Emilia was sleeping right beside him. Add all that to the state of her clothing, and even someone as dim-witted as Subaru could grasp the situation.

"I'm in her debt again, huh…?"

"I wonder about that. This time, Lia might think of it as giving you a hand because your hard work brought results."

Subaru turned in the direction of the faint murmur. Puck crawled out of Emilia's hair and hovered in the air beside her.

"Heya. Good morning, Subaru. Those will hold you back, huh?"

"Maybe not. Feels a little stiff where I'm scarred, but I'm not gonna complain about having my life saved. I'm a guy, so I don't plan on whining just because my body's scuffed up, either."

He didn't intend to turn them into marks of honor from the field of battle, but the deep feelings inside him associated with the white scars would no doubt never fade.

To Subaru, what had happened to the source of his scars was more important.

"Guess it worked out like I expected, but…what actually happened after? To be honest, I don't remember a thing after the dogs went chompy-chomp-chomp on me."

"'Chompy-chomp-chomp' is such a cute way to put it. From what I saw when they hauled you in, it was more like, 'Chomp-munch-crunch-rip-yank-tear'…"

"If it was like *that* I'd be dead already. Five or six extra arms wouldn't cover all that."

"Mm, well, the extra damage you didn't get was why the maid with the blue hair was in a sorry state."

Subaru's throat suddenly froze over at the casual, carefree way he put it. Seeing Subaru react like that, Puck added another thought.

"That's because changing to her demon form makes that girl heal wounds very rapidly. By the time she carried you back to the village, she didn't have more than scratches left on the outside, enough that she didn't even need recovery magic."

"Don't scare me like that, then… Anyway, Rem got back to the village, too, huh? What happened to the last kid with me?"

"You can rest easy about that. All seven children are safe. You really made the right call, Subaru."

Puck said out loud "clap, clap" as he brought his paws together without a sound. Subaru imagined Puck's paws were simply too soft for audible applause, and he twisted his lips at the sight before shaking his head, driving away such idle thoughts.

"Puck, what about lifting the curses on the kids who got back to the village?"

"Don't worry about that, either. Magic healed them a fair bit, so Betty and I will lift those curses in no time at all. They're as good as cured; you have my guarantee."

Puck thumped his own chest as he gave his grandiose seal of approval. Upon seeing that, Subaru let out a deep breath, relieved at the fact that his own actions had not been in vain.

Subaru's hand was still on his own chest as his eyes drifted back to the sleeping Emilia.

"And Emilia…? She pulled an all-nighter?"

"I told her to just be patient and wait, but she wouldn't listen. She even wore down her od to heal you, so could you let her sleep?"

"Od…? What?"

Subaru shook his head when he heard the unfamiliar piece of vocabulary. Puck toyed with a whisker.

"The magical energy that fills the air around us is called mana. Od is the opposite, the magical energy that all living things are imbued with. The total capacity varies greatly from person to person, and drawing on it really wears you out, so I told Lia to avoid using it as much as possible, but…"

Puck's words and demeanor made it easy for Subaru to imagine how Emilia had taken that.

In the first place, calling Puck out during the night was outside the terms of their pact. If calling upon Puck and Beatrice was what it took to lift the curses, Emilia wouldn't have hesitated even an instant.

She helped others, even if it meant getting hurt. That was why he loved her.

"This is someone's house in the village, right? Is it all right if I take a look around?"

If he wasn't going to wake Emilia up, it was best to conclude his quiet conversation with Puck. Subaru was in the process of sliding his legs off the bed when Puck replied with an agreeable nod.

"Probably best to move around a little and see how well the healing took, anyway."

Having received Puck's permission, Subaru slowly began heading out.

Along the way, before he stepped past Emilia, he lowered his head in a polite bow. As he bowed, he looked at Emilia's sleeping face, desperately holding out against his urge to tease her as he made his way outside.

Subaru left his room, poking his head out of the building's entryway when he saw that the village was in an uproar. He murmured, "Ahh, well, guess that totally figures."

The morning sun hadn't even begun to rise, yet numerous human silhouettes stood in the plaza at the center of the village.

It was a small village. The details of even the tiniest disturbance spread like wildfire. Women, children, and the elderly all had looks of concern as they huddled around the stout young men arguing in the center.

They were no doubt the young men who'd pursued Subaru and Rem into the forest. He saw that several were wearing bandages; apparently they'd had casualties, too.

He scanned the crowd, troubled that he couldn't find the face he was looking for.

"—So you are awake, Barusu?"

The voice came from behind. Subaru stopped and turned around. He could guess who it was from the way she'd said his name, but still, seeing her face filled him with relief.

A pink-haired maid—Ram—stood behind him.

Ram had the sleeves of her familiar servant outfit rolled up, and she was holding something akin to a basket in her hands. Judging from the large number of baked potatoes filling the basket, she was in the middle of moving them from point A to point B.

The faint whiff of steam wafting from the potatoes sent Subaru's stomach into a small growl of heightened expectations. He belatedly realized he was really hungry.

"How unsightly, waking up ready to eat after worrying others with such grave wounds. Perhaps you caught rabies from the bites?"

"That's not what these dogs are spreading. Oh, and hey, you worried about me?"

"Just eat."

"Hfwoh!"

Subaru was teasing Ram for her rare slip of the tongue. So she stuffed a hot potato into his mouth. His throat blocked off by the scalding potato, Subaru turned his face up and loudly wolfed the whole thing down.

"I thought I was gonna die there! Tasted good, though!"

"Of course it was tasty. They were freshly baked...no, steamed."

"Oh man, that I'm-so-awesome face ticks me off. Still tasted good, though!"

"Yes, yes. Be quiet if you want another one."

When she handed him the potato, he accepted it, fawning over it like a child.

"Well, I should simply thank you outright concerning the incident last night. Well done."

"Sure didn't come easily... But why are *you* thanking me?"

"When the people of a fiefdom suffer harm, it calls the lord into question. At that rate, the children would have fallen to the Urugarum pack...and so, I believe your actions to have been correct, Barusu."

"Urugarum... Huh."

So that's what the black demon beasts were called.

Urugarum. As far as Subaru knew, it was also the name of a

132   Re:ZERo -Starting Life in Another World- Volume 3

demon beast straight out of mythology. Somehow, the name seemed fitting to him. A single word conveyed that your life was in peril from even a single encounter with the creature.

Subaru nodded as Ram shifted her gaze toward the forest.

"We rewove the frayed barrier last night. Judging from the lack of any issues with it overnight, no Urugarum should be crossing the barrier from here on."

"That's only if no one here crosses past it, right? Not much point to it if a bunch of kids crosses it to play on the other side and a 'puppy' comes back with them?"

"That makes painful listening. I shall have a word with the villagers later."

Ram's unchanging neutral expression gave her last sentence some unpleasant subtext.

Most likely, it was the villagers' duty to check that the barrier was up and running and to report if it was not; their laxness in doing so had caused Roswaal difficulty and no doubt rubbed her the wrong way.

After that, Subaru snatched a pair of steamed potatoes from Ram before they went their separate ways. Ram was heading for the distraught villagers still arguing among themselves. Ram was surely acting out of fondness for the village. It was just like Ram to use steamed potatoes to display that goodwill, too.

"Man, these potatoes are delicious, though. Going light on the salt did real wonders."

Subaru strolled around the village, munching on his potatoes along the way. He was checking both on the condition of his body and the well-being of the children they'd rescued from the forest.

The children were still soundly asleep from fatigue and exhaustion from the now-lifted curses, but the parents and relatives of the children thanked him, almost to excess. Put bluntly, Subaru hadn't done it out of a desire for gratitude, and this sparked a near-terminal case of stage fright. Unable to play the fool to deflect his rising panic, he blushed up a storm and ran for the hills.

Having done a sweep of the village, Subaru thought he'd return to the house and wait for Emilia to awaken—but he realized he had yet to see a certain blue-haired girl's face.

"—"

Suddenly, the sight of the demon girl, laughing loudly while covered in blood spatter, rose from the back of his mind.

It was a spectacularly ghastly sight. And yet, when Subaru remembered it, he felt no fear to make his body tremble.

What was it that Subaru had felt when he saw the pure white horn grow from her forehead? Yes, back then, what Subaru felt was—

But before a word could properly express that emotion, a young girl's voice called out to Subaru.

"—There you are. Just in time."

A thicket swayed, and through it walked Beatrice, the hem of her showy dress dragging along the ground in the process.

"Aren't you going to get that long dress awfully dirty, going outside with it like this?"

"I suppose magical power might repel the sources of grime, such as mud and sand— More importantly, I need to speak with you."

Beatrice gave Subaru's silly question a serious answer and beckoned him over.

She wanted to go somewhere else—meaning, it wasn't something she could discuss with him there. Though that unnerved Subaru a little, he had nothing against Beatrice here. Subaru followed the girl, who was also his savior, then abruptly clapped his hands together.

"Come to think of it, you're here outside the mansion because you were lifting the curses on the kids, right? Thank you."

"...'Tis nothing. I suppose I only did it because Puckie asked me to."

Of course, the reason Puck asked her to was because Emilia asked *him* to. No doubt Beatrice understood as much. Yet, knowing this, she used Puck as her reason once again. She just wasn't a girl who admitted things straight up.

Subaru found himself growing impatient as Beatrice led him to a flower bed right by one corner of the village. With the villagers gathered in the central plaza to discuss the demon beast incident, he couldn't see even a single person randomly strolling around in such a far-flung corner.

"So, what did you bring me all the way out here to tell me?"

Subaru spread both arms out as he spoke. For her part, Beatrice's reply seemed awkward.

"I thought it had the proper atmosphere to deter you from making boorish jokes."

Her gaze seemed to be wandering as she toyed with her skirt, like she was hesitant to say something.

What's with her? Is it that hard to say...?

As far as Subaru was concerned, this plainly wasn't typical Beatrice behavior. She had the air of a little girl afraid of angering her parents.

Seeing that expression, Subaru just couldn't bring himself to drag it out of her. He crossed his arms, leaned back on the wooden fence protecting the flower bed, and waited for her to resume.

The sight of Subaru waiting seemed to spur Beatrice into a decision. She closed her eyes, then gently opened them, gazing straight at Subaru.

"—In less than half a day, you will die."

3

Subaru bit down hard on the words, ground them with his teeth, and swallowed them. He stopped for several seconds as they passed down his throat, into his stomach, and finally flowed through his veins to his brain.

Beatrice raised her eyebrows in surprise at Subaru's reaction, apparently far more silent than she'd anticipated.

"I suppose you are less agitated than I expected. I thought you would be crying like a baby by now."

Beatrice still had that look on her face when Subaru raised his right hand before her, showing her a pair of raised fingers.

"Okay. There are two possibilities I can think of here."

Subaru bent down one of his raised fingers as Beatrice stood silently before him.

"First, this is graveyard humor, a really awful joke. Put bluntly, this really isn't funny, so…if you're gonna bring out a wooden sign that says FOOLED YA! and laugh, go ahead, now's the time."

He closed one eye in an attempt to lighten the mood, but Beatrice's expression went unchanged.

With Beatrice saying nothing before him, Subaru folded the second finger.

"If it's not a joke, there's only one possibility: The curse hasn't been lifted yet."

Beatrice folded her arms as if to lend support to Subaru's hypothesis.

This was the result of white scars from demon beast bites covering his entire body. They still throbbed as Subaru looked at them in a new, ominous light.

"I'll ask just to make sure. You can't lift the curse? You're not holding out on me here?"

He didn't think Beatrice would say, *No one asked me to, so I will not*, but he wanted to ask just in case some sliver of hope remained.

Naturally, Beatrice replied to his question with a shake of her head.

"If it was something I could remove, would it put you eternally in my debt, I wonder?"

"Hey, give me a break here. I'm already up to my eyeballs in debt to you!"

He couldn't repay her for even a smidgeon of it, not last time, not the time before that, not this time, either. Not in that world.

Subaru's reminiscing brought a suspicious look from Beatrice, but he papered things over with a hand wave.

"Mind if I ask why you can't lift the curse?"

"…I suppose you should at least know how you shall pass on. It is a simple tale. There are too many layers of curses, making the curses too complex to lift."

"…Curses have layers?"

Subaru pondered, trying to come up with an image. Beatrice spread both hands apart. Suddenly, the two hands were connected together by a red string.

"A curse is like this red string, I wonder?"

Beatrice took the string she held on each end and tied a knot with it.

"This knot is a curse rite. I suppose lifting a curse is as simple as undoing this knot. But..."

With a deft motion of her fingers, Beatrice increased the number of strings between her hands. The new strings were blue, yellow, green, pink, black, and white. She entwined the new strings into knots and tied the knots into one another.

"If it is only one curse, it can be undone. But if you mix more of them together like this..."

Beatrice held out both hands, offering the knots to him. Subaru slid a hand into the tangle. The string, connecting finger to finger, offered no sign of how it might be unraveled.

"If the curse is like this, too... Aw, crap, yeah, that's a high difficulty level there."

Even if one or two could be removed, at some point it would be impossible to know what should be touched. Of course, given sufficient time, it was probably possible to undo the whole thing, but...

"You said it's set for under half a day from now. What do you figure happens then?"

"I suppose that part is rather simple. In half a day, the demon beasts' rite to seize your mana will activate."

Beatrice raised a finger and pointed it at Subaru as she continued.

"Would the curse's purpose be to drain your mana, I wonder? Its aim is to absorb fuel for the creature's body... In other words, you are the demon beasts' prey."

"So they attack people when they're hungry? That's a wild animal for you—keeps things simple. I suppose I should be grateful their bellies weren't empty before now."

Subaru wanted to lash out and hit something, but unfortunately, his hand was buried in the string. Beatrice watched Subaru glare at the string as he spoke resentful words before she replied.

"Are you not afraid, I wonder?"

"Huh?"

"From your point of view, what I have said is a death sentence. Also, even though Puckie and I have the means to save you, we cannot because there is no time for it."

Optimistically, Subaru had twelve hours left to live. Depending on how hungry the demon beasts were, even that time might be shortened.

Having informed Subaru of the fact that he could not be saved, Beatrice waited for Subaru's reaction. Subaru belatedly thought that Beatrice seemed to want something.

"What's with you—? You want me to blame you here?"

"—"

Beatrice didn't deny it. But she didn't agree, either. Since Beatrice chose silence, Subaru couldn't know what was going on inside her, but he made a pained smile anyway.

"Maybe your and Puck's decision feels a bit inhuman, but it's the natural, logical choice. The risk and effort involved are too much. You two are right. I don't think it's heartless at all."

He really believed that. It wasn't just because he was thinking long-term about his life. Hence—

"—I wanted to ask you something else, though. Do you mind?"

"...What is it, I wonder?"

"Does Emilia know that I'm still cursed?"

That very moment, Emilia was still sleeping in that room, having healed and nursed him to exhaustion.

If Puck and Beatrice had given up, he wondered how Emilia took it. Had Emilia abandoned him, too? That was the one thing tugging at him.

"The mixed-blood girl does not know. I suppose Puckie is not attempting to lift your curse to hide its existence from the girl?"

"...Ah, I see. If Puck starts working on it, Emilia will be able to tell. She'd probably pick up on the fact that my being cursed like this means the chances of saving me are pretty slim, too."

When Puck had realized he couldn't save Subaru, his concern had shifted to Emilia. If he kept his silence until the curse activated, Emilia's heart would bear only the wound of his death. For Puck, who prioritized Emilia above all else, it was a good and wise decision. Puck was tougher than he looked; Subaru had to accept his judgment.

"That aside…"

Subaru switched the subject as he pointed a finger at Beatrice. Beatrice raised her eyebrows, looking at the finger pointed at her, as Subaru declared:

"You don't look malicious enough to go through all this trouble just to hand down a death sentence to me."

"…What do you know of me, I wonder?"

"At the very least, enough that it feels like I know you four times as long as you think I do."

Subaru saw the creases on the girl's forehead deepen further as Subaru's last two weeks flashed before his eyes.

His relations with Ram and Rem were as good as they'd been since the first loop. Putting aside the lap pillow, things were A-OK with Emilia. Now he knew the identity of the shaman, the source of all his ills, and the children's lives had been saved.

Looking back on the previous loops he'd gone through, this one was near full marks. It would count as the best by far if only Subaru could live through it.

"You, Rem, and Emilia healed my wounds, right? That's not the way you treat someone you figure is a goner from a curse and can't be saved."

He felt Beatrice waver. Subaru laughed at how the girl just refused to be upfront.

"Man, you suck at lying."

"It is a fact that the odds of your being saved are incredibly low. I suppose that is why Puckie did not want the girl to have anything to do with it?"

"So that's why you're playing the villain to soak up all my anger. That's way too roundabout for a little girl. So would you tell me about that really-low-odds possibility?"

He formed a circle with his index finger and thumb, showing it to Beatrice in search of a reply.

Beatrice hesitated for a while before sighing in resignation.

"Do you remember when I explained about curses, I wonder? I said there is no way to stop a curse once it has been activated."

Beatrice's words seemed off.

"Yeah, you did say that. That's why it had to be lifted before it activ— No, wait. The premise is all wrong. If that's the case, then… how'd the kids get saved?"

Subaru thought hard, unable to square that knowledge with the available facts.

According to Beatrice, lifting a curse succeeded only against a rite that had not yet been activated. The fact that there was no way to stop it *after* it had been activated was what made it such a scary thing.

The children they'd found in the forest were debilitated. He was certain that the demon beasts' curses had activated. So the reason the children were alive was—

As deductions formed in his mind, a possibility emerged that struck him like lightning.

Subaru lifted his face, turned toward Beatrice, and asked, "What happens to the curse if the caster dies?"

"A normal curse would continue to take effect. But isn't this rite for eating, I wonder? If the eater loses his life, the feeding would logically cease midway."

Beatrice's affirmation rang true to Subaru.

The curses on the children had progressed no further because the demon beasts that had inflicted them had perished. Upon the caster's death, the curse reverted to a simple rite that Beatrice could lift without difficulty.

The night before, a considerable number of demon beasts must have lost their lives. If the individuals that had inflicted the curses on the children had been among them, that supported his deduction.

And that certainty simultaneously gave rise to a new question.

"So that's what it is. There were so many who put curses on me, some are still out there."

Subaru looked over his shoulder at the forest in which the demon beasts dwelled.

His entire body had been battered by the countless fangs of the demon beasts pursuing him. If each and every bite inflicted a curse, there was no way to know how many Subaru carried. More than that, taking out every single monster in less than half a day didn't seem realistic.

That's why Puck and Beatrice had dug in their heels, refusing to tell Emilia the truth.

"Puckie was…"

"You don't need to say it. I know how Emilia is… If she knew, she'd probably try something crazy. That makes me real happy… and also real scared."

Emilia didn't hesitate to help others, even if it hurt her. That was why Subaru didn't consider asking Emilia for help. He didn't want to even think about it.

After all, if by some chance he did lose Emilia right before his eyes, ripping his own body apart a hundred times over wouldn't come close to the pain he would feel.

"The degree of difficulty's totally demonic. Not totally impossible but still crazy. Gotta just give u—"

Are you giving up, then?

Subaru was about to complete the word when the voice emerged from the back of his mind. It was a delicate voice, like a collection of fragments of noise echoing in his subconscious.

He gasped, lifted his face up, and looked all around.

But there was no one there, except for Beatrice and him. Still, the voice continued.

Is there another way to save him? it asked, searching for something to cling to. But somehow the voice was imbued with sorrowful resolve.

"Do you have a headache, I wonder? That is to be expected."

Only that, I wonder? You should do as you please, then.

The Beatrice before his eyes spoke, her words overlapping the different ones she had spoken elsewhere. He didn't know when or where he'd heard them. But the conversation he'd heard somewhere jostled around in his head.

His field of vision narrowed as a ringing echoed like a warning bell. Before he knew it, he began to fall to his knees—

—I will save him.

The voice, echoing with iron resolve, jolted his knees back up. Subaru knew that voice. He knew whose it was and when he had heard it.

"Where…is Rem?"

Subaru hadn't seen the blue-haired girl anywhere that morning. He'd heard she had returned to the village with him, safe and sound.

Beatrice stood silent. Subaru closed the distance and asked her.

"Beako… Beatrice. Where…is Rem?"

"If you were in her shoes, what would you do, I wonder?"

"That's not an answer!!"

Her self-important, roundabout reply made him shout, which in turn made him bend over. His anemic body wavered; Subaru rocked as he looked back on his own actions.

He wanted to tear someone limb from limb. And here was Beatrice, standing there to be blasted by his emotions. He couldn't even manage annoyance with his own wretchedness in behaving exactly as she had expected.

And then…

"I cannot disregard what I heard just now."

Quietly, the emotion in her voice suppressed, Ram walked between Subaru and Beatrice. Looking back, he realized that the pink-haired maid had walked over from the direction of the village square.

"Ram…"

When Subaru called out her name, Ram looked back. The sheer coldness of her gaze made Subaru's breath catch.

He'd somehow imagined as much, but this was the Ram who had cried out in hatred during the loop she'd lost Rem. With the person she loved most, her little sister, in danger, would Ram come to hate everything like she had then…?

"—"

Just when he thought that, Subaru realized it.

The hands Ram held crossed in front of her were shaking a little. She was biting her lip to preserve her neutral expression, desperately trying to keep her emotions off her face.

"My Clairvoyance cannot locate Rem… Lady Beatrice…where is Rem?"

"All I did was present possibilities. Puckie and I do not have sufficient reason to act. Our choices are limited, I wonder?"

"That's not it, is it…? So Rem really did go to…?"

—She went into the forest with the intention of wiping out the entire pack that lived there…by herself.

All to save Subaru Natsuki.

"Why…? Why would Rem go that far for my sake…?!"

Rem had previously taken Subaru's life with her own hands. Even if the relationship between them was better than before, he didn't think they had a connection that made her think his life was worth saving at the risk of her own.

Subaru was having a hard time digesting Rem's decision, when he saw the dramatic reaction in Ram as she stood beside him. In an instant, her expression of grief hardened into determination; she turned toward the forest, ready to run after her little sister without any hesitation.

"—Wait!"

Subaru instantly leaped in front of Ram, spreading his arms wide to block her path.

His demeanor earned him a sharp glare from Ram.

"Move aside, Barusu. I have no time to spare, so I cannot be gentle with you."

"You can't just go without thinking! I've got a bunch of things I have to ask you, and I want honest answers."

"There is no time for anything like—"

"I wanna save Rem, too. If you think of me as one of you at all, listen to me. I want to raise the odds here, even a little."

Hearing that this was about saving Rem, Ram's hard posture wavered just a bit. Subaru, seeing Ram's hesitation, raised a finger into the air.

"There are just two things I wanna ask. Will you be able to tell where Rem is with your Clairvoyance?"

"…Yes, I will. Once I am past the forest barrier, she will be within range of my Clairvoyance. With my vision set on 'Beings on the same wavelength as Ram,' if she is in range, I will find her."

"Different fields of vision to see through, huh…? It's like checking on different security cameras in a monitor room. Anyway, if we can use that to link up with Rem, great."

Nodding at the first condition being cleared, Subaru raised a second finger for question number two.

"So, second question: Ram, are you the type of maid who can fight?"

"…What do you mean by that question?"

As Ram narrowed her eyes, Subaru slumped his shoulders.

"Well, um…until we hook up with Rem, there's no telling how many demon beasts we'll run into. If we can't protect ourselves, this plan isn't going anywhere. Just so you know, I'm total deadweight in combat."

"W-wait a moment. Barusu, you intend to come with me…?"

How Subaru so confidently expressed his own shortcomings brought a rare nervous look over Ram.

"I know that threw you off, but it's mandatory, right? Er, to be honest, if the goal's just making sure Rem's safe, then you don't really need me, but…"

Ram looked even more doubtful as Subaru's line fizzled out. Seeing her expression, he hastily waved a hand.

"I've gotta make it to the fifth day with *everyone*. That's what I've been fighting for over and over. So please, let me do this."

Seeing Subaru bring both hands together in supplication, Ram's lips trembled as if she was at a loss for what to say. But in the end, it was not words that brought an end to that but a sigh.

"If you expect me to fight as well as Rem's horned form, you hope in vain."

"Meaning?"

"Unlike Rem, I am hornless. I can use somewhat violent wind magic, but that is about all."

As she replied, Ram twirled a finger and made Subaru's hair sway with a gust of wind.

If she'd used that magic to interfere with nature more violently just then, she could have sliced off Subaru's right leg or gouged out his throat. The thought of it sent a chill up his spine.

But he couldn't ask for anyone more reliable to have on his side of the fight.

"Beatrice! Ram and I are heading into the forest. If Emilia wakes up before we're back, pull the wool over her eyes, okay?"

"...To bring the younger sister back is to abandon your own life. Do you understand that, I wonder?"

Subaru wagged a finger in response to Beatrice quietly questioning his resolve.

"That's a little off, so let me correct you. I'm *not* giving up as if I'm used to dying. Life is precious, and you have only one. I know you've all worked desperately to save mine. That's why I'm gonna fight for it, even if it looks ugly."

They'd saved a life he had once thrown away when he thought all was lost. It was because so many people had reached out to Subaru that he could do this.

It was only thanks to them that he'd made it to extra innings.

"We'll turn this thing around. It was real awful before, but we still got things this far. I'm doing this because I want to see myself in the sequel... I'm greedy like that."

It was a stupid reason with no legitimate explanation.

It wasn't a direct answer to Beatrice's question at all, but Subaru puffed his chest out to her nonetheless.

"I have no idea what you are thinking whatsoever… I suppose you should just do what you like? I have presented choices. I suppose it is up to you to select whichever choice you prefer."

"And that's how you sent Rem off, huh? Still…thanks, Beako."

He headed toward the forest, his thoughts turning to Rem, fighting within its dark depths even now.

She was a high-maintenance girl who had run off without a word, assuming how others would feel and coming to a hasty, arbitrary decision. Silly and stubborn.

"I mean, geez, I want to help you at least as much as you want to help me here."

He cracked his fist to harden his resolve, heading toward the demon beasts' forest as he made his declaration—a declaration of war against the pack of black beasts that dwelled within, and against the supernatural force that had dragged Subaru into this destiny, just in case it was forgetting about him.

"All right, it's time for the championship bout. Mr. Fate? Game on!"

4

Some fifty minutes after his declaration of war against Fate, they were in the gloomy forest when Ram murmured offhandedly, "Well, you certainly talked a good game."

Ram was walking beside Subaru, looking up at him as he struggled on an area with poor footing.

"It is difficult to hide my dismay at how much deadweight you truly are."

"Do you even know what the word *hide* means…? If you let the other person know what you're hiding, what's the point…?"

And so, Subaru made light of Ram's grandiose, high-handed declaration, adding a sigh at the end.

Subaru and Ram were in the forest of the demon beasts, walking around and searching blindly for Rem.

Consciously slipping past the barrier and walking their way deep into the forest was Ram's idea, knowing full well the nature of the demon beasts. Normally, they never got close to the village because the barrier hurt them, leaving the mountains as their habitat. Naturally, Rem ought to have headed there with the aim of wiping out the beasts.

"That said, the fact that there're just game trails makes it tough going..."

"You may not be accustomed to this, but our meager progress is unacceptable...truly."

"Wait, don't leave me behind that quickly. I understand how you feel, but just a little longer!"

Ram's maid outfit might have been wholly out of place for going hiking in the mountains, but her practiced gait made her marching twice as fast as Subaru's. To Ram, full of concern about her younger sister, matching Subaru's slow-footed pace was a hundred cons and no pros.

At the very least, he couldn't restore his good name by moving so slowly.

"I'm walking wounded with a blood shortage, so I'm getting tired easily... Come to think of it, I didn't have Emilia-tan telling me to come back soon, either!"

"If you have yet to say, 'I'm back,' last night's 'come back soon' remains in effect."

"It, ah, it works that way...?"

Subaru tilted his head at Ram's sophistry and thrust the sword in his hand into the ground like a cane to support his shaky legs as he chased after Rem.

He had borrowed the sword he was using in place of a cane from the young men of Earlham Village.

Subaru had a hard time forgetting the look on the face of the young man representing the others the moment he told them he was heading into the demon beast forest. He had been shocked, and when Subaru brushed off his cries to stop and partially explained the circumstances, the young man lent Subaru his sword.

The sword, supposedly the finest in the whole village, was a simple one-handed blade. Even an amateur like Subaru could manage to swing it. He had accepted the weapon and the villagers had seen them off.

But that wasn't the only thing they had provided him.

"Inside this pocket are…candy, a pretty stone, and… Whoa! There's a bug in here!"

Subaru let out a cry as rummaging through the pocket led to touching something fairly disgusting. Freed from cramped quarters, the winged insect escaped from Subaru's hand; he watched it fly into the forest.

"Just like those little brats to slip something like that in there. I'll give them a good sermon later."

"It is proof that they adore you… What do they see in you…?"

"The sincere eyes of children see how my manly nature sparkles before them. Besides, you're well aware I'm not the only one they like, right?"

Subaru sought Ram's agreement, and Ram concurred.

"…I suppose you are right."

Subaru looked quite satisfied with that, nodding several times.

Ram, too, had seen the children toying with Subaru before they left the village. Subaru connected heart-to-heart whenever he could; to Ram, that was something she only wished she could do.

After the young men had seen them off, Subaru and Ram had been caught by the freshly awakened children. Wanting to thank Subaru and Ram in person, the children had stuffed one sign of their affection after another into his pocket as soon as they noticed him. The piece of candy, the pretty stone, even the bug—these were the children's gratitude in physical form. Subaru could not treat them lightly…though the bug had gotten away.

Subaru repeated what the children had said with smiling faces as he wavered under the pressure of unnecessary gratitude being pushed on to him.

"'Bring back Remrin so we can thank her, too…' Huh."

Where was Rem at that moment? How dangerous a spot was she in? Why was she fighting at the risk of her life?

The children didn't know that. They didn't *need* to know.

After all—

"Don't worry, ya little brats. I'll make sure she's right there with her big sister to lecture you about being bad kids for going into a dark forest to play without saying a word to anyone."

He should probably join them as the stupid boy who'd made trouble for everyone by rushing headlong into the woods and turning into a human chew toy. Wouldn't it be fun to kneel for a lecture from the village chief all night?

Naturally, drawing up that image of the future in his mind brought a twist to his lips.

Then, in contrast to the odd grin on Subaru's cheeks, Ram stopped walking forward. She quietly lowered her head, speaking in a commanding tone without looking back.

"Barusu, wait a little. I will be using Clairvoyance."

She turned toward the silent forest. Subaru felt like sound itself had vanished as he rushed to Ram's side. He drew his sword from its scabbard as he looked around cautiously.

He couldn't let his guard down, for Ram was defenseless while she was using her Clairvoyance.

"—"

Ram lowered her pale face as she silently concentrated on Clairvoyance, also known as the Sight of a Thousand Eyes. She'd explained it as a power that could borrow the vision of other living things, and not limited to people, either. By riding the vision of creatures with compatible wavelengths and using the vision of yet other creatures to further expand her range, she was literally able to look around with "a thousand eyes."

Ram had used that power to scry the forest several times since they had entered, but she had yet to locate Rem.

Apparently the sheer abundance of life made it rather difficult.

However—

"Barusu—there are eyes watching us once again."

"They came, huh…? Should I just walk in front?"

Seeing Ram nod while keeping her eyes shut, Subaru inhaled a little and realized his heart was pounding hard. He gently stepped forward on the grass, leaving the defenseless Ram by herself and making his way up a moss-covered boulder. He stood on top of the rock and took a deep breath.

He banged the iron scabbard against the hard surface of the boulder. As the sound echoed, the forest rustled right in front of him.

"—!"

The silence was broken as the sounds of running across the ground and unified howls thundered against Subaru's eardrums.

He instantly looked back to see a black four-legged beast above his head, leaping out from among the trees. Its fangs were bared and aimed at Subaru's throat, pouncing on Subaru's slow reaction to rip him to shreds.

Subaru instinctively used both hands to protect himself, but the wild beast's speed outpaced his own. Its maw opened wide as it closed in right before his eyes. Just before the tips of its fangs were about to easily puncture Subaru's flesh, bringing blood and his very life gushing forth, a Blade of Wind struck it in the flank, slicing it neatly into two, slaying it instantly. The front half kept going and collided hard with Subaru and sent him flying.

"Whoa!"

An exasperated-sounding sigh reached Subaru's ears.

"I simply cannot understand why you lose your nerve at the sight of a single one of them, Barusu."

Unfortunately for Subaru, he ended his flight by hitting the slope and rolling downward. He stood up, wiped off his scraped-up butt, and glared defiantly at Ram, who was looking down at him from the top of the hill.

"Hey, you! You can cut that a little less close, can't you?!"

Ram twisted her lips as she tossed him a nonchalant line.

"I was too concerned about killing it with the least amount of suffering to think about your needs, Barusu."

Subaru looked at the body lying beside him. It was already a lifeless corpse. Even though he knew it was a dangerous creature, the thought of a living being lying dead like that tugged at his thoughts. Subaru gently brought his hands together in a prayer.

"Your heart will not hold up if it breaks over a single creature, all the more so because your life is forfeited if they are not annihilated, Barusu... Hunting it like this was your idea, was it not?"

"Let me have my hypocritical sentimentality here, geez. It's important for my own peace of mind."

It wasn't so much an issue of sentimentality as it was growing up in different worlds.

Subaru couldn't exactly claim to be a man of deep faith, but he did revere life. His awareness of its value had grown a little stronger over the course of Return by Death.

"So, did you find Rem with your Clairvoyance earlier?"

"No. Unfortunately, she seems to be deeper in the forest. Like just now, it is proving difficult to concentrate on her location with the Urugarum sporadically targeting you, Barusu."

Ram put a hand to her cheek as she said it, looking mystified at how the demon beasts went straight for Subaru. Subaru had a vague suspicion that he knew the answer, but he couldn't bring himself to say it directly—he was weak.

With Subaru's lips sealed, Ram glanced back and forth between him and the beast.

"I suppose it is because you are weak."

"And that's what you come up with?! That's rude."

"It is because you are easy prey, then."

"That's a distinction without a difference, Big Sis."

Ram shrugged; Subaru slumped his shoulders.

It was hard to tell if Ram meant those words or was just needling him. Probably the latter.

Lone demon beasts had attacked them a few times since entering the forest. Either way, Ram had been using magic to strike down the ones targeting Subaru.

It was Subaru who'd established the surefire hunting method. They always went after Subaru, even when Ram was defenseless while using Clairvoyance. At first, Ram had had her doubts about it, but that was then.

—Subaru halfheartedly thought that now was as good a time as ever to bring up a different subject.

"Can I ask you what *hornless* means?"

He'd kept wondering about the term he'd abruptly heard just prior to entering the forest. He could guess up to a point. Ram took the word in as she continued looking down at Subaru from above.

"It is what it sounds like, a disparaging term employed by fools to mean a demon without a horn."

The word *demon* brought to mind the sight of Rem from the night before. He would never forget the sight of her covered in blood, laughing hysterically, with a white, faintly glowing horn on her forehead.

She looked like a demon straight out of the fairy tales.

And Ram had called herself hornless. In other words, Ram's forehead—

"I lost my one and only horn in a minor skirmish. I have had to rely on Rem for everything ever since."

"...Probably was a bad thing to ask, huh?"

"Why?"

As Subaru scratched his face, Ram tilted her head as if she was genuinely mystified.

"Er, well, I don't know how big a horn is to someone who's a demon, but I'm guessing it's a pretty big deal. I thought it might've been pretty insensitive to ask."

"Even if that is the case, there is no getting it back now. Well, you can rest easy."

Ram spoke down at Subaru, putting him in his place before lightening her tone very slightly.

"I may not have been calm about it then, but I am now. I lost my horn, but I gained a life in its stead—I suppose that is not what Rem thinks, however."

Her voice had a painful overtone before she cut things off, a wave of her hand indicating her intent—she was entering Clair-voyance again. By the time Subaru climbed up the slope, Ram was already deeply enmeshed in viewing the world through the eyes of others.

Ram's eyes were closed, her breathing ragged, and she had a con-siderable cold sweat on her brow. Both of her legs trembled, looking like she'd run them ragged over the course of the long day; more than once, she looked like she was getting dizzy and was about to totter over. Using Clairvoyance to borrow the vision of other beings simply put that great a strain on her body.

But no matter how painful it was, not the slightest sound of weak-ness passed through Ram's lips.

When you really got down to it, Ram and Rem were twins who greatly resembled each other. If pushing themselves hard was what it took, they'd do it without a moment's hesitation. When you con-sidered Emilia and Beatrice as well, the mansion's girl squad priori-tized others just a little too much.

"Man, this makes me feel even guiltier for being a weakling..."

He kicked the grass at his feet. That was a major miscalculation, for a piece of grass leaped into his mouth and the dirt flew right into his eyes.

Spitting out the earth-tasting grass, he cursed his own extremely hesitant nature. But he relaxed a little, thinking that even such stu-pidity was fitting for him.

Even though he knew it wasn't a good thing to disturb Ram's con-centration while in Clairvoyance, he asked, "Ram. You're worried sick about Rem, right?"

Ram, her concentration focused on aligning herself with other people's vision, belatedly replied, "Of course I am. Certainly that girl is much stronger than me, but that is no reason not to worry."

"...Yeah."

"Even if she is better than I am at everything, I am still her older sister. That will never change."

Until then, Subaru had seen Ram as someone who used her

younger sister for the sole sake of making things easier on herself. He'd gotten it all wrong. Calling it a foolish misunderstanding didn't come close to cutting it.

Ram understood her own position far more keenly than Subaru ever had. She was well aware that she couldn't live up to Rem's constant boasts.

Subaru, seeing how Ram had accepted it, could only harden his own resolve.

He scratched his head, murmuring as he stretched to loosen up.

"I really figured we'd have met up with Rem by now, but..."

Maybe Ram felt how Subaru seemed unable to calm down. At any rate, she abandoned her fruitless Clairvoyance and brought her mind back in full. She promptly put her sweaty hair in better order as she cast Subaru a suspicious glance.

"Barusu, what do you plan on doing?"

"The way things are, I'm just baggage, exactly as you said. I told you before we headed into the woods... I'm gonna make myself useful and help save Rem."

He wasn't waiting to be sure of his guess, but based on prior events, he gave it about 70:30 odds in his favor. Of course, the remaining 30 percent weighed heavily on his mind, but...

"I've gotta play the hot hand here. Ram, you ready to cross a somewhat dangerous bridge?"

"I am alone with a young man in a forest full of demon beasts. As a maiden, there is surely no greater danger."

"Oh, now you've said it, Sister."

Subaru laughed, then took a deep breath and reopened his eyes.

If Subaru's thought proved true, he could turn the situation around. Even though he knew it was necessary, it didn't quell the fear in his heart.

He knew he was a scaredy-cat. Even so, there were some things he couldn't run from.

If Subaru was right, this was one of them...

"Ram, actually, I—"

—He began to speak of Return by Death.

Subaru acted like he was about to break the taboo, putting into words that which it was forbidden to convey.

Before his eyes, Ram looked like she was wondering what Subaru was saying when her expression froze.

No—time itself had stopped.

The world lost color, sound vanished, and the very concept of time came to a grinding halt.

It was a world where everything had stopped. Suddenly, the sole exception to the rule appeared.

"There you are."

His murmur did not actually create a sound, but he hoped his invective still reached that which hovered before his eyes. If even a fraction of his emotions communicated, that would give him great satisfaction indeed.

In the frozen world, the only thing unaffected was the black cloud. The cloud that had suddenly emerged before Subaru shifted into a silhouette of an arm to call his bluff. It formed fingers, then a wrist; the biceps emerged to complete a full right arm. Though the previous arm hadn't even reached an elbow, this one materialized all the way up to the shoulder.

"—"

Subaru's breath felt like it caught inside him as the cloud, more distinct than the first time around, slid its black fingers forward. They moved past the thin flesh of his chest, stroked his rib cage, and went straight toward his heart.

Even though he knew it was coming, there was no way he could endure pain so far past his limits. He had no words with which to express the mad screams inside his head from feeling his heart directly grasped.

The long suffering, the time of unbearable anguish, continued.

His heart rhythm was thrown off. His blood flow was cranked to the limit, making his entire body scream out. It was such torture that he felt like he was gushing tears of blood, biting down on his teeth hard enough to break them. For Subaru, the only thing he could sense in this world was pain. All he was allowed to do was continue to writhe.

The agony seemed to last for eternity as his field of vision was dyed pure white—

"—Barusu?"

When he heard his nickname, Subaru realized he had fallen onto his knees and butt. He hastily wiped off the saliva that had spilled from the corner of his lips and rose back up.

"Man, daydreams are bad, bad stuff."

"It is because you forced yourself back from injury too soon. If it is too hard, you should return to the village. If you have some other way to find Rem, at least tell me that before…"

Before completing her sentence, Ram gasped, and her expression changed as she looked all around the area.

The only sounds were those of the quiet forest: tree branches swaying from the wind and leaves rustling as they rubbed against one another. Ram listened carefully as she looked back at Subaru.

"What did you do, Barusu?"

"…I rolled the dice a little, pain and all."

Despite how extreme the pain had been, not even a single trace of that remained in his body at that moment.

Even as Subaru silently reviled the wounds carved solely into his mind, he was grateful for the saving grace that his body still had enough endurance with which to act.

After all—

Within the deep verdant foliage, the rustle of the wind began to lose its tranquility. Ram frowned and looked to her right.

"The wind is astir… The scents of beasts approach, many of them."

He looked that way, too, and saw multiple red points of light approaching from deeper in the forest. Based on the number of eyes, there were about five demon beasts running their way.

Ram made a small click of her tongue.

"And we haven't even found Rem yet…!"

"Well, don't worry about that. She's not that far, so we'll hook up soon enough."

"How can you be certain of such a thing?"

Subaru shrugged in the face of Ram's sharp gaze and rebuke.

"Rem's goal is to wipe out the demon beasts here in the forest, right? As long as I'm here, they're going to keep coming to try to eat me. That'll bring Rem running straight to me in time."

He'd been thinking of it from the beginning. And he'd also thought it strange from the beginning. Why did the demon beasts prefer Subaru as their target for the curse during every loop?

When Subaru repeated those four days, the demon beast always cursed Subaru when they'd met in the village. That wasn't so much unavoidable fate as the operation of some *other* compulsion.

Subaru's existence provoked a reaction from the demon beasts. Subaru had deduced the answer as to *why* from the exaggerated reactions he'd received from other sources.

"In other words—it's the stench of the witch."

Demon beasts were enemies of all mankind created by the witch. And they seemed to be intensely sensitive to Subaru, who carried the scent of the witch. That was no doubt why they'd gone after him and not Ram since they had entered the forest together.

If all it took was a whiff of the witch to compel the demon beasts to appear, he'd make full use of that. He'd lure every demon beast in the forest to put their curses into Subaru, a grand feast that would bring Rem running in after them.

He called it Operation: Subaru Chew Toy.

When he'd previously tried to tell Emilia about Return by Death, Beatrice had made an offhanded comment in the aftermath that gave him the clue he needed to draw up his plan. Apparently, the appearance of the dark cloud had thickened the stench of the witch hovering around him.

That haze was probably related to the witch in some way. Somehow, the scent of the witch around Subaru was related to the power behind Return by Death—but it was not the time to think about such things.

All he had was anguish he could not speak of to anyone, ferocious pain without anyone who could hear him complain.

In the face of fast-approaching danger, the sheer exhilaration of turning the tables on the hand Fate had dealt him made the corners of Subaru's lips warp into a malevolent grin.

—*Yeah, I've finally shot an arrow off at Fate for putting this loop together!*

Cheering inside his mind, he re-gripped his one-handed sword, positioning himself to face the oncoming tide. And to Ram, who stood by his side, he stated in a high-pitched voice, "So, since you're super reliable in a fight, please and thank you for that!"

"After this, when you look back objectively at what you said, please beg me to kill you."

A sigh trailed behind Ram's voice as she slammed a Blade of Wind into the throng approaching from the front.

—The cast had been changed for round two in the battle against the demon beasts.

5

He kicked off from the ground and leaped forward.

He trampled on the large, undulating root beneath him, slamming his feet into it as hard as he could.

He had been truly mistaken to think that there was no sure footing when moving through forests and mountains without any proper roads. All he had to do was run down the natural game trails and not hesitate in his judgment as to where his heels should touch down. Trusting the stoutness of his shoes as he stepped forward made a huge difference in progress.

His breath was ragged. The sweat on his brow was getting into his eyes, so he made painful blinks to give the sweat somewhere to go.

He was sprinting full force, tilting his body forward to reduce wind resistance even the tiniest bit. But the sounds of his pursuers' footsteps did not diminish. They rang out right beside him, as if mocking Subaru's attempt to escape. The chances of getting away were virtually nil.

His lungs hurt, and he gasped as if desperate for oxygen. Subaru's mouth was open in an unsightly fashion. And to top it off—

"What a horrid face… I shall tell your home village on you."

"I'll remember that later, damn it!!"

Subaru immediately regretted his unnecessary use of oxygen as he continued to carry Ram in his arms as he ran.

About ten minutes had passed since he'd used the stench of the witch for Operation: Subaru Chew Toy. As Subaru had planned, the demon beast pack had gathered around them. Amid exceptionally harsh combat, the two of them finally…had no option but to run through the forest for their lives.

"And I believed you could fight them, geez!"

"I did fight them. My endurance simply didn't hold up as well as I had hoped."

"What about being ready to cross a dangerous bridge there?!"

"It was a bridge too far. We would have fallen before crossing it."

Ram had a comeback for everything Subaru had to offer.

Her mana had been depleted from repeated combat; she wasn't even in any state to properly move her limbs.

The demon beasts had treated Subaru's release of the witch's stench as a written invitation, arriving one after another, their numbers soon exceeding anything they could handle. The only word he could muster was *regret*.

Ram had used her wind magic to take out some seventeen fiends. Things had gone swimmingly until that point, but Ram suddenly lost her strength and collapsed. Subaru, scared witless right beside her, picked Ram up, carried her, and started running for the hills—

"Nothing changes with you… Still, I appreciate your inability to prepare."

"You're cheeky for a girl being carried around! And don't talk too much! Looks like you bit your tongue…and my strength's…not… gonna…hold…!"

Subaru could boast athletic ability that scored well above the norm, but that was all indoor stuff. Outdoors, his stamina issues were substantial. He'd never dreamed of running a marathon back in school.

Even with his pathetic stamina, he wrung out everything he could in that life-and-death situation. That said, it was only a matter of time until his endurance ran dry...

No doubt the demon beasts pursuing them were well aware that Subaru was at the end of his strength. They'd nipped at his heels as if they truly enjoyed preying on the weak, which further fueled his flight instincts.

"Looks like it's finally time to unleash the power hidden within m— Ow!"

Subaru let out a painful yelp as demon beast fangs sank into his right shoulder.

One of the bastards toying with him had run ahead of them. The sharp pain buried deep in his shoulder and thrust into his brain, making his head feel like it was about to burst. He desperately twisted his body in an attempt to shake the beast off him—

"—Barusu!"

"Oh cra—!"

Right after Ram spoke from within his arms, the forest suddenly opened wide, and Subaru's feet were slicing through the air.

His feet clawed at the sky as a floating feeling assaulted him, as if every internal organ were rising inside him. The next moment, his heels dug into the slope; Subaru and Ram lost their balance as they slid down together.

"Bastards tricked me...!"

He should never have underestimated them as *mere beasts*. Even though repeated contact with them had given Subaru an appreciation for their intelligence, when push came to shove, he'd been unable to shake his impression of them as *just animals*.

As a result, the seemingly viable path he'd followed had literally led him off a cliff.

"Damn it all!!"

Subaru's yell made his throat tremble as they slid down at an even sharper angle. He held Ram tighter as he thrust the drawn sword in his left hand into the cliff.

"Owwww, ow, ow, ow!"

His left side scraped against the ground as the sword he'd thrust into the cliff twisted, stopping them from sliding farther. When he looked, the cliff ended a short distance below; had he been a single second slower, they would have surely met their deaths.

"Whoaa!"

When he looked up, several demon beasts pursuing them were rolling down beside them.

The beasts, moving with too much force to stop, yelped like domesticated dogs as they vanished off the edge of the precipice. Their bodies mercilessly smashed against the sharp, rocky ravine below; the sound of their bones breaking reached even Subaru's eardrums.

"Ah, we came very close to needing condolences ourselves..."

"Arm...hurts...!"

Ram complained as Subaru's arm tightened around her.

Her body was light, but when added to Subaru's own weight, the burden on the sword thrust into the ground, and on Subaru as he gripped it, was more than two hundred pounds. His limit would not be long in coming.

"It will of course be dangerous if we fall down the cliff. Can you climb, Barusu?"

"I'd love to tough it out...but the demon beasts up there are still a *problem*," he said as he put more strength into his left arm. He let the blade, thrust in at an angle, support their weight as he tried to somehow get in a more stable position, when...

"—Ah," both said together.

The same moment, the high-pitched sound of steel breaking rang around the area.

The blade thrust into the cliff snapped, leaving the end of the sword stuck in the slope.

He hastily thrust the warped blade into the ground anew, but the dull edge didn't penetrate very deep.

He clung to the slope with all his body, resigned to however scraped up he might become, but friction alone could not slow two people. His efforts proved fruitless as the blade popped out. They began to fall once more.

"Aaaaa! We're done for—!!"

"—You owe me for this, Barusu!!"

Subaru fell headfirst, every hair on his body standing up as he recalled flinging himself over a cliff. Even so, he never abandoned his duty as a man, continuing to hold Ram in his arms to try to shield her from the fall.

Ram let him handle the physical work and twisted in his arms to aim her hands toward the ground.

"—El Fulla!"

Mana welled up in Ram as she chanted, causing a powerful gust of wind to erupt at their estimated landing point. As they fell straight down, Subaru's body hit the ascending air current and rode on the pressure underneath them; he managed to get them upright again as their fall slowed further.

We can do this, he judged while the world spun all around them. He focused all his strength into his legs, biting down hard enough to split his teeth as he endured the impact of landing.

"Nguuuuuuh, aaaaaa—we made it!!"

—They had endured.

He labored to leap onto his numb, incredibly unhappy legs as he looked up at the cliff from which they had fallen. He was aghast at the height—over thirty feet, the rough equivalent of jumping out from the fourth floor of his high school. That, combined with the hardness of the ground, made their very survival quite a feat.

"You totally turned into my Buddha there, Ram. If it wasn't for your wind magic there, we'd be—"

It was when Subaru tried to express his gratitude for Ram saving his life that he realized she wasn't moving within his arms.

Ram's head drooped as a thin line of blood trickled down from her nostril. Her eyes were closed, her breaths shallow, and the only sounds she made were painful moans.

"Ah, er, Ram? Uh, geez, this is bad."

He gently rocked her body and called out to her, but Ram made no reply.

From the beginning, she'd been exhausted from using Clairvoyance and fighting the demon beasts. No doubt Ram had really overdone it with that spell, putting her mind in a precarious state.

"Ah, crap. My timing really is shitty..."

Subaru cursed his own impulsiveness as he re-embraced Ram more carefully. He laid her down beside him, awkwardly slid the broken blade into its sheath, and looked up.

Even the demon beasts couldn't leap down the edge of a sheer precipice after them. Surely they'd circle around to resume their pursuit. He'd hoped that would give them the advantage in the meantime.

"Oh, come on, you've gotta be kidding me!"

The very moment Subaru looked above his head, a large number of rocks flowed down the slope that they'd barely survived falling from—and riding atop them was a pack of demon beasts, with a pup deploying its mana leading the way.

Subaru recognized the demon beast pup: He was absolutely certain it was the one that had first cursed him in the village, and the one that Rem had delivered a powerful blow to when it chased the children the night before.

Seeing the way the other demon beasts followed it, as if it led that whole pack in spite of its size, Subaru couldn't keep a dry laugh away.

"I'm starting to hate you, Lady Witch—that perfume of yours is overkill."

Duly lodging his complaint, Subaru checked on his numb legs as he prepared to flee once more. He prayed that the demon beasts would show them contempt and not pounce the instant they landed—

"Er, wha...?"

A moment before Subaru started running, he tilted his head, sensing that something was off.

The demon beasts sliding down the cliff looked wrong. They began to flinch while on the rolling rocks, and the instant they hit the ground under the cliff, they began to scatter in all directions.

"Huh? Uh, I'm over here, guys…?"

The sight of them scattering like little spiders was a bit much for him to take in.

The heck's going on here…? The moment after he thought it, the explosion atop the cliff brought the answer.

"—Heh?"

When he looked up again, the change atop the cliff surprised Subaru, but he instantly understood.

—A human silhouette now stood on the precipice far above them.

It was a girl wearing a servant's outfit, her blood-drenched ball and chain held low as she glared down the incline with eyes that had lost all trace of sanity.

The moment his eyes met that murderous gaze, Subaru broke out in a cold sweat as he experienced a bad feeling like no other.

In an instant, the demon leaped off the high cliff to land on the ground far below.

Subaru's breath caught. Here he was, deep in the forest surrounded by demon beasts, face-to-face with a demon girl, one arm around a girl he had to protect at all costs—and he had arrived at the final stage wielding nothing but a broken sword.

"This is just…a tiny bit unfair, don't you think?"

His plea died on the breeze blowing through the forest, unheard.

It was, as they say, a do-or-die situation—

6

Ram and Subaru had entered the forest of the demon beasts fully aware of the danger, but since they had cooperated together to take down the beasts, they had arrived deep in the forest without a scratch. The idea was to find Rem, who would be miraculously unharmed, and lecture her for being a loose cannon in a safe, peaceful, happy reunion. And, using Subaru's knack for drawing the demon beasts to him, they'd use Ram's and Rem's sisterly powers to take down the demon beasts one after another, liberating Subaru from the curse. End of story.

"That's how I imagined it, but, yeah…"

In a pathetic voice, Subaru mused about how his smooth-sailing scenario was now in tatters.

Subaru didn't see a single shred of friendship in Rem's eyes as she stood before him. All he sensed was pitch-black bloodlust.

Though he couldn't be sure, she didn't look like she was in any mental condition for them to talk things through.

The pressure rolling off her made him hesitate to even blink. He didn't know what might happen if he took his eyes off the threat in front of him for even a split second.

—That very thought brought a strained smile to Subaru as he realized Rem viewed him as her enemy. *What the hell am I doing all the way out here, then?*

"Heya, Remrin, it's your pal Subaru! Your buddy!"

Unaware that his face had gone stiff, Subaru nonetheless managed to call out with a cheerful voice. Perhaps he thought that calling to Rem might bring her back to her senses, but…

Rem turned her head toward him, locking on with a look so sharp that he could practically hear it.

"If you give me steamy looks like that, I'm gonna get singed…"

Subaru felt the entire weight of her attention on him. Perhaps he had failed. Rem's dreadful appearance certainly warranted that thought.

The familiar servant's outfit on her was fully covered in blood spatter. A coat of fresh blood dampened the dried blood below it in a gruesome two-tone pattern, sporting blackish red and vivid red.

Her nails were long and sharp enough to rival those of the demon beasts—perhaps an effect of her horned form. Under her right hand was her iron ball for "self-defense" and a pool of blood and little bits of flesh, an exceptionally ominous combination.

He'd somewhat expected to find Rem like this, so he was able to keep hold of his senses, but if Subaru had met this Rem in a dark alley, it was safe to say he'd be 100 percent certain to piss his pants.

That was how terrible Rem was in her ghoulish madness—and yet, in the midst of it all, the white horn protruding from her forehead had maintained its purity and beauty. To Subaru, even though the horn was the very symbol of Rem's malevolent demon state, it was the only thing that seemed out of place in contrast to the rest.

But the circumstances did not permit Subaru such leisurely thoughts.

When he looked, he saw scattered demon beasts waiting behind the shadows of boulders and among the trees of the forest. No doubt the beasts were watching their every move.

He'd be lunch the instant he showed them the slightest opening.

Rem standing before him, the demon beasts standing behind—his life was truly dangling by a thread.

Subaru couldn't move. The demon beasts couldn't move. The entire situation would hinge on Rem's next action.

He took a deep breath, closed his eyes, and looked straight back at Rem once more.

He didn't know if he could make Rem's eyes waver, but he had to give it everything he had and leave no stone unturned.

Then—

"Sister…"

Her voice was tired and faint. However, the sound and its meaning thrummed in Subaru's ears. Her lips quivered, and she seemed out of sorts as her eyes fixated on the side of Ram's face.

Even amid a frenzy sufficient to make her lose her sanity, Rem still recognized the sight of her other half, the sister she loved above all. Subaru sighed in astonishment.

"If I didn't know better, I'd say you had a sister complex. If that brought you back to sanity, I'm all for—"

"—Let her *go*."

She interrupted his words as she flung the iron ball at him with the force of a typhoon.

It was close to a miracle that he'd managed to bend his body to the left in time. It was perhaps fortunate that Subaru's knees were a little wobbly, having not yet recovered from the earlier hard landing.

The spikes of the iron ball grazed his right shoulder as it passed. The anguish clawing out his flesh sent his brain into hysteria.

Biting down to hold back a pain-filled shout, Subaru advanced at an angle.

"That hurt, damn it!"

Subaru turned his gouged shoulder before sidestepping the chain as it lashed downward. A moment later, the chain violently slammed into the spot where Subaru had just been, leaving a snakelike trail on the ground.

If Subaru had been any slower in dodging, his back would have borne an identical mark.

He shuddered, imagining his flesh rending as he looked at Rem. But Rem looked no different from before. Her eyes were steeped in enmity without having regained their sanity.

"Horned form isn't the problem; it's whether or not you can control it..."

That was Subaru's guess based on Rem's current demeanor.

If that was the case, the issue was *how* to restore her sanity. She'd been in a frenzied state the night before, too, but her mind had been more Rem than mad demon in the moments before he'd blacked out.

Perhaps the sight of Subaru gravely injured before her eyes would be enough of a shock to snap her back to lucidity.

"Maybe I should try getting hit by the iron ball once? Wait, I'll be mincemeat then..."

Repeating the conditions from the night before would surely bring Rem around, but by then Subaru would be dog food.

"—"

Ram might have understood the situation, but the girl in his arms was a long way from conscious; he'd been trying to shake her awake, but that was probably going to take some time.

Time that Rem and the demon beasts surrounding him weren't likely to permit.

Subaru licked a drop of sweat trickling down his cheek, using the moisture on his tongue to lubricate his lips.

If no new option presented itself, he'd just have to try everything.

If charging forward was the only way, then that was that. It was the Subaru way.

"Hey, Rem! Don't just look at your sister in my arms here, look at me! My name is Subaru Natsuki! The absolutely useless newbie doing odd jobs! The doe-eyed manservant at Roswaal Manor! I probably caused you and Ram a lot of trouble, but we got along some of the time, ri— Whoa!"

He was in the middle of appealing to Ram's memories and emotions when her short temper put an immediate stop to it.

The whirring iron ball snapped and shattered the trunk of every tree in its path, smashing branches along the way as Subaru made a leaping forward roll to evade. He dodged her next attacks with a pretty hop-step-jump and looked back.

"It's rude to beat someone to death midsentence! I saw my family's faces before my eyes there... Ah, here we are!"

As Subaru yelled, Rem leaned forward and murmured, "Give Sister back...!"

But out of the blue, Rem yanked back the iron ball she'd swung with one arm alone, using the momentum to spin her body around on a dime when...

"—!"

...Rem's backward spinning kick connected with the torso of the demon beast leaping at her from behind. With a roar equal to that of a bomb, the demon beast exploded; even from some distance away, Subaru could clearly make out its innards sailing through the air.

That's what you get for trying to profit from the misery of others.

The demon beasts had formed a second wave to attack behind the vanguard, but the gruesome sight of that death made them stop in their tracks. But this was folly, no different from offering up one's belly in the face of one's predator.

She unleashed a single horizontal attack that smashed together the bellies and skulls of the next two beasts. Rem, unconcerned by the flying blood and flesh, charged in the wake of her attack. One of the beasts drew its head back, so she crushed one of its front paws; now that it had stopped moving, she used her other foot to kick it in the head, snapping its neck.

Her heel continued up, then back down into the torso of the next beast. A third pounced at Rem to avenge its comrade, but she gripped its throat below its wide-open maw and hurled it high into the sky. The demon beast arced through the air, curling its tail as it made a faint yelp. It flew farther and farther, then closer and closer, until finally smashing against the hard ground with a sound resembling that of an overripe fruit.

Slaughter followed slaughter. It was carnage for the sake of carnage, a massacre even by massacre standards.

It was already plain that the beasts could not compare to the destructive power of the single, mighty horned demon who had descended upon them.

Yet even so—

"Damn, numbers really are a weapon all their own."

Though the demon beasts saw their brethren cut down one after another, they showed no sign of disengaging. They bared their fangs, brandished their claws, and howled menacingly as they sprang at Rem.

Even as they were blown away, crushed, smashed, and dismembered, adding to the pile of demon beast corpses, they carved shallow wounds into Rem's body little by little. When Subaru saw that the maid outfit, drenched in blood spatter, was reddening not just from the outside but fresh bleeding from the inside, he realized the tide had begun to turn against them.

The battle before his eyes between horned demon and demon beast was extremely intense; they no longer paid any heed to Subaru and Ram whatsoever. Both sides were leaving low-threat opponents for later as they concentrated their rampages on their mortal enemies.

If Rem had been dominating the battle, Subaru would no doubt have let her hunt the demon beasts to extinction without it weighing on his conscience. But her situation was gradually getting worse.

"—"

Rem's arms flung about, mowing down demon beast torsos. She gasped in pain as claw after claw reached her own body. Blood scattered; lacerations carved into her white skin.

Subaru couldn't just sit and watch.

There was a way. All he had to do was butt into the fight. But charging in to join the fray directly would only get him wrapped up in the typhoon and blown back the way he came. For him, interjecting meant drawing the horned demon's and the demon beasts' attention to something besides one another—it was the only way to save Rem.

He resigned himself, spread his legs, took a deep breath, and looked right at Rem.

—*I can do this. Girls have charm, boys have courage.*

"Don't make that scary face, Rem. Smile. I've Returned by—"

For the second time that day, the world ground to a halt, and the black cloud brought another banquet of screams.

Even though he'd resigned himself to the extreme pain that would arise, it was not pain one could endure. All the more so because this time, it was not just a right arm but a left arm that emerged with it.

Perhaps the completed right arm had developed a taste for this. Before Subaru's unmoving, wide-open eyes, the right hand slid past his rib cage and brushed against his internal organs as the left hand split off.

The right hand went for his heart; the other caressed Subaru's cheek like it was fond of him.

—Terror welled within him, and the next moment, pain shot through his every nerve.

He ceased to be himself. From the top of his head to the tips of his toes, he had a horrible, unendurable sense that something was *wrong*. His brain boiled in a tempest of negative emotions; his consciousness faded in and out.

And yet, the soft touch of the palm on his cheek bore warmth that brought relief when he felt like his mind and body were about to melt. But Subaru knew a feeling of beyond that, so—

"I'm...*back*!"

His vision was blurred. His soul had been whittled down. None of the pain and suffering had carried over to the real world.

No time had passed. Rem and the demon beasts were in front of him, at each other's throats just like before.

—But the instant Subaru returned to reality, a great change came over the field of battle. Rem and the demon beasts poured all their attention onto Subaru; it was as if some anomaly had emerged then and there that could not be ignored.

No doubt the cause was that, just as Subaru had planned, the witch's stench was erupting from him.

"—!"

Rem roared. The demon beasts howled in unison. Subaru, too, yelled at the top of his lungs.

With split-second timing, he evaded the claws of the leaping demon beasts and the iron ball slamming toward him, as if his life, his very soul, had been set on fire.

—And so the great melee began.

7

As the unquestionably odd one out in a battle of horned demon, demon beast, and ordinary boy, Subaru paid attention to every detail of the melee as he bobbed and weaved.

His conduct was exceedingly simple. He'd hold his position as the battle grew more intense, making no effort to increase the distance, dodging only the sparks that fell in his direction—end of story.

"—"

Once again, the demon beasts pounded by the iron ball became wall paste before his eyes. Heedless of their comrades' deaths, three demon beasts teamed up to attack Rem without pause, aiming to inflict greater wounds upon her. But such crude intelligence went to waste, for her hand knocked them away; once they were immobile, they became easy prey for the iron ball's descent.

Subaru glanced at the spectacle as he shifted his hold on Ram, in danger of falling out of his grasp, and jumped back. He barely evaded the fangs of one demon beast, only to dance right into Rem's range of attack.

And when Rem realized Subaru was closing in, she instantly moved to intercept. Subaru came to a very abrupt stop to escape the thrust of her iron handle, then leaped back and ducked to avoid the lash of the chain that followed, with the iron ball passing over his head to change the head of the demon beast chasing behind him into a spectacularly blooming crimson flower.

Subaru heard the body crashing down behind him as he threw shame and honor to the wind and crawled on the ground, cockroach-style, to escape immediately. Rem, hot on his heels, found her path obstructed by demon beasts. Escape successful.

Subaru held his distance as he rewarded himself with a single sigh of relief for the quick thinking that had saved his life.

"—Hah! I'm actually doing pretty well here!"

He'd desperately bounded away to avoid being bitten, foisted the pursuing demon beasts on the maid girl, and had crawled like a bug to escape the angry girl's wrath. If his actions were ever recorded for posterity, he would want to die then and there, but he focused on the fact that his conduct was intended to keep him alive.

At that moment, things were unfolding according to Subaru's plan.

The situation could be worse—they were at least buying time and reducing the number of demon beasts. When he glanced up, he sensed the eyes of demon beasts all around the valley. Once they spied the battle, they joined the fray one by one. The demon beasts were obeying their instincts in response to Subaru's spreading the stench of the witch throughout the forest.

This could work. He saw a chance for victory. That, at least, was what Subaru thought.

"—Uh?"

Subaru engaged in more evasive action when he suddenly felt dizzy and tilted heavily. It wasn't that he'd been careless with his steps. He was suddenly assailed by a feeling of lethargy as a chill ran through his entire body... He *knew*.

"The curse... At a time like this...?!"

Subaru looked up to try to see if the demon beast from which the curse hailed was one of those surrounding Rem. But he had no way to tell which was the caster. Besides, it was unlikely the demon beast had triggered the curse just to make Subaru suffer.

It was the simple result of being faced with the menace of Rem and craving the mana with which to fight her. And Subaru was right there with them, rite ready for activation, his mana there for the taking. A simple reason but also a fatal one.

The curse got the better of Subaru, making him lose his balance and crash to the ground. If the demon beasts bit Subaru to death, it was only a matter of time until they weighed Rem down by sheer numbers. But more than that, the very reason Rem had entered the forest would be—

"—Aah!"

A great shout echoed loudly enough to rend the air and split the ground as she swung down, her fist turning one demon beast into dog food.

In a single instant, with incredible, explosive force, Rem had broken through the monster ranks to kill a demon beast far away from her. The sight shocked Subaru and the beasts alike. When Subaru recovered, he immediately realized it.

—He was breathing easier. The lethargy had abated. He had been freed from the effects of the curse.

"—Rem."

"—!"

Rem returned to butchering the demon beasts surrounding her as if she hadn't even heard Subaru call her name.

Subaru watched the blue-haired girl in the midst of combat as it keenly sunk in that, though she wasn't lucid or in a state to recognize who Subaru was, Rem had saved him by turning that demon beast into paste.

She hadn't mistaken the sight of her beloved older sister. Nor, apparently, had she forgotten the reason why she'd plunged into the forest in the first place.

If that's the case..., he thought.

Subaru scraped his mind for the thing that only he could do. He thought that he should be faithful to his original goal, not resort to a roundabout plan like this.

"In other words, I'll have the heartthrob maid sisters, Ram and Rem, send that curse packing!"

If Subaru could accomplish *that*, he might yet be able to get out of the situation alive.

Furthermore, to do that, he needed to bring Rem back to sanity in a real sense. Subaru's business was not with the murderous demon but with the superficially polite, quick-to-jump-to-conclusions girl whose running off on her own caused everyone else so much trouble—Rem.

"—The horn."

Suddenly, Subaru heard a voice from within his arms.

Ram, still in his embrace, faintly opened her eyes, giving Subaru an unfocused upward glance.

"You're...awake?!"

"I think my timing here is quite...excellent..."

Ram was smiling a bit. Subaru smiled back half seriously as he replied.

"Yeah, you've got awesome instincts, Big Sis. What do you mean, the horn?"

Ram pulled her chin in with a look of annoyance.

"It is that horn that has led Rem astray... A single, powerful blow will...bring her back..."

"You're sure that'll work?"

"Fairly. Largely. I believe that it will."

"That's kind of vague, you know?! But I wanna believe you."

Subaru cut off his words and looked at Rem.

The white horn jutted out from Rem's forehead to a length of some four inches. If Puck stood on her forehead, he and the horn would be around the same height.

A single blow—there.

"Doesn't that seem kinda...impossible?"

"Use your intellect and courage and just do it."

"Well, I do kind of have a way to do this that involves intellect and courage, but..."

Subaru's unexpected reply made Ram raise her eyebrows. He smiled weakly at her, as he had difficulty putting it into words.

"It's probably gonna give you a scare."

"If it brings my little sister back to sanity, I shall not be upset."

"Really?"

"Really-really."

"You swear on Rozchi?"

"...You must really not mind dying to pick *that*. Yes, I swear on Master Roswaal."

It was because Ram had said it in such a thoroughly valiant way that Subaru respected her view so highly.

Before them, Rem slowly turned in their direction. The bulk of her attention was trained on them, with the remainder toward the demon beasts surrounding them to warn her if they came close.

In contrast to Rem, on guard for attacks from every direction, Subaru was focused solely on smacking that horn.

Namely—

"Aaaaand, off you go!"

"—Ah?"

Ram had a distant look of shock on her face as Subaru lifted her up by the hips...and chucked her forward.

No doubt that the thought he'd *throw* her had never entered her mind.

Ram looked aghast, but Rem was equally so. Rem, still in her horned form, stood agape for a brief moment before reaching out as her older sister flew through the air toward her.

The iron ball fell from Rem's grasp as she welcomed her big sister with open, bloodstained arms. In an instant, her expression, so hard and painted over with hostility and bloodlust, changed into something much softer.

—Subaru sprang forward to not let that instant go to waste.

The same moment he hurled Ram forward, Subaru lowered his body and charged. Rem's gaze was aimed up, preoccupied with her big sister, while Subaru approached from the blind spot closer to the ground.

His feet slid as his right hand drew his sword from his waist. In one motion, he sliced through the wind as he slid the blade out of the scabbard, aiming it at the horn on Rem's forehead—the timing was perfect. Even Rem could not respond in time to the sudden attack. But—

"—Ah?!"

Through a combination of the blade's broken tip and Subaru's own timid, halfhearted step at the end, the blade missed a direct blow to her horn, passing a few millimeters short.

Subaru was appalled at having let his tiny moment of opportunity slip through his hands.

"I chickened out! I didn't have enough courage for the last part!!"

His body swam as he got nothing but air.

Subaru's momentum carried him past her, exposing his back, and Rem raised her left hand to stab him. The long claws on her fingertips would surely go right through Subaru's back and stick out the other side.

He regretted dying one step away from success, and at Rem's hands at that.

The very moment he thought it—

"Whoaaaa—?!"

The ground beneath his feet exploded, with the resulting cascade of rocks vaulting Subaru straight up.

The scattering rocks pelted his body all over. Skin breaking and bleeding, Subaru looked down from midair to see the cause of his pain.

South of the point where the ground had exploded under Subaru, he saw the demon beast puppy in a low crouch. The Urugarum had kept a low profile since leading the pack down the cliff, waiting for its opportunity to take Subaru and Rem out in a single cascade of rocks. And so, seeing Subaru create an opening, it had spectacularly intervened with the goal of sending both him and Rem flying.

However...

"—!!"

...its plan was foiled when Rem roared and stomped onto the ground from which the rocks were erupting. Force canceled force, ending with only her blue hair heavily disheveled. She'd canceled out magical force with raw violence—smashing the spell with brute force.

The cascade of rocks ceased, and Rem's shoulders eased as she held her big sister preciously in her arms.

Subaru, still above her, had vanished from even the furthermost reaches of her mind.

Buffeted by the magic spell, Subaru whirled head over heels with no idea which way was up. But his right hand kept the sword firmly in its grip even then; fortunately, he landed not against the rock wall but merely on the hard ground.

And Rem stood right below him, her head exposed, not noticing him whatsoever.

There would be no better chance, nor no chance after. It was now or never.

He gripped the single-handed sword's hilt with both hands and swung with all his might.

He had arrived at this point at the end of a long string of coincidences.

Opportunism for the win. Miracles were awesome. Even if purely by whim, sometimes God did good work—although God's work would also have helped tremendously with the previous attempt.

And now he was right above Rem, unnoticed, her head fully exposed...

He made a strained smile. There was no time. Rem was close at hand, and so was a slow, leisurely world with her.

He saw the horn. He swung the sword past its apex with all the energy he could muster.

"Laugh, Rem. Today, I'm more demonic than any demon!"

The blade flashed straight down, aimed at the white horn—

The high-pitched sound of steel striking steel sharply echoed through the demon beasts' forest.

The next moment, Subaru crash-landed, his own painful yelp merging with the echo.

INTERLUDE
REM

1

Compared to her older sister, the girl named Rem had a very difficult everyday life.

Even among humanoids, the might and mana possessed by the demon race were head and shoulders above the rest. Their robust bodies and the quality of the mana they employed granted them peerless fighting strength. They boasted the title of the mightiest of all humanoid races.

The single weakness the demons possessed was their crushingly low population. A race dedicated to producing the mightiest individuals did not give breath to great numbers, and so, despite their strength, the demon race was obliged to dwell in poor villages deep within the mountains.

Because they were a race dwelling far from human habitation, there were strict taboos among the demons to protect their limited numbers.

To their race, twins were abominations. This was one of the unbreakable laws of demon kind.

By nature, demons are born with two horns on their head. In tranquil times the horns are hidden, but when circumstances change and their demon instincts awaken, the horns appear on their heads and consume mana from the surrounding area. Their horns draw in and control mana from the atmosphere, greatly heightening their combat capabilities. This purpose made them the pride of their race.

But twins were born with only one horn each.

Among demons, the "hornless" were considered the dregs of society. Losing even one was cause for ridicule. Twins lacked something deeply precious from the moment of their birth. What else could they be but abominations?

And so, it was taught that twins were to be discarded immediately.

The fate of this pair of twins ought to have ended then and there. And it would have, had one of the twins not displayed her gift from the heavens with a tremendous burst of magical power the very moment the chief, having made the bitter decision, was about to render judgment by his own hand.

2

The older twin was named Ram; the younger, Rem. Both occupied the lowest rungs on the ladder among the tribe.

Their daily lives were far from pleasant. Even though their lives had been spared, they were still twins. Both were treated as hornless from the beginning and raised inhospitably by their people.

In spite of their connection by blood, their own parents acted distantly toward them. Their fellow tribesmen did not hide their contempt for the two "abominations." For both of them, it was the worst childhood imaginable.

The hostility continued until the demons realized what they were capable of—or more precisely, until the older of the twins became aware of it herself.

The most accurate term describing Ram during childhood was *wonder child*. She had talent that exceeded even that of great demons throughout their storied history. Indeed, their entire race was enthralled by the beauty of Ram's horn, which allowed her to use a vast amount of mana in spite of her youth. Her demeanor was as forthright as the single, pure white horn on her forehead, lacking any hint of becoming drunk on her own might and potential, making it seem natural for their brethren to bow their heads before her.

It was very special treatment for a girl who was not yet ten years of age.

Even their cold and distant parents, even their kin who had openly scorned them, even the chief who had tried to slay the twins shortly after birth—all were speechless before Ram's authority. She was destined from birth to become the pinnacle of the horned demons, the mightiest of all humanoid races.

Members of a race that prized individual strength were flawless in their politeness toward an individual with such power. And yet, Ram never once used the tribe's reverence for her own benefit.

All Rem could do was stumble down her older sister's path to glory.

She had no abilities above the norm. Her mana supply was strictly average, with her body's capabilities in line with what a normal demon with only one horn could do. Compared to Ram, she did not have a shred of confidence; she cowered behind her sister's back like a shadow.

That was how the young Rem coped. That was how she protected her immature heart.

It wasn't that she was jealous of her older sister. She admired her. She adored her.

It wasn't that her parents hated her. They loved the younger as well as the older.

It wasn't as if their people had spurned Rem. Of course they had high hopes. She was *her* little sister.

Her sister, kinder than anyone; her parents, full of expectations; all her kin, cheering her on to excel like her twin—these were the little cuts that chafed Rem.

No doubt it was the direct consequence of her and her sister looking like two peas in a pod. Yet even though their heights and faces were identical, their qualities as demons were on completely different scales.

Of course, Rem strived to change those circumstances. It may have been no more than shallow, clumsy trial-and-error efforts by a young child, but Rem tried any and every way of getting closer to her older sister, to beat her in even a single area.

But Ram was simply better at everything.

And so, Rem was still a young child when she learned that the sister to whom she was closest, the sister she loved more than anything, occupied an area that she could never, ever reach.

She could never stand by her sister's side. Ram would always walk ahead of her, bathed in the light of the world. Rem's place was behind her sister, cowering behind her back, peeking out once in a while, only to shrink away from the dazzling light.

Once she gave up, she could accept the sufferings of daily life, like a reed bending with the wind.

—She wondered how long she would have to bear her own weak capitulation.

3

One night, Rem awoke, unable to sleep well because of the heat.

She slid off the wooden bed and pulled the blankets off her sweat-covered body. When Rem looked around, she suddenly realized that her older sister, always sleeping beside her, was gone.

I have to look for my sister right away, she thought.

If her sister was awake, she had to follow behind her majestic gait. To do so without fail, even for matters as trivial as waking up briefly to pee, was Rem's obsession at the time.

I have to go outside—but only then did Rem belatedly notice the source of the warmth—flames that enveloped her home.

When she touched the doorknob, she yanked her hand back from its heat. At that moment, the truth sank in. Rem's sleepy sense of smell was awoken by the scent of something burned; her forehead felt itchy as her horn grew, appearing fully.

Instantly, she used her solid body to break the door down and dash out of the house enveloped in the hellish flames. She didn't know why this had happened, but she obeyed her instincts to flee, to get outside.

Rem kicked apart the brittle fence and rushed from her home to the outside world.

Even then, a single, fanatical thought ruled in her mind: *I have to leave the house and have Sis tell me what to do.*

But then, that thought fell by the wayside at the sight awaiting her once she left the house.

In the center of the village was a pile of burned bodies. The burning houses and flame-swept trees had turned her familiar world into a reddish hell in one night.

When Rem saw the faces of her parents among the corpses swallowed by the flames, she immediately abandoned all rational thought and fell to her knees then and there.

Rem remained kneeling as a group of men dressed in black robes calmly surrounded her. Even up close, the deep shadows of their hoods hid their faces until they were very close; even then, they were not faces she recognized. However, when Rem did not sense a single trace of goodwill from them, a smile came over her that seemed alien on her cheeks.

That smile was the one that hid her despair for the good of everyone else.

The figures did not respond in the slightest to the expression or the pain behind it.

The shadows approached her, raising their hands and swinging the glimmering silver blades within them down at the girl—but their heads flew off in the next moment.

Blood. In a single moment, four lives had been taken with such skill that the heads never raised a shout, never even realized what had happened.

The familiar feel of the mana pulsing against her skin instantly told Rem it was the work of her sister. She stood up.

If her sister was here, Rem had to follow her lead.

She didn't even need to look around. Her eyes located her older sister immediately.

The face identical to Rem's own was warped with grief. The older sister ran over to embrace the younger, sighing with relief and relaxing her body when she realized Rem was unharmed. Rem hugged her sister back, never feeling more pathetic, or happier, in her life.

—Rem did not clearly remember what happened next.

She thought that she'd leave everything up to her sister.

That was best. That was right. Sis always chose the finest option among all available possibilities.

And yet, they had been surrounded before she realized it.

Even with silhouettes so numerous they formed a wall, Rem looked at them in a daze, still believing that Sis would somehow overcome.

Her sister pushed before her, straining herself yelling. Tears flowed from her cheeks; her body seemed to shrink as she made a desperate plea.

When they threw her sister to the ground, Rem felt troubled. To look down at her sister was to contradict her way of life. To stand behind her sister, to hide behind her back, was what brought meaning to her existence.

Her sister screamed. She returned to her feet and spread her hands out before her. She unleashed the mana. The power would flow through her sister, and invisible blades would descend upon the world, slicing everything around them.

But the moment before unleashing it, her sister turned around, embraced Rem—then, an impact.

And then, Rem could only watch.

She saw steel flash at her sister's head from the side. She saw a white glimmer dance in the reddened sky.

She saw the severed horn spin round and round and round.

She saw blood gush out from her sister's forehead. She heard someone's high-pitched scream.

She listened to the cries of the sister she adored, the sister who had shielded her and taken the blow for her, as the beautiful white horn that she had so envied tumbled through the sky.

—*Finally. It finally broke off.*

That was the thought she had.

4

Rem did not understand the details of what occurred after that point.

What she did grasp was that at some point, they'd lost consciousness, only to awaken far from home with a huge mansion all around her, and that her sister, who had lost her horn, was there with her.

Her sister had regained consciousness first and was overjoyed to see Rem awaken, but Rem was lost in thoughts of her twin, whose abilities ranked lower than the average person's now that she had lost her horn.

On the surface, her behavior was largely unchanged, but there was no trace of the talent she had commanded in every area. Now that she struggled with even minor things, Rem had many opportunities to help her.

And so, one would think that Rem would develop a superiority complex toward her now universally inferior sister—but one would be wrong; the inferiority complex took root in Rem's spirit even deeper than before.

In other words, Rem felt shame at the fact that her sister had gone from beloved by the whole world to having to endure life at the bottom.

Rem's guilt was spurred on by the admiration she had for her older sister. Had Rem's heart been filled with only jealous thoughts, no doubt it would not have been so. But Rem loved her sister. And she was not so shrewd or self-serving to live and forget the thought she'd had that moment when her sister's horn was broken.

"I have to do everything in Sis's…Sister's place…"

Rem changed how she addressed her older sister and put her days of hiding in her shadow behind her. Rem's battle had begun.

In all things, in all duties she was assigned, all she could think was, *Sister would do* this. She'd always been right behind her sister, watching. Her sister's judgment had never failed.

Even so, the results were always less than she expected. That was natural, for her sister was incredible. With a flawed little sister like her, even both of them working together could not reach the same place.

Rem had to blaze the trail that was properly her sister's to have blazed, to have walked, to have led her down, and to lead her older sister along it by the hand.

—There was no longer any individual life for the girl known as Rem.

To Rem, the only thing she could do was "live the life Sister would have." That she could not fulfill such a role made her unable to believe that she had any real value.

Days and months passed. There, in the mansion that had taken them both in when their homeland was burned away, the gap between their reality and Rem's ideals wore at her day after day.

It was not that she minded her role as a servant. The lord of the manor had benevolently given them a place to stay, and moreover, she adored her older sister enough that she did not mind offering up body and soul.

If problems arose during these untroubled days, Rem took full responsibility.

You have done well, the master would say in praise. She had heard such words from her homeland many times over.

Don't force yourself, her sister would say to Rem out of concern. But even forcing herself was not yet enough.

Why do you push yourself so hard? one irresponsible person had asked Rem.

—That was obvious.

Because she was inferior in anything and everything. Even if she pushed herself to the breaking point, whittling away her soul and burning her body to ash, she would never reach that which ought to have been.

—What could she do to atone?

And so, Rem dedicated her life to cutting open the path that her sister ought to have walked herself but that Rem had stolen from her.

For Rem was a substitute for her sister in all things and nothing more.

5

With her obsession strengthened, the seven years wore upon Rem.

Others dutifully commended Rem on a daily basis for her earnest hard work, though to Rem these efforts never yielded satisfactory results. Even Margrave Roswaal praised her as a capable worker, to the point that he commanded her to serve at his side during that significant time when the royal selection was underway.

And yet, all the praise she earned filled Rem's chest with vague unease.

The days and months had not made her sense of guilt fade away; indeed, they had only reinforced it—and she continued to live her life for the sake of her older sister.

And then, Lady Emilia and Sister had returned from the royal capital, bringing a foreign element into the mansion.

"My name is Subaru Natsuki. Zero work experience! Pleased to meet you!"

The wounded lad had been brought into the mansion because he had saved Emilia's life. Upon waking, the young man negotiated with Roswaal and gained for himself the position of apprentice servant in no time at all.

Naturally, Rem was gripped by a deep sense of distrust toward the youth of uncertain origin. In particular, she could find nothing to like during the first two days, when the young man had plastered a smile on his face and worked constantly to win her and her sister's favor.

Furthermore, there was a scent wafting around him that triggered memories in Rem that she could barely endure. It was the scent of the witch—the miasma that surrounded only a few beings in the entire world.

Ever since her homeland had become a sea of flames, Rem's nose had learned how to pick out the scent.

She did not know why. She knew only that it triggered abominable memories and that seven long, bitter years had taught her that nothing good came from that which accompanied the scent.

She had been unable to make her antipathy plain in front of Roswaal and Emilia, but instead, she had often found herself staring at the young man while he seemed at war with himself.

Now that she had lost her horn, Sister had no need for any relationships other than her one with Roswaal, whom she adored. To Rem, who had stolen her sister's proper place, there was nothing more important than protecting the place her sister could be at ease. And Rem would show no mercy to those who threatened their home.

As far as anyone else could see, the boy showed no sign of untoward behavior whatsoever. Yet even as her sister told her that they should only watch, Rem thought he should be driven out of the mansion as soon as possible.

By the time something happens, it will be too late. Such was the conclusion Rem had formed at the time.

—And then, she saw Subaru sleeping on Emilia's lap.

Rem gave Emilia's opinion on the matter a great deal of weight, but internally she was still struggling to think of how she should treat the person known as Subaru.

Rem, who had strictly observed Subaru's every action because he was an outsider, understood that he tried his utmost in everything he did—including the sarcasm. It was in complete contrast to his frivolous manner.

And seeing him struggle so hard to produce results in spite of inferior ability reminded her of someone, but she couldn't put her finger on it.

From the following morning onward, she saw Subaru's demeanor and behavior in a different light. The strained atmosphere evaporated; how he approached everything changed, even if his technical skill had not.

He had gone from striving without a tangible goal to burning with desire to accomplish something. Naturally, his approach to work changed as well. He still held others back, but the quality of his work did rise a little bit.

Rem, who welcomed no changes to her environment, still regarded Subaru as a troublesome interloper, but she felt like she should at least not regard him as an enemy.

Then, when Roswaal was absent, disaster struck.

"—Worst case, the whole village might get wiped out."

Rem, ordered by her older sister to accompany Subaru, half doubted the extreme scenario he'd suggested so seriously. However, when they reached Earlham Village, the children really were missing, and the barrier that should have blocked off the forest had been breached and was no longer functioning.

"Rem, let's go. We have to do something."

Rem had recoiled at Subaru's invitation to go into the forest to rescue the children from their plight.

Of course it was strange. Rem could not grasp why someone so powerless would act so desperately for children he barely knew.

Subaru was not being reckless. He was well aware of his own weakness. And still he did not hesitate to ask others for the things he lacked. *What incredible arrogance*, she had thought.

They had gone into the forest, found the children, and used magic to save them. Even when Subaru wanted to go deeper into the forest to find the missing last child, Rem was not surprised.

With eyes that said he was useless, an expression that said he didn't measure up, a voice that bit back the urge to give in many times over—Subaru never stopped struggling.

When Rem watched Subaru head into the forest by himself as she healed the children, her heart fluttered furiously. She was filled with warmth that words could not express.

After Rem had handed the children over to the young men of the village, relying on the miasma of the witch to reach Subaru once more, she had found him in a life-and-death situation, surrounded by a pack of demon beasts.

Seeing the sleeping girl in Subaru's arms had cleared away all Rem's doubts.

As Subaru ran, Rem leaped into action, running interference for him against the attacking mob of demon beasts. Blood and pain toyed with her, but Rem felt light, as if a weight had been lifted from her heart.

Not once had she imagined that trusting someone, trusting Subaru, could feel so good.

The next moment, Rem had sustained an impact that plunged her mind into darkness. In its place, her demon instincts took over, and she began an indiscriminate slaughter.

She learned the pleasure of making flesh fly apart. She felt delight at indulging in her power, completely forgetting her goal.

Her demon instincts demanded more blood, more lives—

"—!"

The collision against her back had sent Rem flying, dulling her reactions.

Something was holding her down. When she looked behind her, she saw Subaru's face. The relief on it snapped Rem from reflex to rational thought.

She saw a ferocious demon beast right next to him, its fangs drawing near. She needed to jump, to reach out, to save him—so thought Rem when suddenly, the miasma tickled her nose.

That made her delay her decision by a single moment.

And then…

"—Gaaaaah!!"

…Rem finally realized that she had not changed at all.

She had committed the sin from long ago…again.

CHAPTER 5
ALL IN

1

—When Rem regained consciousness, her feet were not planted on the ground.

There was an arm firmly around her waist. Someone was carrying her. She did not think that the rough manner was any way to touch a girl. Though that was indeed the case, the owner of the arm was sprinting recklessly, with not a shred of concentration for anything beyond that.

"—Barusu, go right at the broken tree in front! You are slow!"

"Don't...demand the impossible... I'm—*haghh*—running...as hard as I can...here!"

Two familiar voices, one more intimately so, were yelling at each other from close by.

The intense up-and-down shaking jostled Rem's head back into consciousness.

"...Subaru, what are y—"

"—! Rem...you're awake?!"

Subaru kept running as he voiced his delight and glanced down at her. Rem looked up at him, her mind still rather hazy, when something unexpectedly caught in her throat.

The side of Subaru's face was wet with blood. Maybe he'd cut his forehead? The scars all over his body from the night before had whitened; at some point, new wounds had been made on top of them, staining both with fresh blood.

Ram, her pink hair swaying as she ran beside Subaru, made a faint, pleasant smile toward her.

"...I am so glad, Rem... You are one high-maintenance girl..."

Ram's words were few, but only those who really knew her knew this particular smile. She reached out and stroked Rem's blue hair. A moment later—

"Fulla!"

She conducted the Blade of Wind incantation and used the resulting attack to slice through the trees—and cut the demon beast charging at them into discs to nourish the plants on the forest floor.

For a moment, Ram seemed dizzy; her steps went astray, making her lightly bump into Subaru's body.

"Owwwww! Ram, you know better than to touch my right shoulder, geez!!"

"...Be quiet. You would have been bitten if not for me. You can at least be a wall for me to lean on."

"At least pick the other should— Owww!"

Subaru was half in tears as he cried out in fierce pain.

Ram put her weight on Subaru as she bled from the scar of her lost horn. Rem watched both of them as the current situation slapped her in the face.

Why was she in a place like this? Why were they protecting her?

"Wh...y...?"

"Ah?"

"Why...did you not just let me be?"

She trembled as she voiced the question. Subaru stared down at her with a look of disbelief as Rem's quivering lips continued.

"You and Sister coming made it meaningless. I...I have to do this myself... I should be the only one getting hurt..."

"It's a little late for that. Ram and I are all beat up already! Hell, maybe more than you are!"

Subaru was prone to exaggeration, but he seemed to believe every word of that last sentence. She wondered what Ram thought of that, but her beloved twin did not enter the conversation. Rem felt like her sister had left her out on a limb as she desperately tried to find the right words.

"It…it is my fault. I hesitated last night, that is why… I have to take responsibility… If I do not, I cannot face you or Sister…"

"Now may not be the best time for it, but we're actually, you know, talking! That's seriously awesome…"

"Really, you should not have been bitten at all—"

Though Subaru didn't look like he was listening, he apparently heard her words loud and clear. His face went stiff, looking at Rem as she confessed her sin.

Rem's shortcomings had caused Subaru to risk himself to shield her during the forest battle the night before. When she saw the fangs had punctured and ripped Subaru's flesh, bathing him in blood, she could only gape at what her conduct and judgment had wrought.

The same scent as on that day long ago, when everything had been burned away, had hovered thickly around Subaru. And Rem had caught a whiff of it, leaving her unable to move.

"It is because I hesitated to reach out to you that you nearly died. And then your body suffered too many curses to lift. That is why I—"

"You went off to deal with it by yourself to atone for it, right?"

Just as Subaru nodded in acceptance, Rem drew in her chin, once again acknowledging her own sin.

Rem was prepared to be scolded and scorned. Subaru should have given her a tongue-lashing before she had set foot into the forest again.

She had not let him because she had not a moment to spare to save Subaru. That, or she was unprepared to face the consequences of her weakness.

—Rem, resenting her own frail heart, thought it must surely be the latter.

She was prepared to accept whatever words he struck her with, however stern they might be. After all, that was only the punishment she deserved for the crime she had committed.

"Rem."

"Yes."

—Subaru's face was truly right before her eyes.

"*Bonk.*"

"—?!"

The hard *smack* sound of bone upon bone sent sparks into Rem's vision.

For an instant, the sharp pain narrowed Rem's field of vision as she put a hand on her forehead in confusion. When not in her horned form, her flesh was no hardier than an ordinary human's.

No doubt others would be able to see a faint, reddening bump from the impact to her brow.

Rem's eyes were still wide, with no idea what was going on, when Subaru looked down at her.

"To begin with, are you an idiot? No, you *are* an idiot."

"Barusu. You split your split forehead and it is bleeding again."

Ram butted in to speak. Subaru shook his bloodied face.

"I'm an idiot, too. I know that already! But your little sister's an even bigger idiot!"

Rem realized that Subaru had head-butted her. She didn't understand the significance at all.

"Now look here, in my homeland, they say, 'Three women make a market.' Not that that has anything to do with this. But they also say, 'Three heads are better than one.'"

What's sagacity, anyway? Subaru murmured to himself after he spoke. "Er, anyway," he said, twisting his neck as he continued, "it's like how it's easier to snap an arrow with three people than a person might think."

"I am guessing you are using that somewhat unlike the original..."

"A-NY-WA-Y! Don't think about it all by yourself and rely on the people around you! You understand what I'm saying, right?! If you had your heart grabbed like m—"

Subaru was about to say something when his expression changed to one of pain.

"That was over the line, huh…? Th-that's a little strict, ain't it?"

"What are you talking ab—? Wait, Subaru, the scent of the witch is suddenly much thick—"

Rem pinched her nose, twisting her body away from the repugnant smell.

Right beside her, the horrible, abominable stench wafted about. What had suddenly caused it to—?

But Subaru moved to set Rem's misgivings aside with a statement of his own.

"Well, I need you to switch gears on that for now. I'll switch gears, too."

Rem was agape, but the serious look on Subaru's face told her to push that question down the road. Subaru looked ahead as they ran, the tension and caution in his eyes growing stronger.

Simultaneously, Ram, again running beside him, put a hand to her painful forehead as she began to chant.

"Ram, the villa— No, the barrier's good enough. Which way is it to get there?"

"If we can slip past the pack before us, we simply need to sprint to the left, but what are you planning?"

When Ram asked, Subaru let out a long *mmm* sound as he made a sour face.

"How about I push Rem onto you and I cruelly run off to the barrier on my own?"

"You intend to let me flee with Rem while you lure the Urugarum away? Understood."

"Can you *not* spoil what I was trying to hide?! It's embarrassing!!"

The speed of their run did not abate as Subaru and Ram sparred with their words back and forth.

When she heard what they were saying, Rem felt a feeling of despair, like the whole world was turning black before her.

"I cannot...save you like that... Pl-please stop this. If you do this, I..."

"Luggage should be seen and not heard! It's all right, I'll get past the barrier and hook up with you there. After that, I have a special plan you don't know about to take down the demon beasts all at once. It'll be big, an easy win!"

She had no idea what "special plan" Subaru had prepared. To be blunt, she wondered if there even was one.

Was he simply papering things over? Subaru slipping past the pack by himself was all but impossible in the first place, she thought.

"You need to do no such thing... I will wipe out the demon beasts all by myse—"

She couldn't let Subaru do anything rash. Rem tried to move her arms and legs. But her limbs merely dangled, refusing to obey her commands. The most she could do was wiggle her fingers and move her tongue around a little. Nothing was working as she was accustomed to.

"Where is my weapon...?"

"Like I could carry around a heavy thing like that! I'll buy you a new one later, geez!"

Pain shot through Rem as she realized she was unarmed and unable to move, so there was nothing she could do but be protected by others. The thought drove her to despair.

Subaru gently handed Rem off to Ram.

"Don't drop her."

"I believe I have more strength than you possess in one arm, Barusu."

"Why'd you make me carry her, then?!"

"You never told me to, did you, Barusu?"

"Seriously, that's your answer?!"

Subaru slapped his own face for missing the opportunity.

Rem looked up at Subaru from her sister's arms, shaking her head at the unbelievable reality. She'd said so many mean things about him. Why was he going this far?

"Subaru, why are you going this far to...?"

"—Good question."

Her inquiry sent Subaru into thought for but a single moment. He raised a finger and smiled.

"Because you're the first girl I ever went on a date with. I'm not so cruel that I can just turn my back on you."

As he spoke, he gently petted Rem with the same hand.

"Well, I'm gonna head off for a little bit. Take care of Rem, Big Sis."

"I pray that you meet with us safely, Barusu."

With that brief exchange, they suddenly parted ways, with Subaru running one way and Ram another.

Ram ran right. Subaru ran left.

The Urugarum pack coming from the front hesitated at their prey splitting up, but only for a moment. They immediately ran off in pursuit of Subaru.

"—Sister!"

"Barusu is risking his life to buy us time. I shall make good use of it."

Sweat formed on Ram's brow as her tone made plain she had no margin for error. The combination of wounds and fatigue slowed her down considerably. Compared to Rem in horned form, it was nothing.

When Rem thought of that, she regretted what she had done enough that she wanted to cry.

If Rem could have returned to horned form, she'd have had the power to get them through this, not only to save Subaru but to carry her older sister out of danger. She could do it all.

And yet, at the most critical of moments, she was unable to even bring out the demon within her.

It was her own halfhearted weakness that had brought Subaru and her older sister here and held them back.

In contrast to the regret-filled Rem, Ram had not hesitated when Subaru offered himself as a decoy. No doubt that was because she valued Rem's life above Subaru's and, indeed, even her own. Knowing that Subaru's ploy would buy them time and increase their odds of survival, she had accepted without the slightest falter.

Though Rem thought her beloved older sister's judgment was correct, she suddenly rebelled against the idea.

Why was Sister so strong, strong enough to cut anything and everything away? What incredible part of her allowed her to make such a horrible decision so easily? Rem wanted to see for herself.

"Sister... Subaru... Subaru is—!"

"Rem. We cannot turn back. It would put his resolve to waste."

They were the words of her beloved sister. Her sister was always right.

If Rem followed her, she would surely be safe, for Ram had always been right.

—Then why did what was right feel so empty...?

"—Sis!!"

"—!!"

Ram's expression greatly trembled in response to Rem's heartfelt shout. Ram bit her lip, her eyes wide open as her feet came to a stop. Rem instantly twisted her body, escaping her sister's arms to fall to the ground, rolling as she looked behind them—and saw Subaru's back as he ran.

Far away, his run was much too slow to be called a sprint.

She saw his black hair and his wounds all over. She saw the sway of his listless right arm, devoid of strength, and the way Subaru appeared to be hiding his emotions.

Towering before Subaru was a giant, sheer black demon beast. Judging from its size compared to the rest of the pack, it might well have been the leader.

Under that fearsome gaze, surrounded by predators, Subaru ferociously ran.

No matter how much she stretched out her fingers, no matter how much her heart quaked, she could not reach his back.

And yet, Rem shouted, as if pleading.

"—Subaru!"

She did not know if her voice reached him.

All she saw was Subaru on the run, his left hand drawing the dimly glimmering sword as if responding to her call.

2

He didn't understand it himself.

Since when had he become a man stubborn enough to do something crazy like this…?

No matter how much he wanted to put on a brave face and not make the sisters feel like they owed him, this was completely, thoroughly *not* like him.

With his back turned to them, the look on his face crumbled the instant he knew they could no longer see it.

He keenly felt both extremes of pain—dull and sharp alike. His mask had fallen to pieces, Subaru's magnificent face scowling as his tongue pathetically hung out like that of a dog.

"It hurts… It hurts. It hurts, Mommy, Daddy, Emilia-tan…!"

He invoked the three most important people in his life as he glanced at his dangling right arm.

The intermittent numbness in his shoulder was from his crash landing after his blow to Rem's horn. He hoped dearly it was merely dislocated.

One way or another, he couldn't rely on his right arm for combat. With one less weapon at his disposal, Subaru had no idea how he was going to face the enemy standing before him.

As Subaru ran, he found the demon beast pup standing in his path—the one that had been the bane of his existence more than once. Subaru wondered if it had a grudge against him to be so darned persistent.

"I'd like this to be the last time we meet…"

Subaru kept running as he girded himself for the cascade of stones the demon beast would surely unleash. If that hit him when his guard was down, there was no way he'd get away with just a dislocated shoulder.

Shaking off the unpleasant image of being whittled to death by a thousand stone cuts, Subaru mentally simulated dodging at the exact moment the stones would be unleashed. He gave the demon beast a half-resentful, gimme-your-best-shot glare when—

"Uhh?"

He suddenly sounded quite clueless.

Subaru could scarcely believe his eyes at the scene unfolding before him.

The demon beast pup made a small howl before curling up its little body further. It seemed to be gathering all its strength. Before Subaru, whose eyes were narrowed with no idea what was coming next, it…

"—!"

The fur ball suddenly grew with explosive force.

Poof—in the blink of an eye, it grew from the size of a cute, huggable domesticated dog to something larger than the largest breeds, to the point one might call it jumbo sized.

"I've seen this in manga a lot, but *seriously*, where does all the extra mass come from?!"

The reply to his question was a howl that seemed to make the entire forest shudder.

It used its hind legs for support as it vigorously sprang off the ground. The demon beast then struck together the claws of both its raised paws, revealing them to be sinister weapons that could slice through human bone with the slightest graze.

"Oh, so you're *not* gonna settle this with magic? What did I ever do to you…?"

Subaru shuddered at its decision to fight their final battle mano a mano as he looked around, searching for any avenue of escape—but demon beasts in pursuit were cutting off the back and the sides, making escape a difficult proposition.

"Man, coming after me instead of the beautiful sisters… You guys have seriously demon-cursed taste… Damn it all!"

Once he noticed it, his steps slowed as the beasts surrounded him. Apparently, Subaru had brought every demon beast in the whole forest running. His decoy operation was a huge success.

He didn't have time to have a nervous breakdown or piss his pants while begging for his life.

With all avenues of escape cut off, his only option was to run straight forward. In other words, he had to take the giant demon beast down one-on-one.

He fumbled in his side pocket. He felt a rock...a piece of hard candy...something that felt sticky and icky...and...

"All I can do now is trust in Puck...!"

He took *it* out and tossed it in his mouth as he prayed to the gray cat with all his might.

There wasn't much time before Subaru would reach the demon beast. They would clash in mere seconds.

That was when...

"—Subaru!"

...he heard it.

That moment, Subaru heard someone call his name.

It had a painful echo, drenched in sadness as if the whole world were about to end, knowing that whether Subaru lived or died determined whether her heart would shatter—perhaps it was insensitive of him, but Subaru was happy.

I'm too pathetic. A pervert. A two-faced jerk.

It wasn't like he couldn't guess how the girl felt as she cried out his name. The fact that he smiled nonetheless was proof he was totally mad.

He smiled, and smiled, and when he was done smiling, Subaru's left hand drew out the broken one-handed sword.

The demon beast roared before him. Subaru put all his weight behind the sword as he, too, yelled out. Their voices raised a pair of discordant war cries. Soul clashed against soul.

A moment before they were within each other's reach, Subaru inhaled deeply. He pictured the center of his body. He focused on the region between chest and waist, imagining a gate connected to the outside, just above his navel.

"—SHAMAAAAK!!"

The magical invocation permeated the air. The next moment, a black cloud erupted around Subaru.

The cloud enveloped Subaru and all the demon beasts. The decisive battle in the forest was now sealed within the darkness.

3

Within the black cloud, the world was incomprehensible.

The shape of the world, its color, its scent—none of these things could be discerned here.

The single firm, solid sensation came from the soles of his feet touching the ground. If not for that, surely he would not have even known which way was up inside the darkness.

He could see nothing. He could hear nothing. He could understand nothing.

So this was the end of the world.

As Subaru felt his feet pressing against his shoes, he searched for something within the haze. Surely there was something that awaited him within the black cloud, something he had to do.

—Something, something, something, something was *missing*.

Faced with a world of incomprehension, he had to remember the world of *comprehension*.

Why had this nothingness come? Who had brought it? What were the conditions for ending it?

Remember, remember, remember the world beyond, the world that was firm under his feet.

His command to his brain made thoughts erupt like sparks.

He couldn't make it another step. His feet were drained of all strength. Sooner or later, the incomprehension would crush him, making him doubt even the sensation of his soles. If he could see that coming, the answer did not lie outside him.

If the answer was not outside his body, it must lie within. Even if he could not bring the oblivion outside him to heel, he could call upon his internal organs, all subconsciously functioning even then.

The roles had been assigned. It was time to *move*. And so, finally—

"—!!"

Suddenly, he felt like his entire body was on fire.

The unendurable sensation of heat ripped through Subaru's body, bringing not words from his throat but a bestial cry… No, he *thought* it had. He did not understand even that.

He didn't understand. He didn't understand, but his feet, once drained of strength, moved once more.

Forward. His feet moved in the direction he believed to be *forward*.

Awareness, oblivion, awareness, oblivion, awareness, oblivion, over and over and over, until finally—

4

The instant Subaru broke through the black cloud, leaping outside it, his sword hit something extremely thick. The sword in his hand was ripped out of his grasp. Subaru lifted his face and bit down his shock.

Before his very eyes, the huge demon beast's head remained thrust into the black cloud—and the single-handed sword Subaru had been grasping was deep in its chest.

The surprise blow left an ugly feeling lingering in the middle of Subaru's hand—the feeling of plunging a dull blade into the flesh of a living creature. The psychological shock was greater than he'd anticipated, giving rise to what was almost an eerie, out-of-body feeling.

The demon beast, still in the world of incomprehension, couldn't even feel the blade in its body.

Even as Subaru glanced at the contradictory spectacle of a dead beast that didn't know it was dead, he shamelessly ran, putting distance between them while he still could.

His head was heavy; his whole body was sluggish. It was the after-effect of using magical power without complete command of it, and thus burning excess amounts of mana.

In the first place, using that magic should have spewed out all the mana in his body, leaving him on the ground and unable to rise again, but Subaru had played his trump card to get around that.

"—Thanks a million, brats."

Subaru spat out the tiny remnants of the fruit's skin still in his mouth as a small smile came over him.

He'd spat out a bokko fruit, a recovery item that brought strength back to a body devoid of mana. It was amid the completely useless things the kids in the village had pushed on to him when he was heading off to rescue Rem. He had no idea where they'd found one.

The instant he was sure he had one, his head had been able to muster that plan alone. If he bit down on it at the exact moment he used his magic, maybe he'd be able to move afterward. He'd gambled his very life on it, but the scales had marvelously swung Subaru's way.

Putting his back to the demon beast trapped in incomprehension, his feet took him in the direction the barrier ought to have been.

Subaru was a beginner with insufficient mana, so he had no idea how long his Shamak would keep going. He couldn't think of any other way to buy time, so he had to get as close to the barrier as he—

"—Ah?"

But Subaru's scheme was instantly foiled by a single claw that grazed the back of his left thigh.

The sharp pain heralded the bleeding. Subaru let out an anguished groan as he fell to his knees. But Subaru's mortal foe would not permit him to kneel.

Its thick paw violently grabbed Subaru's neck, the tips of its claws digging in as it easily hoisted him up.

"Damn it all..."

Before his very eyes, he saw the gaping maw of the huge demon beast, open wide enough to swallow Subaru whole. Its fangs dripped with blood as its stinky breath hit Subaru's face. He could only smile desperately at the depth of the creature's grudge.

"Go to hell, why don't you—?!"

He yanked the sword out of the demon beast and plunged it into the creature's mouth with all his might.

"—!"

The fatal blow delivered to the inside of its mouth sent the demon beast roaring and flinging Subaru's body away.

Subaru tumbled across the ground, holding onto the sword, then held it before him as he looked up at the demon beast.

"Yeah! How's that, sucker?! Bite on that!!"

The demon beast shook its head, facing Subaru in a berserk rage. Subaru, his body drenched with blood, taunted it with trash talk.

With blood all over their faces, they only had eyes for each other. They were whittling down each other's lives.

They both understood. None of this would end until one of them slew the other.

They stood off against each other. A single spark would be enough to set them off.

The confrontation between man and beast—no, two beasts—was on the cusp of beginning. But the square impact of the fiery shot that rained down from the sky put it on permanent suspension at the sound of a man's voice.

"—Ulgoa."

"Whoaaa?!"

Subaru shielded his face as the shock wave enveloped his body and blew him back.

All of a sudden, the ground in front of him exploded into flames. The high-temperature impact enveloped his entire body with a ferocious wave of heat.

Subaru, lying on his side, shook his head as burns added to the wounds already peppering his flesh.

"What the hell just…?"

The hot, parched air seared Subaru's throat as he looked up…and saw. His cheeks stiffened in shock.

—Before Subaru's very eyes, the huge demon beast was wrapped in a pillar of fire. It was burning.

The flames licked its entire body. The demon beast's paws shuddered and tore at the ground in agony. With the air scorching its lungs, the demon beast could not make a sound as it writhed within the crimson sea and finally dropped to the ground with a heavy *thud*.

All that was left behind was a clump of blackened flesh that had lost two-thirds of its mass.

"—"

The unforeseen end of the demon beast was not all that surprised Subaru.

Flaming shots like the one that had burned the demon beast to death rained down from the sky one after another, plunging into the black cloud. From outside the spread of the darkness, Subaru could not see for himself the full power of the flames upon landing. But he could guess what they were doing.

Inside the impermeable darkness, the demon beasts were being destroyed without even realizing.

Subaru could no longer tell if that was cruelty or mercy. However—

"Myyy, my, myyy, who would have thooought that a mere Shamak, used chiefly for smokescreens, could be employed with this much impaaact?"

The man who had directed the demon beast's fiery-death scene floated down from the sky, a flippant smile on his face.

His long indigo hair swayed in the wind. His eyes were oddly colored: one blue, one yellow. He wore a bizarre outfit over his tall, slender body. The clownish lord, mightiest magic user in all the kingdom, Roswaal, had arrived.

Upon landing, Roswaal brushed off his pant legs and swept his long hair behind him as he looked down at Subaru.

"Ohhhh, you look rather teeerrible, I must saaay."

"You're super late to the party, Rozchi. How many times do you think I thought I was gonna die there?"

It was definitely more than a handful.

After flinging his abuse, Subaru lost his strength; he fell down then and there, not even strong enough to get up on his knees.

"You sure figured out where I was, though."

"Ah, that is because of what Lady Emilia pounded iiinto me at the viiillage. She said, 'Even if it's crazy and reckless, if he's backed into a corner he'll probably use magic, so don't you dare miss it from the sky.'"

"Damn it, Beako…you let Emilia figure it out real quick."

Apparently Beatrice had not been up to the task. Perhaps it was for the better, given how Roswaal had miraculously entered the fray at the last moment.

Subaru thought over the circumstances when a voice sounded in his ears.

"Master Roswaal—!"

He saw Ram, who'd taken a detour around the burning black cloud, cutting through some thickets. Rem was leaning on her shoulder as Ram's expression melted in Roswaal's presence.

"I am sorry to have caused you so much trouble."

"Oh no, that is quite fiiine. Indeed, you have done veeery well in my absence."

Blushing hard at the words of praise, Ram pressed a hand to her chest as she made a solemn nod.

Watching the exchange between them, Subaru let out a deep sigh of relief.

"—Subaru!"

Rem suddenly rushed over and embraced Subaru, drawing a sharp cry from his throat.

"Guh!"

Before his eyes, blue hair swayed right next to his face. The soft sensations in so many places made Subaru understand the circumstances. In any other context, he'd be overjoyed, but he had no such leeway at that moment.

"Rem, my body's banged up all over the… Ah, my mind's kinda…"

Maybe she couldn't control her feelings, but she was hugging him with all her might. Every wound on his body began to cry out as Subaru desperately tried to pat Rem's back to appeal to her. But—

"You're alive. You're still alive. Subaru, Subaru…Subaru!"

Rem was too overcome with emotion to notice how Subaru was reacting.

He felt her press her face against his chest and her warm teardrops flowing down her cheek. A wide range of ticklish sensations struck him, well beyond the capacity of Subaru's brain to deal with.

In other words—

"Oh man…not this…again…"

As Subaru spoke, his head slowly tilted forward, his neck no longer able to support itself.

His mind grew distant. The voices grew faint. Finally…

"Go ahead and sleep. When you awaken, I must thank you quite earnestly. At the very least, rest assured I shall eliminate that which threatens you."

...someone's voice sounded in his ears, serious and devoid of clownish affect.

Feeling a deeper sense of security, Subaru gently let go of lucidity.

Until the moment he fell asleep, he reveled in the warmth of the embrace and the relief of finally receiving it.

Subaru's consciousness sank into a river of unconsciousness.

EPILoGUE
TALKING ABOUT THE FUTURE

1

Subaru's mind was invited to the land ruled by the black shadow once more.

There was nothing. Only his consciousness seemed to hover in space. Subaru dimly realized that he existed.

There was no one. There was nothing. Nothing began. Nothing ended. It was a world of no being at all.

Subaru felt like he had been cast into the sea at night. He let his mind float with the fickle sensation.

Abruptly, a change came over the world of darkness.

In front, directly ahead of Subaru's mind, someone stood.

The shadow grew vertically. Before he knew it, a human silhouette stood before Subaru.

He couldn't see its face. The shape was indistinct. But he vaguely thought that it had the shape of a woman.

The shadow wavered and slowly reached out a hand.

For some reason, when her fingers gently grazed his mind, Subaru wanted to weep. The wave of strange emotion washing over him suggested that he had always been waiting for her to do so.

He had an instinctive desire for the wriggling shadow to embrace him, to swallow him whole—and then it stopped. Something had stopped it.

Subaru's mind realized that there was another shadow, its white fingers embracing him from behind.

Her touch felt soft, and not just warm but hot.

The instant Subaru felt that heat, the shadow before him rapidly faded away.

He faced his front. His heart trembled. He shouted ferociously. But the world of nothingness had no sound.

He was left behind as the shadow became distant, fading, fading away.

Finally, the shadow serenely stretched her fingers out toward Subaru, who was nearly in tears.

"—*ve you.*"

Even the words he could not hear faded, and the world fell apart.

2

When Subaru awoke, the first thing his eyes took in was an unfamiliar, ornate ceiling.

Unlike his bedroom, the chamber he awoke in was ornamented more than most parlors; even the ceiling was decked out to excess. Perhaps it was mandatory in an aristocrat's mansion, the better to show off the master's authority to other parties.

At any rate, to a boy like Subaru, born and raised in a small city, it was distinctly uncomfortable.

Subaru blinked several times in the moments it took him to arrive at that thought after waking.

"—It seems…you are awake?"

The voice came from the edge of the bed, and at point-blank range.

Subaru turned his head, which rested on an exceptionally soft pillow, and narrowed his eyes upon the girl sitting right beside him.

"I suppose in one sense, having a maid by your side when you wake up is a man's cherished desire."

"…Considering my degree of carelessness, this is the least I can do to atone."

"Man, that's such a negative thing to say, Rem. *More to the point…*"

With Rem's eyes downturned, Subaru sat up, punctuating each movement with a word as he took his right hand from under the blankets and lifted it up. It was firmly in Rem's grasp.

"Did I do this? If I just grabbed you and didn't let go… That's kind of embarrassing. It's like when I was a kid and wouldn't let go of my favorite towel."

"Er, no, that's…"

When Subaru posed the question, still holding Rem's hand as he glanced at her, he saw her cheeks redden just a bit.

"I…did it."

"Why? I mean, I sweat a lot when I sleep, so my palm's probably pretty nasty, too."

"Subaru, I…"

"Yeah?"

As Rem's words faltered, Subaru had a warm feeling as he quietly watched her, their hands still joined.

There was no rush involved, so Rem took several breaths before looking at Subaru with upturned eyes.

"You seemed to be suffering while you slept, so I…"

"You held my hand?"

"Yes, because I am weak and full of flaws. Hence, I do not know what I can do for someone when this happens. Since I did not know, I did the thing that would have made me happiest."

Her halting, fumbling words suggested that this was linked to some kind of embarrassing memory. However, Subaru gave his hand a smile as Rem made her feelings clear.

It was like that hand had rescued Subaru from a bad dream, as if he were a little kid. No doubt someone had held Rem's hand on some night when she seemed about to cry. Subaru couldn't help but be happy, even giddy, that she had done the same for him.

With no reason to let go, their hands remained together. Subaru kept soaking up the warmth as he inclined his head.

"Anyway, care to tell me what else happened before I read the sequel?"

"Yes. How much do you remember, Subaru?"

"Rozchi made fire rain from the sky, and you were worked up and bear-hugged me. That's it."

"…So, what happened after, then…?"

Haltingly, Rem explained the aftermath in a businesslike fashion.

After Subaru lost consciousness, Roswaal had mopped up the demon beasts in the forest. The effect of Subaru's stench of the witch worked fine even with him out cold, so Roswaal had used him as bait to lure out the demon beasts, and then incinerated the remainder in the forest.

"Then the curses on me…?"

"In this case…the casters were the demon beasts that bit you. You need not be concerned about dying from those curses any longer. Master Roswaal and Lady Beatrice and the Great Spirit have already taken care of everything."

"So all three are guaranteeing it, huh…? Well, I'll believe it this time."

He'd been bitten almost everywhere else, so Subaru put a hand on his breast as he sighed with relief.

Apparently the time bombs in his body had been successfully defused. He grimaced as he recalled just how many times he'd almost died and what pain and suffering he'd gone through to achieve this.

"Master Roswaal also calmed the agitated villagers in person. Things have mostly returned to peace and quiet."

"I see. So the brats are safe, huh? But they're probably worried sick about their beloved Big Bro Subaru coming back all beat-up, heh-heh."

Subaru was lightening up the mood when Rem made a murmur rich with meaning as she pulled down the blanket covering him.

"—Yes…so it would seem."

What? thought Subaru, suspicious of Rem's demeanor, but his expression soon changed to surprise.

Under the blankets, Subaru was dressed in a gown just like the one he'd worn on his first day at Roswaal Manor when he'd been severely injured. He realized there was something odd on the parts of the gown below the waist, namely...

"There are scribbles all over it...like on a cast for a broken leg!"

"The children Master Roswaal graciously invited to the mansion wrote these things."

"Geez, those little brats...!"

Subaru clicked his tongue as he looked over their notes to him. In the first place, they were written upside down from Subaru's point of view, and it wasn't good handwriting to begin with. But since they were written in the I-script Subaru had learned, he eventually read everything.

"Thanks for bringing Rem back." "Thank you very much." "You look crazy, but you're cool." "Do aerobics with us like you promised." "Love you."

Subaru grumbled as he leaned back against the pillow, looking toward the window.

"Geez, those brats... It's so stupid. I don't even like kids..."

He was glaring toward the village and the children there who had written such things. He was looking forward to paying them a visit as soon as he could.

Then he'd give those happy, prank-playing children a real chewing out.

Rem warmly watched how Subaru's words contrasted with the look on his face. Then her expression wavered, her lips trembling.

"Setting aside the past, I need to speak to you about your body."

"Mm, ah, suppose you're right. Setting aside the curse, I pushed it pretty far, huh?"

It was only as he spoke that he realized his right shoulder, the same side as the hand Rem was holding, was in its socket. Even when he put weight on it, there was no ache. He felt no malaise from the scars all over his body where fangs had punctured his flesh. *This world's healing magic can do anything*, thought Subaru.

"Subaru, I am sorry."

In spite of Subaru's optimistic judgment, Rem bent forward at the waist and bowed her head before him.

"Hey, hey," Subaru said with a wave of his hand, not able to grasp why Rem would be apologizing to him.

"Lift your head up, Rem. My body's fine; there's nothing bad about it. I'm in perfect condition."

"That is…not true whatsoever. Certainly the visible wounds have been healed, and fortunately, you need not be concerned about aftereffects hindering normal, everyday life. But…"

As her words broke off, a bitter shadow came over Rem's face.

"The scars remain…not only on the body but the heart as well. Also, due to repeated healing, your body's mana is on the verge of running dry."

"Ahh, that's why my body's a little sluggish… But that's not a big problem, is it? Scars on the body are a man's medals as long as they're not on the back. And I'm pretty tough when it comes to mental scars."

Subaru pointed his thumb at himself as he smiled to drive away Rem's pangs of guilt.

He wasn't making it up. If his heart had been naive enough to have been broken beyond repair, he'd never have made it to that morning to have Rem holding his hand like that.

After all, he'd undergone wounds to his spirit that could very well have made him unable to look Rem in the eye again.

Subaru gazed at Rem intently.

She had short blue hair. Her face was more the "lovely" than "pretty" type. At first, he thought she showed little emotion on her face, but she was coming around on that bit by bit. He wasn't afraid of her. He wasn't afraid of her at all.

There was a Rem who had made Subaru loop more than once, but here was a Rem happy from the bottom of her heart that he had come back alive. It was all by chance.

There was the Rem who ran amok for her sister's sake, the Rem who acted rashly to protect Subaru, the Rem who ran off before switching to Berserker Mode so that she wouldn't cause friendly fire—

"You may look like you have it all together, but you really aren't the calm type at all, are you, Rem?"

In everyday life at the mansion, Rem had exceptionally sound, rational decision-making ability. But in a fast-moving crisis, Rem's thoughts also moved quickly, making her hasty and rash.

Subaru wasn't really one to talk about snap judgments, but in Rem's case, it was scary how she held a hammer only to see every problem as a nail. Subaru had experienced that firsthand.

When Subaru pointed that out, Rem froze for a moment before making a listless, low bow.

"I…understand."

Her murmur seemed like the first drop to break the dam of feelings she held inside her.

"I am powerless, talentless, and a reject of the demon race. That is why I could never live up to Sister. I was so slow-footed compared to Sister, and I could not think of any way to catch up beyond running faster."

Rem covered her face with her free hand, continuing her confession as if squeezing it out of herself.

"Sister did everything better. Sister never blundered. Sister never wavered. Sister was right about everything. Sister… If it was Sister, she…"

Rem's words trailed off as she meekly looked up at Subaru.

What rested in her eyes were not tears but hollow resignation and despair.

"I was always Sister's…substitute. I've always, always been inferior. Truly, I am a good-for-nothing. I could not catch up to Sister no matter how much I chased after her."

—Faint tears abruptly welled up in her eyes.

"Why was I the one to keep my horn? Why wasn't it Sister? Why was Sister born with only one? Why…? Why were Sister and I twins?"

Rem's lips trembled as she sought meaning for her very existence.

The tears welling in her eyes rolled onto her cheeks, making Rem's pale flesh glimmer in sorrow.

Subaru held his silence. Rem seemed unable to bear the quiet, hastily wiping the tears off her cheek. She spoke rapid-fire, trying to take back her preceding statements.

"I…I am sorry. I said some very odd things. Please forget them. This is the first time I have said such strange things to anyo—"

"Hey, Rem."

Subaru called her name, cutting her words off midway.

Rem was afraid of what Subaru would say now that he had broken his silence but lifted her face nonetheless.

And so, Subaru said to her…

"From everything I've heard from you, you're a pretty big idiot."

"—Eh?"

"I can think of three stupid things about you. Can you guess what they are?"

Rem's eyes quivered, unable to grasp the meaning behind Subaru's words. Subaru smiled at her reaction and raised a finger in front of Rem.

"Can't be helped, then. The first stupid thing is…you're going overboard given the fact that I was actually, you know, saved. You see me waving right before your eyes, right? I have both legs on and everything."

Subaru wiggled his scratched-up legs. Rem realized that Subaru was speaking in regards to her confession but meekly shook her head even so.

"That is…justifying after the fact…"

"A wise man once said, 'All's well that ends well.' To be honest, I think my version's a lot more on target than trying to grade every part along the way. That leads me to the second stupid thing, which is you trying to carry everything on your shoulders by yourself."

With a wink, Subaru raised a second finger.

"Now, I'm super happy you flew off the handle like that for my sake, but everything has a time and a place. To begin with, if you'd talked to other people about it, we'd probably have come up with a better way."

Where hunting the demon beasts was concerned, it was crystal clear that Subaru had a point. Rem, unable to refute him, lowered her eyes as if ashamed of her own impulsiveness. Of course, his criticism was something that could be said only in hindsight. But Rem did not realize that even the tiniest bit, nor did she realize Subaru was sticking out his tongue just a little.

"As for the third... You know what it is, Rem?"

"I...do not understand at all. I am always insufficient; I can never reach as far as—"

"Yes, that. That's the third stupid thing."

Subaru pointed at Rem and how she never missed a chance to put herself down.

Then he raised a third finger and waved the three about.

"Rem, just because she's your older sister, you build her up and put yourself down to where it almost kills you... I don't think Ram's always in a stronger position than you, okay? Her stamina's worse than yours, her cooking's lousy, she slacks off work, she makes snide comments... I suppose she thinks a little too much, too?"

In Subaru's mind, Ram's specs were a long way from the pillar of perfection Rem spoke of. She was an older sister with talents behind her younger sister in every area. Surely the sisters themselves were well aware of this. That was what Subaru supposed, but Rem shook her head, rejecting his suggestions.

"N-no...you are wrong. Sister is truly... If she had her horn, you would never judge her so—"

"But Ram doesn't have her horn. So I don't know a Ram like that."

Subaru, cutting off Rem's attempt to firmly deny herself, continued.

"The Ram I know is just like I described. She can't hold a candle to you in cooking, sewing, cleaning, politeness, or the way she talks—well, I don't think that last part is a bad thing, really."

It wasn't bad to butt heads with her over her haughty manner of speaking from time to time. To Subaru, the distance between him and Ram was more comfortable.

"It's probably only you who's worked up about whether she has a horn or not. Comparing someone else's good points and your own bad points just gets you bent out of shape."

"—"

"Whatever she doesn't have, you have. So accept it already... You're gentle, a hard worker, always doing your best, and your breasts are bigger than Ram's, too—"

"—!"

"Ow! Hey, don't smack me with tears in your eyes like that!"

Subaru recalled his brief conversation with Ram in the forest. There, he had learned that Ram wasn't particularly hung up any longer on what she had lost as a demon, to the point where he believed Ram wanted Rem to get over it, too.

—Subaru was not arrogant enough to think that was a problem he was capable of fixing. In the end, Subaru was just a mouthy young man lacking the length or depth of life experience to handle the job. A lecture from someone like him wasn't going to get him anywhere.

He put no pressure on himself. He imagined no gravitas in his words. It was simply something in him that refused to compromise: the idea that, in the end, you didn't get the answer from someone else—you had to just roll up your sleeves and do it yourself.

So Subaru was simply conveying to Rem his exceptionally simple feelings about the matter.

"If it wasn't for you, I'd be dead and dog food right now. I'm safe and sound because you were there. I'm alive now thanks to you. That's your doing, not your sister's."

"...Truly, Sister could have done it better."

Subaru poured cold water on her weak rebuttal as he brought his left hand over his right, which still held Rem's hand.

"Maybe she could have...but you were the one there for me."

When Rem gasped and lifted her face, Subaru put enough gratitude into his voice to make himself blush.

"I'm glad you were there for me, Rem. Thank you."

"—!"

A choked sob escaped Rem's throat at his words. After that, Rem turned her face aside so that Subaru would not see the look on it.

"I...I have always been a substitute for Sister..."

"Stop defining yourself with lonely words like that, all right? You and Ram are different genres. I mean, she's the older sister and you're the younger sister—sometimes you're gonna clash."

There would always be differences between the two. Each had their unique good points.

Whether Rem understood what he was saying or not, Subaru's encouragement made Rem squeeze her eyes shut.

"Well, I haven't really asked why she lost her horn, and since I didn't ask I don't know. I don't know, so I don't want to talk like I do know, so..."

Subaru put his left hand on the upper part of his own forehead—patting it right where Rem's horn grew out of hers.

"Ram doesn't have her horn, and you have yours, so you can just do whatever she would need a horn for. You can just be two demons getting along great. There's nothing stronger than love between beautiful sisters, right?"

"...Ah..."

"So I mean, you said you were a substitute, but Ram has no substitute for you, does she? I mean, if you weren't there for her, can you imagine the state she'd be in?"

Rem, aghast, didn't know this, but Subaru had seen such a future. He had seen Ram, despairing at the death of her younger sister, go mad and use all her remaining strength for the sake of vengeance.

"...But..."

Yet even so, Rem did not simply nod in agreement.

"I get it. So, how about we do this? You have an idealized Ram inside you that you can never compare to no matter what you do. Let's take that ideal Ram you have on a pedestal and send her packing."

"That is...easier said than done. I have always compared myself to—"

"That's why I want you to listen to how I rate her. My rating's based on reality, not the ideal. Just so you know…I don't have any talent for reading the mood at all, so I just call 'em like I see 'em, no flattery or mercy. What you see is what you get."

Subaru smiled at Rem, grinning as he stroked her blue hair. It tickled her, but she merely narrowed her eyes, drawing a small sigh out of Subaru.

"Where I come from, they say, 'Talking about the future makes a demon laugh,' so…"

Rem said nothing and merely tilted her head a bit as Subaru continued caressing her head and speaking.

"Laugh, Rem. Don't make a glum face. Laugh. Let's laugh and talk about the future. Let's make up for all that living in the past you've been doing and talk about what's to come. I mean, even if we start with tomorrow."

"…Tomorrow?"

"Yes, tomorrow. Anything's good, all right? Like, whether it'll be Japanese or Western food for breakfast tomorrow, or even if you're going to put on your right shoe or your left shoe first. It doesn't matter how trivial, there'll be a tomorrow, so we can talk about it. How about it?"

Subaru spread his arms, prodding Rem for an answer.

Rem hesitated to reply for a while before lowering her brows with a conflicted look.

"I am…very weak…so I will most likely lean on you a great deal."

"What's wrong with that? I'm weak, too. I'm not very smart, I'm not good-looking, and I can't read the mood, which gets me down even when I'm the one saying it, but I still get by because the people around me help me. We just have to lean on one another and move forward."

She had been unable to see a path for her to walk because she insisted on putting anything and everything onto her own shoulders. The least Subaru could do was offer his two empty hands and make the walk forward that much easier.

Even so, he'd just been extra baggage himself more than once… but if you couldn't see ahead by yourself, you just needed someone to share the burden with as you moved forward. That's how he felt, anyway.

"So let's laugh, hug each other, and talk about tomorrow. I've always dreamed of laughing with a demon and talking about the future, anyway."

"...You truly are possessed by a demon."

"You bet."

Subaru closed one eye with the corner of his lips curled up. Rem apparently couldn't resist making a small smile herself.

She laughed, and as she laughed, tears poured out of the corners of her eyes. The seemingly endless tears poured out, flowing and flowing, but Rem continued to laugh even so.

Rem laughed, Rem cried, Rem buried her face in a pillow to suppress her laughing, sobbing voice. Even so, her mirthful, tearful voice quietly filled the room.

Subaru gently caressed Rem's hair the whole while, his right hand grasping hers.

Softly, softly, he stroked her hair.

3

He thought back to the days he had repeated over and over in his first week at Roswaal Manor.

Subaru had a place at the mansion with a good relationship with Ram and Rem. The children of the village had been saved, and the demon beasts in the forest had been wiped out, eliminating that danger. It was a grand adventure spanning some twenty-odd days.

Yes, it should have been cause for celebration. And if not for the girl using a finger to toy with her silver hair, in a sullen mood as she laid into Subaru, it would have been.

"—It's not that I'm upset. No, I'm not *upset*. All that happened was the patient I'd been nursing was gone when I woke up, and when I was going to go looking for him, I found out I'd been tied to the chair and left behind. No, I'm not upset about that *at all*."

A flood of cold sweat poured down Subaru's brow as he silently listened to Emilia's rant.

It had already been some ten minutes since Emilia had come to the room, but most of that time had been chewed up by a mix of lecturing and venting.

Her initial visit was out of concern for Subaru's condition. When she was certain he was fine, she had sighed with relief and switched gears to leveling her complaints on the spot. That was Emilia's personality for you.

"I'm...not upset...so..."

"Yes, Emilia-tan, you're right to be upset with me. I'm very sorry."

"Sheesh, I *said* I *wasn't* upset. But since you apparently feel guilty I have no choice... I will accept your apology, Subaru. Really, don't make me worry like that."

After Subaru gave in to her pressure, Emilia accepted the apology and punctuated her last sentence with a broad, charming smile.

It wasn't even remotely fair. How could she say things like that and make that kind of face at the same time?

After he'd made up with Rem, the maid had left, and Emilia had taken her place. The moment she'd arrived, he'd largely expected how the rest would go, but now that her lecture was finished, the way there was nothing in her purple eyes but concern for Subaru made it really hard for him to calm down.

"I have to say, Subaru, you sure get hurt a lot. And the reason you got hurt was that you came to the mansion, too... I mean, it's only been four days."

"Hey, it's not like I want all these injuries. I guess you could say the world kind of has it out for me...so, if I can at least have Emilia-tan fawning over me, it's all good!"

"I fawned over you plenty and you just ran off. You can fend for yourself next time."

"*Nuaaa!* I let my chance slip away! Damn it, if only Beako had done a bit of a better job!"

Subaru shouted in anger at the coldhearted girl, having not seen a single trace of her curly hair since his recovery. Emilia pouted as Subaru's words made her remember how he'd left her behind.

"I told you, when I woke up after falling asleep in the chair I was tied up in it. I was flabbergasted."

"No one uses *flabbergasted* anymore…"

"Don't make light of it… Puck tried to keep me from going after both of you, too. I don't know what would have happened if Roswaal hadn't come back. Understand?"

Faced with Emilia's tight-lipped anger, Subaru could only feel ashamed of himself.

Just as he had imagined, Puck attempted to keep Emilia from putting herself in danger. Apparently Beatrice had abandoned any thought of convincing her early on and had moved straight to physical restraints. Having both of them impeding Emilia must have been pretty hard on her mental state.

Subaru knew that was exactly how he'd feel if it'd been him left behind like that. Even so, if he'd had to do it all over again, no doubt he'd have left Emilia behind once more.

"You've saved me again, though."

"Eh?"

"I said, you've saved me again, even though the whole point of bringing you to the mansion was to thank you for saving me before. Thank you *very* much."

Emilia put her hands together for emphasis as her face broke into a radiant smile.

Subaru, bearing the full effect of it, finally felt something go *plunk* in his chest.

"Err, that's fine, really! I just did it because I wanted to, and it's not like this has nothing to do with me, either. Yeah, that's right. I…did it."

As he said it, it really sank in. That was what had fallen inside his chest. Having repeated events over some twenty days, Subaru had finally made it to the end.

After having his heart broken and crushed so many times, his hand had finally reached that which he had long sought. He was finally able to register that feeling of *I did it!*

"That's what you say, but that won't put my conscience at ease. I'm sure Ram, Rem, and Roswaal are all grateful to you, too."

"That so…? All right, let me take advantage and have my contract with Rozchi amended so that Ram and Rem are *my* personal maids for a while, *muah-ha-ha*. And *then*!"

Subaru put his hand over his mouth as he made a lewd laugh. He then swayed his body left and right as he drew closer to Emilia, thrusting a finger toward her, making her recoil ever so slightly.

"Am I going to get an Emilia-tan reward, too?"

"Goodness, if I can afford it. If it is within my power, then… Wait, last time, you asked me for my name."

"Heh-heh. Do not underestimate my greed. This time I am a man unaffected by anything so weak. I am aroused by greed and avarice and a vortex of libido!"

Though he never even got up from the bed, Subaru posed, furiously spreading his arms up at an angle.

Perhaps seeing Subaru worked up to that degree made Emilia believe the subject couldn't be avoided. She sat down, properly facing him.

As Emilia awaited the inevitable, Subaru browsed the "Emilia Reward List" in his brain. He carefully went over options ranging from the bittersweet to nighttime adventures, selecting one.

And so…

"All right, Emilia-tan, let's go out on a date."

…he would redo the promise he'd made with Emilia so many days before.

" 'Date'…?"

"It means we head out together, see the same things, eat the same food, share the same memories together."

"…You're fine with that?"

"I'm *fine* with that."

How many hardships had Subaru gone through to go on his long-desired date with Emilia? Along the way, various other intentions had piled up with it as he leaped over one hurdle after another, but he'd finally cleared the last obstacle and reached his wish.

Hence, the promise was a fitting way to tie all the loops together.

"I want to brag about you to the brats in the village, Emilia-tan. Plus, the flower bed's just awesome. To me, it'd be special just to have a casual stroll there together."

"I think your definition of *greed* is a bit different than for most people."

"Don't say that. My shamelessness will freeze that cute smile on your face yet. Oh yeah!"

Subaru's teeth glinted as he did a thumbs-up and a wink.

"Yes, all right already, I'll go on a 'date' with you."

The promise having been made, Subaru clapped his hands together and exulted.

"Yessss! And that's why E M F (Emilia-tan's Majorly a Fairy)!!"

Subaru, seeing Emilia sigh at his enthusiasm out of the corner of his eye, directed his hopes for a speedy physical recovery outside the window, toward the village where they would have their promised date.

Visions of a glittering future danced when Subaru abruptly thought of the demon beast forest.

The curses that inhabited his body had lost all their effectiveness. The demon beasts had been eradicated—the end of a long chain of events beginning with a single one slipping past the broken barrier.

This time, matters had ended with one species wiping out the other. The events left a bitter aftertaste that he didn't fully understand.

He remembered how he was in a daze as he thrust his sword into the demon beast's body. The memory was fresh, and the sensation of taking a life lingered on his hands.

He wondered if he would forget that sensation someday. Surely the passage of time would make the ache in his chest subside. But until that day came, what could he do...?

"Subaru."

"Yeah?"

He looked back when she called his name.

He wondered what Emilia would think of the meaning behind Subaru's distant, absentminded gaze.

Emilia rose to her feet and opened the curtains. Light flooded into the room all at once. Emilia's silver hair was enveloped by vivid, dancing light that left him spellbound.

Finally, as Subaru sat in silence, Emilia smiled at him out of the blue.

"When we go on the 'date,' let's bring back a flower bouquet."

"—Sure."

Subaru covered his face with his palms. There was no winning against that smile.

He thought, before the day came when he forgot, he ought to carve it into his chest so that he could not.

He knew it was hypocritical and would only force the pain on to him, but he felt it was the right thing to do.

He felt like Emilia's pretty smile was telling him so. So he did.

Emilia and Subaru continued to spend time together with smiles on their faces.

—Having finally and truly reached it, the morning of the fifth day continued to gently shine down upon them.

INTERLUDE
A PRIVATE CHAT UNDER THE MOON

About half a day had passed since Subaru and Emilia had promised to go on a date together.

The man's gentle voice contained a masculine eloquence that was the product of years of experience.

"First, I must thank you for your service during my aaabsence. The situation was salvaged thanks to your efforts."

His tone was casual, but its firm, unwavering resonance made Ram's shoulders tremble.

"I do not deserve such praise. Besides, in the end it was settled by your own hands, Master Roswaal—"

"I mind not. Incinerating harmful beasts in the forest is no great expenditure of tiiime."

Roswaal waved a hand, speaking as if it was a trivial matter.

Ram was well aware that his claim was not false modesty, hyperbole, or an empty boast. She could not say a word to refute him.

They were speaking to each other in Roswaal's study on the uppermost floor of the mansion. As always, their nocturnal chats involved only the two of them.

"Leaving past events aside, let us speak of something more construuuctive. For instance, what shall become of young Subaru from here ooon, I wonder?"

"…His body is most certainly largely healed. Lady Beatrice made many complaints, but she fully exerted herself to heal him, so…"

"I wonder what illness has befaaallen her. I have known her for quite some time, and the boy is the first time I have seen her become so involved. Surely she could not have…? Ah, surely not…"

Roswaal closed his blue eye as he discarded the implication of his own words. Ram pretended not to hear the quiet portion at the end, not wishing to disturb her master's thought process as she said, "Either way, if not for Lady Beatrice, I doubt we could have saved Subaru."

"Perhaps we should call that young Subaru's good fooortune. Indeed, there are few more accomplished healers than Beatrice. I am embarrassed to say that I specialize only in the infliction of harm."

Roswaal shook his head and tilted it to the side a little. The corners of his lips formed a thin smile. It was a transparent, mild expression, the sort that would perfectly conceal his pleasure or displeasure from anyone but himself.

"Howeeever, I am guessing, from your stating this as the preface, that his condition is not so rooosy?"

"Yes. Barusu has had his gate forced back to life after running dry twice in a short period of time. On top of that, he has been healed from life-threatening injuries, so…I wonder how well his gate can function after being forced open and abused like this."

"Is this the diagnosis of Beatrice and the Great Spirit?"

"Yes."

Roswaal folded his arms and closed his eyes as he mulled the report over.

Damage to one's gate, and thus, one's ability to use mana, was a fatal affliction for any magic user. Roswaal, bearer of the title of court magician, keenly appreciated the state Subaru was in.

"Though gates mend differently for each person, it would take years no matter what. He will face a very difficult choice."

Ram nodded at Roswaal's conclusion before voicing how Subaru's condition was even graver still.

"It is not merely an issue of his damaged gate but the remnants of the curses as well."

"—I thought the danger of activation has passed?"

"The casters…in this case, the Urugarum…have been eliminated, so there are no casters to activate the curses…but the rites for them still remain in Barusu's body."

"So they are intertwined with such complexity that even Beatrice cannot unravel them… My, my, that is a curse in an altogether different sense… I suppose this means we must reward his service all the mooore."

Though the rites remaining in the absence of their casters was some cause for concern, there was essentially no danger of their activating. However, Subaru's body had taken the bullets that, in the worst case, would have spread to others still, those not only in his employ but also, more importantly, Emilia.

As a result, Emilia's participation in the royal selection had been preserved. It was, in every way, service that merited a reward.

"Incidentally, Ram…concerning the iiissue of the demon beasts, did you check on what I asked you to?"

Roswaal asked with a meek look that was quite rare to see on him, and it threw Ram off a fair bit. He awaited her reply as she touched her forehead. Her finger prodded the old wound beneath her headdress. Ram felt the faint throb of the scar as she made her report.

"As far as I have determined from the corpses that remain, the demon beasts were all hornless."

Roswaal exhaled at Ram's reply. He leaned back against his chair.

"The demon beasts I mopped up were the same. Howeeever, that makes this something far larger than an issue of mere noxious beasts, does it nooot?"

"A demon beast with its horn severed will obey the one who severed it. That would mean some fool directed the beasts toward your manor or your lands in general, Master Roswaal."

"It is no doubt relaaated to the royal selection. Like the invitation to Garfiel's land, this has interfered with us considerably."

Ram raised her eyebrows at the invocation of the well-known name.

"Gar…Garfiel, you say?"

Roswaal had a conflicted look as he shrugged. His behavior was aloof, but Ram was acutely aware that this was no small matter. Indeed, it was a battle with low odds of victory. They needed every card they could add to their hand.

Ram knew very well that she was one of those cards. Her inability to do anything but watch Roswaal battle alone chafed at her.

"Let us return to the matter at hand. Do you have an educated guess as to the 'ringleader' who severed the horns?"

"…Tentatively. But the trail has already gone cold. One of the children Barusu and Rem supposedly brought back from the forest vanished from the village the next day."

When she'd asked about the girl with braids who the two had brought back, they had said the villagers all claimed they didn't know the girl. According to the children, she became part of their group at some point, but they couldn't say when.

When she pressed further, they told her that it was that girl who had first brought the demon beast pup to the village, and it was she who had later brought the children past the barrier with her into the forest. She was all but certain that girl had been the ringleader.

"First the Bowel Hunter in the royal capital, now the Beast Mage here. Certainly a strange cast of characters."

"Yet they cannot best you no matter what they throw at you, Master Roswaal."

"My, such a cheeky thing for you to say. Come."

When Roswaal smiled and beckoned with his hand, Ram cut across the ebony desk to be at his side. As she did so, Roswaal reached his arm around Ram's small body, pulling her atop his lap. Then—

"Because I could not be here last niiight for you, it must have been hard on you."

"I know that you are very busy, Master Roswaal. Even if you leave my needs for later…"

"Ram, I have always tooold you…"

Ram's eyes were downturned when Roswaal lifted her chin with a finger, turning her face toward his with a smile.

"You and Rem are among those beings precious to me, so few I can count them on one hand. Indeed, if some terrible fate had befallen you in this incident, I am not confident I could have restrained myself."

His finger remained on Ram's chin as the dramatic words Roswaal tossed at her put an enthralled look on her face. Heat seemed to fill Ram's eyes as she gazed at Roswaal from close up.

"To Master Roswaal, Rem and I are—"

"Yes, to me, you and Rem are precious, vital, and irreplaceable..."

As their words piled upon one another, so did their feelings as Roswaal beheld Ram with his yellow eye, pausing for a brief moment...

"...pawns."

So spoke Roswaal to Ram in theatrical style.

His words did not carry the slightest hint of guilt, for he was stating what he regarded as pure truth.

And Ram, upon hearing her existence described as that of a pawn...

"—Yes."

...her cheeks reddened as she nodded back.

Ram's demeanor was perfectly docile and full of adoration as Roswaal pulled her even higher on his lap.

"Nooow, then, shall we begin? You pushed yourself quite considerably, yes? You are quite mana-depleted, even though I told you to take it easy."

"I am very sorry... Please."

Ram untied the headdress atop her pink hair as she acknowledged Roswaal's words. Roswaal slid a finger past her hair to where a faint white scar rested on the upper reaches of her forehead.

—It was the last vestige of her life as a wonder child among the demon people.

Roswaal grazed his finger across the scar like it was a beloved, wonderful thing.

"—The blessings of the stars upon thee."

Four glimmering colors flowed along Roswaal's arm and converged upon the tip of his finger to become a white light. The light coursed down his finger and poured into Ram's scar.

—The technique to transfer mana directly to another demanded exceptional skill.

If the elemental composition of the mana was not perfectly balanced, the mana would harm the recipient's body when converted back into energy. It was a "therapy" that Roswaal could employ because he was attuned to all four major mana affinities and was accomplished at using them all at a very high level.

For demons, the horns on their foreheads formed the pipeline through which mana passed in and out of the body. Their horns, which functioned much like stronger, finely tuned gates, were the foremost reason the demons were a powerful race.

But Ram had lost her horn due to external factors, leaving her body unable to draw in mana or emit power as her body demanded, a loss all the graver because Ram's body was top tier, even by demon standards.

Left to her own devices, her body would simply wither away. These private nighttime chats were a daily event so as to prevent that from happening.

Ram felt her body come back to life as mana poured into her through the horn scar. She let herself luxuriate in the sweet feeling of warmth filling her body from the inside out when she said out of the blue, "Ah, I forgot something. There was something else I need to report to you, Master Roswaal…"

"Mm? And what would thaaat be?"

Roswaal continued the treatment with one eye closed while Ram sank into thought for a while. She seemed to be at odds about how to word it exactly.

"Rem has…fallen in love with Barusu."

"Mm?"

"It would seem Barusu has…grazed all of Rem's weak points."

Rem was the younger twin sister. As her older sister, Ram was painfully aware of her younger sister's state of mind. Put another way, she knew all too well that it was not in Rem's nature to be honest with herself.

"Rem has, has she? Weeell, perhaps it is not so mysterious. After all, she does not serve me out of loyalty, unlike youuu."

Ram remained quiet before her master's assessment of her younger sister in silent agreement. Unlike Ram, who loyally served Roswaal without asking anything in return, Rem viewed that as a betrayal of the self.

To Rem, Roswaal was very much "Sister's patron." Since her sister was her very purpose in life, Rem's thought process never extended beyond that. It was that line of thinking that made Rem so reckless and rash when it came to defending her community; take your eyes off her, and she'd eliminate anyone she viewed as a threat to it without a second thought.

Ram believed Subaru had been saved because he'd gained Rem's trust before she could assault him.

Of course, all that being said, Ram still regarded Rem as the cutest little sister in the whole world, someone more important than Ram herself.

—But if someone asked her if Rem occupied the highest pedestal in her heart, Ram could not simply nod and agree.

"Regardless of Rem's feelings, you shall remain firmly in my hands, Ram. Where you go, Rem shall invaaariably follow. You seeee, things shall be as before. Nooothing will change."

"I…suppose so, though now that there is one more precious thing to Rem, the chance of her acting rashly is even greater, one might say."

"Let us cross that bridge when we get to it. This is important work for tomorrow, after aaall."

As Roswaal jested, light faded from his palm. The treatment was over.

Ram felt full not only of life but also disappointment as she slid off Roswaal's lap. After Ram rose from his lap, he rose from the chair.

"Things shall be busier from here on. It shall require much labor, but I am counting on you and Rem, yeees?"

"As you wish. I am yours, Master Roswaal, as I have been since that fiery night."

Ram grasped the hem of her skirt and bent her knees in a reverential curtsy.

Roswaal noted her display of loyalty as he crossed his hands behind him and walked toward the window. He glanced at Ram, following beside him, as he opened the curtain.

When he looked up at the sky, and the full moon floating within it, Roswaal narrowed his oddly colored eyes.

"We must be victorious in the royal selection, no matter what... for the sake of my goal..."

As he murmured, he reached out his arm, wrapped it around Ram's shoulders, and pulled her close.

Able to feel the warmth of his tall body for a second time, Ram closed her eyes and leaned into him.

She listened to the voice of the man beside her, her lord and master, the man she had given her soul.

"...For the day the Dragon dies."

AFTERWORD

Hiya! Nagatsuki here! Tappei here! People call me The Mouse-colored Cat!

Thank you very much for purchasing *Re:ZERO -Starting Life in Another World-*, Volume 3! It's awesome that you've read this far, so thanks a million! Volume 3 is the last volume being published in consecutive months. I'm not sure any brave souls out there decided to take the plunge starting with this one, but if so, go ahead and try the others with the pretty girls on the covers. Volumes 1 and 2 should be right beside this one—and if they're not, ask the clerk to order them!

And if that line gets us even one more sale, the fate of the entire work could be changed forever!

Along with the same direct marketing as in the Volume 2 afterword, I want to thank you from the bottom of my heart for sticking with our story so far.

The first volume was the tutorial. The second was more like, "This is how the series goes." This, the third volume, wraps up what I hope is a hearty three-month consecutive publication schedule with the message: "This series is *interesting*."

I passed on the view of Ikemoto the editor, who wanted a safe publication schedule to slowly grow the series, and ignored his admonition that "we're looking at a new horizon here, an achievement never done before!" as I dashed forward, with Otsuka-sensei the illustrator rising to the challenge of my unreasonable requests, with Kusano the designer doing all-nighters to humor the selfish author's selfish project goals—just kidding! The editor said, "Do it!" Your dear author worked desperately to make it happen. Now I have sympathy votes! Thank you very much for buying this!

Now, setting aside minor tales of such hard labors, the "main series" begins with the next volume.

The royal capital becomes the dramatic stage once more, with the world beginning to expand from the narrow confines of the story up to the end of Volume 3. The cast of characters will approximately double, with cute girls and cool guys coming out of the woodwork. Otsuka-sensei looked almost dead from the heavy character design workload, but he's all right—his face says, "I made it because of all the messages from the readers cheering me on!"

Of course, messages of goodwill are welcome for not just Otsuka-sensei but also the author, Nagatsuki, too. You can even send me "I want to be an author!" messages. You can message me on Twitter. You can comment on my blog. You can make your own Re:ZERO fan site and spread the word. You can run for election, take the political world by storm, and get my novels published as textbooks for school. It's all good.

Impressions, cheers, critiques, commentaries—anything goes. You can read the Quick Response Code at the back of the book and talk directly to the publisher, MF Bunko! It's all good! Bring it on!

Since I've run out of other things to babble on about, I'll move on to customary words of thanks.

Ikemoto the editor, you really took good care of me. Publishing three volumes in three months is all thanks to you. I think both of us had a change in the look in our eyes over those three months, so I await the return of the gentle-looking Ikemoto during the interval that now follows.

Otsuka-sensei, thank you again for such beautiful illustrations. In particular, your "lap pillow" illustration was E M D beyond words. I enlarged it and used it to cover my bedroom ceiling. Thank you, thank you!

Kusano the designer, as usual your mighty designs stand head and shoulders above, mercilessly laughing down at my expectations. Thank you very much. Beako is one seriously dangerous Beako.

Volume 3 is also the product of the cooperation of many others, with their efforts having brought us to a successful back-to-back-to-back monthly schedule. I think I caused you all a lot of trouble from my unfamiliarity with various things, so thank you very much for helping me this far.

I would be most content if you stuck with me from here on... forever.

For that, dear readers, please stick with me...forever. Please and thank you.

Tappei Nagatsuki, February 2014
(Stress relief through direct marketing!)

Emilia

エミリア

"The main series is about to start, so let's preview the next volume! Isn't it a little late for me and Emilia to be do one?"

"Hmm, I think we should be *very* grateful for being given this chance to appear like this, just the two of us kind of exhilarating."

"No one uses *exhilarating* anymore…but with the back-to-back-to-back publishing done, the next volume ways down the road, right? How about we shoot the breeze?"

"*No*, you have to do your work properly. The three-month publishing schedule is done, but the Monthly Comalive man said… The, ah, *Re:ZERO* Project will continue, yes?"

"*Re:ZERO* Project, huh? The back-to-back-to-back and the Visual Complete are done, but Monthly Comalive decided to serialize a short novel! Wait, it's a comic magazine, why's it publishing short novels?"

"It seems to be a new thing for them. Also, apparently the story involved will take place during the time betw Volume 3 and Volume 4. With the uproar at the mansion and the village resolved, peaceful days should returned, but something new stirs up the mansion…so they said. It sounds like a lot of fun!"

Subaru Natsuki

ナツキ・スバル

"The way you said that just now makes it feel more worrying than fun, though!"

"And from the fourth volume on is the 'episode' when the story really begins. This is around when it made big [wav]es in its Web novel days."

"Emilia-tan's going one way, withdrawing from the royal selection, and I'm going the other, riding on taking [care] of the demon beast mess. So when we get back to the royal capital, we see other royal candidates face-to-face… [And] I get treated like an intruder. Rough stuff!"

"When it comes to weirdos, I don't think anyone is going to get the better of you, Subaru…"

"Didn't hear that, fingers in my ears. So, *Re:ZERO -Starting Life in Another World-* is taking a little break with [the n]ext volume, due in June!"

"Errr…thank you very much for buying Volume 3. We would be very happy to have you with us for Volume 4 [and b]eyond… Is that all right?"

"[T]M D!"

Re:ZERO

‒Starting Life in Another World‒